THE SISTER PREACHERS

OTHER TITLES BY GALE SEARS

Finding Baby Jesus

The Fifth Favorite

One Candle

Three White Dresses

Belonging to Heaven

Letters in the Jade Dragon Box

The Silence of God

The Route

Christmas for a Dollar

Upon the Mountains

Until the Dawn

Autumn Sky

BASED ON THE TRUE STORY OF

THE FIRST SISTER MISSIONARIES IN 1898

THE SISTER PREACHERS

GALE SEARS

DESERET
BOOK

This book is lovingly dedicated to the past, present,
and future sister missionaries throughout the world,
who enrich the tapestry of proselyting.

Visit us at deseretbook.com

Library of Congress Cataloging-in-Publication Data

(CIP data on file)
ISBN 978-1-63993-015-9

Printed in the United States of America
Pub Litho, Draper, UT

10 9 8 7 6 5 4 3 2 1

Preface

It has been a blessing to research and write about the first single female proselyting missionaries for The Church of Jesus Christ of Latter-day Saints, Sister Amanda Inez Knight and Sister Lucy Jane (Jennie) Brimhall. Both in their early twenties when called, these young women were daughters of prominent Provo, Utah, families: Inez was the daughter of Jesse William Knight and Amanda Melvina McEwan. Brother Knight was a wealthy mine owner who used his money for the good of the community, the Church, and Brigham Young University. Jennie was the daughter of George Brimhall and Alsina E. Wilkins. Brother Brimhall was a man of letters and scholarship and served in many school administrative positions, including as president of Brigham Young University.

As you travel with Inez and Jennie on their 1898 journey from Provo to England, you will discover their pioneer status in this ecclesiastical experiment and note that the rules governing their conduct were unlike the structure now in place for the tens of thousands of present-day sister missionaries, whose service encompasses the globe. You will also find that the structure for elders in the field today differs from their counterparts in the late 1800s. From Inez Knight's journal we learn that the early missionaries did not have a strict curfew and were free to attend the theater, and the sisters were allowed to "walk out," or go strolling, with their male counterparts. Also, the young single sisters did not receive temple covenants prior to departing for their fields of service.

Though this book focuses on Sister Knight and Sister Brimhall and pulls information from their journals, I have also blended in stories from other sister missionaries from the 1898 to the early 1900s British Mission—namely, Sister Josephine Booth and Sister Liza Chipman. It was my desire to keep the story concise by focusing on the two main characters, while including valuable experiences and lessons garnered from others. For those wishing to learn more about the book's two central figures, Sister Knight's journal is available at the Church History Library in Salt Lake City and snippets of Sister Brimhall's journal can be found in the *History of Utah* series, in private correspondence, and in other sources. Many of these sources and others are found in the bibliography.

Some of the historical information is woven into letters—tender correspondence which served as vital strands of connection between missionaries and their families. These handwritten missives carried not only information but also emotional expressions.

This book contains several recipes. Recipes have always been generational links between women, whether they be among family members, friends, or neighbors. Most of the recipes included in *The Sister Preachers* are from the 1860 English cookery book *Mrs. Beeton's Book of Household Management*. Though unique to the period, the recipes are workable for those adventurous souls wishing to step into history.

There are fictional characters and events woven within the historical material to add texture and depth and to move the story forward. If there was need for clarification or definition in a chapter, I referenced additional information at the end of the chapter in the notes.

Chapter One

Elder William Knight knew if he died in this back alley in Manchester, England, his mother's heart would break, his father would attempt to find solace in his ledgers, and his fiancée, Jennie Brimhall, would weep as she boxed her beautiful wedding dress for the attic. *Jennie.* Why had his terrified brain conjured that sweet image? Her visage was often in his thoughts, but it did not belong in this grimy place.

Elder Knight heard running footsteps and shouts from the main street and pushed himself back into the shallow alcove of the fishmonger's shop. He hated fish. He needed to escape the stench before he retched, but more footfalls and angry voices rooted him to the shadows.

"Oye! Whot say we skim this side alley for the Mormon rat? Me and Charlie'll frisk it, and the lot of you go after the other un."

The other one? Will knew the toughs were referring to his brother, Ray, and he prayed for his protection. Hopefully he could make it safely to the train station and back to Liverpool.

Commitment to an ideology was easy when unchallenged, but here, with a thick fog gripping the dark street and a gang of thugs promising injury, commitment became a test of courage. The heavy footfalls of his pursuers echoed in the narrow alley. *They're coming closer!* Unthinkingly, Will fumbled for the shop's door handle. *Stupid to think it would open*. The knob turned, and the door moved inward. He quietly pushed the door open and stepped inside, closing it quickly and turning the lock. He crouched down behind the door and worked to still his breathing. His assailants moved past the shop and out of the alley, their taunting and murderous voices fading into the night. Will's heartbeat slowed, but then he heard someone coming from rooms behind the shop, and it stopped altogether. He closed his eyes as he had when a child. Perhaps the person would miss seeing him. He heard the hiss of a gas lamp and a startled yelp.

"Whot ya doin' there?"

Will's eyes flew open, and he focused on a young woman threatening him with a rolling pin. "Turn down the lamp!" he hissed.

"Whot?"

"The lamp! Turn it down please. It may mean my life."

The young woman reached up, and the light faded.

"Thank you."

"Yer awful polite for a burglar."

"I'm not a burglar, and I wish you no harm."

"Ya be American?"

"Yes," Will answered from his crouched position.

"Get up, then," the woman said.

"I don't think I will."

The woman took a step forward, holding the rolling pin in front of her like a sword. "So whot ya doin' in here?"

They were speaking in lowered voices, but Will still feared the ruffians might hear and return. "I'm hiding. Your door was unlocked, and . . ."

"Hidin'?"

"Yes."

"Somun after yer money?"

He stood and spoke in a normal voice. "After my life, I think."

The rolling pin lowered. "Yer life?"

"Yes." From the dim light coming through the shop windows, he noted the well-worn dress and headscarf of the young woman. "I'm sorry I snuck into your shop, but I was desperate."

"Why was somun after yer life?"

"It's a long story," Will answered.

"Ya did break into our shop, ya know. If me husband and Da weren't down at the pub, they'd be makin' ya tell the tale."

"I'm a preacher."

"Whot?"

"Not so loud," Will pleaded.

The young woman chuckled and lowered her voice. "A preacher? You?"

Will gave her an affronted look. "Yes, me. Why not me?"

"You seem to be all of a pup in the basket," she said with a grin. "And whot? The bloke thought ya was preachin' a bunch of tripe?"

"A gang of ruffians, actually."

"A gang of ruffians? Pshaw! Yer rippen' me bonnet."

"Listen," Will said in his most conciliatory voice. "I'm grateful that you let me stay here to avoid the ruffians, but I think it's time for me to clear off."

The young woman reached to turn up the lamp, and the small dreary shop became visible, along with Will's face. "Now that I get a good look, I'm thinkin' yer not a burglar."

"Thank you for that." He turned to open the door.

"Stay 'way from the park. That's where gangs 'ang out at night. The park and the pubs."

"I'll avoid both." He slowly opened the door and peeked out. The smell of the alley wasn't pleasant, but it was better than the shop. Will lifted his hat. "Thank you again."

"Caw. Ain't you fine." Will stepped into the doorway. "Ah! Jus one more sum'in'!" the shop girl called.

Will turned back. "What's that?"

"Come back in the daylight and buy some fish."

Will gave her a half grin. "I will, absolutely," he said, tipping his hat.

"And preach me some of your tripe," she added with a chuckle.

"It would be my pleasure," Will said, moving out onto the cobblestones. *I would love to share the gospel,* he thought. *But I will absolutely not be buying any fish!* Will laughed softly as he put on his hat and headed for the main street and the train station. He soon lost himself among the carriages and horses and the press of people searching out supper and drink.

Will stepped into the conference house just in time to see Mrs. Reed, the cook, applying a wet cloth to the back of his brother Ray's head.

"So glad you made it back, little brother!" Ray called. "I was just about to send out a posse to find you. How did you escape?"

"Fish."

"Fish?"

"I'll tell the exciting tale at supper," Will said, walking to his brother's side. "What happened to *you*?"

"Ah, just a rock."

"*Just* a rock?" Will evaluated the injury. Mrs. Reed had managed to stop the bleeding since the cut was superficial, yet the large goose egg looked painful. Will laid a hand on his brother's shoulder. "Sorry."

Ray reached up and gingerly touched the lump on the back of his head. "Good thing it wasn't a bigger rock."

"It's no laughing matter," Mrs. Reed scolded as she gathered the medical supplies. "You need to report this to President McMurrin."

"Along with the dozen other times we've been attacked?" Will asked sarcastically.

Mrs. Reed gave him a narrowed look. "*Because* of the other times."

Will felt the reprimand and nodded. "You're right, Sister Reed. We'll write him straightaway."

"Good. Now, get to your studying and that letter. I'll call when supper is ready." She left for the kitchen, mumbling to herself about impudent elders, injuries, and rabbit stew.

"She's a dear old thing," Ray said, standing. "Clucks around like a mother hen."

As the two brothers headed for their room, Will recounted his narrow escape—thanks to the young fishmonger.

Ray entered and threw his satchel on his cot. "We will not be sharing *any* of the facts of this attack with the family. Agreed?"

"Agreed." Will went to the desk and secured paper and his fountain pen. "Remember what we wrote to them when that angry street vendor threw rotted fruit at us?"

Ray grinned. "Dear parents, today we met a lovely street vendor who invited us to lunch."

Will started laughing. "So do you want to write the fabrications, or should I?"

"You do it. My head hurts," Ray said, sitting on his cot and placing his satchel on the floor. "I'm going to lie down for a bit before supper."

"All right, then. If you trust me."

"Of course. Just tell them about the good food we're eating, the friendly people, and how much we miss home."

"Well, that last part is true," Will said with a sigh.

Ray laid his head carefully on the pillow. "Yes, that last part is indeed true." His next words were soft and drifting. "Oh! And write a warning to Inez that she'd better be taking excellent care of my horse."

Will sat at the desk and picked up the pen. "All right, first a letter home, then after supper I'll write the letter to President McMurrin, and maybe one to Jennie."

"Jennie? That one is going to take a lot of imagination," Ray said.

"I'll tell her that the lilacs should be blooming soon and that I met a fishmonger who wants to hear the gospel."

"She'll like that lovely half-truth," Ray said on a yawn.

Good thing my Jennie will never have to know the difficult life of a missionary, Will thought to himself. He put the pen to the paper and began writing.

Dear parents,

Having a jolly time in England . . .

NOTE

Anti-Mormon League: In the mid-1800s a British apostate by the name of Jarman wrote a spurious book about his brief time as a member of The Church of Jesus Christ of Latter-day Saints. People in the British Isles were joining the Church in great numbers, and Mr. Jarman made his living vilifying the Church and forming anti-Mormon leagues, whose members harassed the Saints and tried to sabotage missionary efforts.

Chapter Two

"The ivory petticoat or the white?"

Jennie looked up from her mending to scrutinize the proffered undergarments. "The white is lovely, but the ivory is much more practical for travel."

"Ivory it is, then," Inez said, hanging the white petticoat in her chiffo-robe and folding the ivory into the steamer trunk. "Of course, we'll never compete with the French fashions."

"I don't know," Jennie answered. "Some of the seamstresses in Salt Lake are quite capable." She snipped the thread from the button she'd been securing and held out the blouse to her friend. "This blouse is *very* elegant. It was made by Christine Bose, wasn't it?"

"Yes, but that was nearly three years ago," Inez said. "I'm sure it's out of fashion."

"I think not," Jennie countered. "I can see you walking on the Champs-Élysées in that blouse, your blue pinstriped skirt, and your yellow-and-blue hat."

Inez sat on the bed and gave Jennie a squeeze around the waist. "And you in your gray skirt and vest, with the pink blouse . . . perhaps carrying a parasol."

"Mademoiselle Knight and Mademoiselle Brimhall on the Champs-Élysées!" Jennie said breathlessly.

"First England and France, and then perhaps Germany," Inez said, a note of wonder in her voice.

"I would love to see Switzerland too," Jennie added.

"And Austria and Italy!" Inez said laughing.

Jennie joined her. "Why come home at all?"

"This trip *is* a dream, Jennie, and we are the luckiest girls in the world."

"Lucky?" Jennie responded. "I worked hard for every mile of this trip."

Inez stood and took a skirt from the bed. "Oh, piffle. Your father is sending you, just like mine."

"Yes, because I worked hard securing my pedagogy degree and then spent many months teaching," Jennie answered.

"I know. I'm just teasing," Inez said, hanging her skirt in the trunk. She sighed. "I think it's amazing how everything has fallen into place for us to go on this trip."

"I think so too!" Jennie agreed. "Who would have thought our parents would let us go without a chaperone?"

"Who would have thought they'd say yes to the trip in the first place?"

"I suppose they saw how much a trip abroad meant to us."

Inez smiled. "We've only been talking about it since we were fifteen." She gave Jennie a knowing grin. "Besides, I think my mother really wants me to check on Ray and Will."

"To make sure they're well?"

"To make sure they're not dodging their missionary duties."

Jennie laughed. "I can't see Will dodging *any* responsibility."

"Says his dutiful fiancée." Jennie blushed. "And, here's another miracle of the trip," Inez added. "Look how your health has improved over the past few months. Your father said you couldn't go unless your health improved, and look at you—fit as a fiddle."

Jennie nodded. "That *has* been a blessing."

Inez went to look out her bedroom window. "A few weeks from now we'll be looking at the fair green hills of England."

"So stop dreaming and finish packing!" Jennie scolded. "What's left?" She eyed the assortment of clothing on the bed.

"Just a few more things," Inez said, turning from the window. She picked up a hat and placed it in a hat box. "I can't decide which shoes to take."

"At least you have choices," Jennie said with a shrug. "I have only one decent pair, as 'frugal' is the Brimhalls' middle name."

"Well, that won't do! We'll just have to go shopping when we get to England."

Jennie sighed. "Do you think Elder Knight will mind seeing me in my old, scuffed shoes?"

"I think he will be thrilled to see you even if you're wearing worn-out work boots and a flour sack," Inez teased.

Jennie shrugged. "Well, after I sent the letter with news of our final itinerary, his response seemed . . . " Her voice drifted away.

"What?"

"Less than excited."

"Oh, you know Will—moderate, pragmatic."

Jennie smiled, but Inez noted that it was half-hearted. After a sigh, Jennie said, "Well, that's true; he is pragmatic, but I also think he and Ray might be so involved in their mission work that we'll be a distraction."

"I certainly *hope* I'm a distraction!" Inez stated. "I have every intention of being a distraction. I haven't seen my brothers in months and months—Will for over a year, so they can both give me a few days of their time without complaining."

Jennie laughed, and the tension eased. Just then Inez's father came to the open doorway. "How goes the packing?"

"Almost finished, Father," Inez said.

"We're having a family council downstairs, and your presence is required."

Jennie stood. "I'll be on my way home then."

"Actually, Miss Brimhall, you are also requested. Your parents are here."

"My parents? Here for *your* family council?"

Mr. Knight smiled at the shocked look on Jennie's face. "It is a combined family council." He turned to the door. "Come as soon as you can."

"Yes, sir," Inez and Jennie said together.

Mr. Knight spoke as he stepped out into the hallway. "Oh, the stake president is also in attendance."

The young women stood in perplexed silence. Finally, Jennie turned to her friend. "What do you think is happening?"

"I have no idea."

The two girls checked their images in the mirror, straightened their skirts, and headed downstairs, hoping their curiosity would be given adequate satisfaction.

"A mission?"

"Yes, Sister Knight, a mission."

"To Great Britain?"

President Partridge smiled. "Yes."

"But . . . women, I mean . . . single women don't serve missions," Jennie stammered.

"Well, it seems that is about to change, Sister Brimhall," President Partridge said. "As I understand it, the First Presidency has received letters from several mission presidencies, especially President McMurrin from Great Britain, requesting single sister missionaries."

"I do not wish to seem impertinent, President Partridge, but do you know why?"

He evaluated the two young women. "The mission leaders in England have indicated a growing animosity toward the Church, spurred on by the distribution of anti-Mormon literature."

"But hasn't that always been the way of things?" Inez said.

"Yes, but this vitriol comes from apostate members of the Church in Britain, and sadly, many of the notions concern the women of the Church."

Inez glanced over at her friend and noted the guileless expression on her face.

"The preaching of these groups declares that women in Utah are slovenly, uneducated, and downtrodden."

"They don't know us then, do they?" Inez said with a smile.

The president shook his head. "They also say that Utah women are kept behind high walls."

"I'd like to see anyone try and keep Inez behind a high wall," Jennie said.

Inez tried to control her jollity. "Surely they don't believe such foolishness, President Partridge."

"Many *do* believe it. They also believe that here in Utah, women are slaves to their husbands, and if they don't do exactly what they are told, they can be killed."

Jennie and Inez sobered immediately.

"What an invention," Inez protested.

"A lie," Jennie stated flatly.

"A lie indeed," President Partridge concurred.

Inez looked at Jennie and saw her face drain of color. She turned back to President Partridge. "So what do the mission presidents think *we* can do?"

"I believe Sister Elizabeth McCune may have played a part in this."

Inez leaned forward. "Sister McCune of the Salt Lake McCunes?"

"Yes," President Partridge said, securing a chair and bringing it to the side of the settee. He sat down and spoke directly to the pair. "Several months ago, Brother and Sister McCune went to tour Europe and to visit their son in the Great Britain Mission. Sister McCune attended several street meetings with the elders and noted the opposition and harassment. It seems that at one meeting some men were making insulting comments about the deprived and addlepated women in Utah. Sister McCune stepped forward and announced to the crowd that she was a Mormon woman from Utah, and she had a very different story to tell."

"Good for her," Inez said.

"Good indeed. The entire mood changed, and people began asking her frank questions about her life in Utah and the faith she professed. President McMurrin was at the meeting and, without warning, announced that she would be speaking at the London conference in the evening."

Inez sat straighter. "And that's what they want us to do? Speak in conferences . . . "

"And talk to angry crowds of people?" Jennie interrupted, giving a worried look to her father and stepmother, Flora.

"There won't *always* be angry crowds," President Partridge encouraged.

"Well, I feel a shoddy example of Utah womanhood compared with Sister McCune," Inez stated bluntly.

The president stood and replaced his chair. He turned to face the girls.

"I have no doubt that you two will be remarkable examples of faith, and it seems the First Presidency of the Church feels the same."

After a long pause, Inez spoke. "When would we leave?"

"The same day already scheduled for your tour. Only now you will be joined by a group of Saints also heading east."

"Are they all going to England?" Jennie asked.

"No. Some are stopping in New York and Philadelphia, but there are several who will cross the ocean with you."

Inez looked over at her parents. "And how long will we be away from home?"

"That I don't know, Sister Knight. I think the Prophet will keep a close eye on your work and evaluate your length of service."

"President Partridge, I . . . I would like time to discuss this with my parents, and to pray," Jennie said simply.

Inez felt calm relief wash over her. *Thank heaven for my wise friend.*

The president smiled. "Of course, Sister Brimhall, but the time for your departure draws near, so don't linger. Now, if you'll excuse me, I need to speak alone with your parents for a moment."

The girls were quiet as they made their way back to Inez's room, and they continued their silence when Inez shut the door and it was just the two of them. Jennie moved to Inez's dressing table and picked up her friend's well-worn Book of Mormon. She stood quietly, leafing through its pages. "What are we going to do?" she breathed out on a sigh.

Inez sat on her bed. "Just as you said—we're going to pray about it."

"And then?"

"Well, I have a fairly sure idea I will be going on a mission," Inez stated.

Jennie turned quickly. "Really?"

"Yes."

"But how can you be sure? It will take days to figure this out."

"We don't have days."

Jennie let out another big breath of air and sat down on the bed beside her friend. "I know, but I am not one to make hasty decisions."

"Our parents will help us. And the Lord." Inez gave Jennie a forlorn look. "But if you will allow me to be perfectly honest, I don't think you'll be going."

Jennie was stunned by this statement. "Why not?"

"Well, you would not serve as much of an example for the Church now, would you? Far too slovenly."

Jennie laughed. "Well then, *you* certainly cannot go, as ignorant and uneducated as you are."

"And you're as homely as a post."

"And you're as stubborn as a mule."

"And don't forget clumsy," Inez added.

"Oh indeed! How could I forget clumsy?"

Inez looked around at her lovely bedroom with the damask curtains, crystal lamps, and silk coverlet on the bed. "And then, of course, we are both downtrodden."

Jennie nodded in agreement and took Inez by the hand. "Terribly downtrodden. Both of us—totally unsuited." She gave the hand a squeeze. "You have always been able to come right to the point, my friend."

"Exactly! We are totally unworthy of this calling, so it has to be some sort of mistake—a big mistake."

The girls were on the verge of convincing themselves when Brother Knight's voice came up the stairs to them. "Sister Brimhall! Your parents are ready to leave now."

The girls stood abruptly, and Jennie brought Inez into an embrace. "Oh my! This day has not ended with the same expectations as it began."

Inez shook her head. "No, it hasn't."

Jennie stepped back, took a deep breath, and moved to the door. As she opened it, she turned and fixed Inez with a half grin. "There is just one problem with your theory, my dear Inez, about this call being a big mistake."

"And that is?"

"I don't think the Lord makes mistakes." Jennie moved out into the hallway, leaving Inez alone to contemplate her statement and what it meant for their futures.

NOTES

The call: Inez and Jennie's call to abandon their tour of Europe to serve a mission in England is recorded in Inez Knight's journal. At one point in their mission, the girls were given permission to take a three-week tour of Europe. For the sake of continuity, I did not include this holiday in the story.

Elizabeth Ann Claridge McCune: Elizabeth Claridge was born in Bedfordshire, England, on February 19, 1852. Her parents joined the Church and immigrated to Utah in 1853. As an adult, she married A. W. McCune, a rich mining magnate. They became one of the notable families of Salt Lake City.

Brigham Young Academy: Inez Knight and Jennie Brimhall were both graduates of the Brigham Young Academy, which later became Brigham Young University. Jennie received a degree in pedagogy and went on to teach at the academy. Jennie's father, George Brimhall, served as the institution's first president and thereafter as president of Brigham Young University, to which Inez's father, Jesse Knight, contributed sizable donations.

Chapter Three

Inez could not find her gloves. She looked in her wardrobe, on the side table, even under the bed—to no avail. The pesky things showed up when she grabbed her hat off the bed. She snarled at them for playing hide-and-seek when there was no time for games. She changed her shoes from travel to decorative and back to travel, poked herself in the eye putting on her hat, and nearly fell down the stairs in a frenzied attempt to avoid stepping on the cat.

During this pandemonium, her father efficiently readied the carriage and loaded her trunk, her mother assembled a boxed supper of favorite foods, and her two younger sisters, Jennie Pearl and Addie, sat in the parlor, weeping. Inez now stood staring out the open front door, fighting the urge to run back to her bed and hide under the coverlet. She stepped out onto the front porch and looked east. An orange sun was pushing its head above the snowcapped Wasatch peaks, and Inez held her breath to ward off emotion and tears. She wondered if Jennie was looking at the same sky and feeling the same feelings. *England? What was the Lord thinking?* Inez tugged at her gloves and adjusted her hat. She had never ventured far from home—the canyon outside of Provo for summer camping and picnics, St. George to do genealogy, and last summer a trip to California with her family. On that adventure Jennie had come along for companionship and convalescing. The prior winter had not been good to her friend—pneumonia with its attendant weakness and worry. The winter they'd just come through had been milder, and Jennie had caught only a slight head cold, which she'd thrown off quickly. Her father and stepmother, Flora, had fretted nonetheless. *How brave of them to let her fulfill this call,* Inez thought.

Her father brought their four-person open-air carriage to the front of the house. "Woah!" he called out to the two sorrel mares. He gave Inez an encouraging smile. "Are you ready, Daughter?"

Inez put on a show. "England will not know what to make of me."

William Knight Sr. chuckled. "That is most assuredly true."

Inez moved to the edge of the porch. "Thank you for your blessing last night. It will be a great comfort to me."

Her father cleared his throat and spoke in a low rumble. "It will comfort me also." He smiled and gave her a wink. "It's one thing to send your sons off to foreign adventures—a tad more difficult to send a daughter."

Mrs. Knight came onto the porch at that moment with Jennie Pearl and Addie in tow. "Indeed," she said, shutting the door and handing Inez the supper box.

"Oh, I will keep Ray and Will in line," Inez said. "I've packed a stick in my trunk in case they've forgotten how to be good." Jennie Pearl and Addie laughed at that, and Inez gave each a one-armed hug.

"Well then, it's time to go!" her father called out heartily as he hopped down from the driver's station to help the ladies into the carriage. "You sit up here with me, Amanda Inez," he said extending his hand to her. "I want a few more minutes to lecture you about duty and commitment."

"Oh, then I think I'd rather sit in the back with Mother and the girls," Inez responded, snatching back her hand.

He kept his hand out. "All right, I repent. No lectures. Just your company will suit me."

Her chest tightened, and Inez set her jaw against the emotion. She took her father's hand, and he helped her up. She was relieved when he turned away to help the rest of the family, for tears were leaking out of the corners of her eyes. Inez took a deep breath and tried to compose herself. *I must think of this as leaving on my tour,* she told herself fiercely. *I'll be meeting Jennie at the train station, and we'll be off on our escapade. Just a pleasure trip abroad—nothing more. Not months away from home—perhaps years. No unfriendly confrontations or the terror of speaking in public. No strange foods or strange accents. Just a pleasure trip.*

Inez started when her father hoisted himself onto the driver's seat. "Are you all right, Daughter? You look a thousand miles away."

"More like five thousand."

"Ah." He slapped the lines on the horses' rumps. "Walk on, Captain! Walk on, Magic!" The horses pulled, and the carriage moved forward.

Inez fought the urge to turn and look back as each clop of the horses' hooves carried her away from home. She tried to think of Big Ben and Westminster Abbey, but her mind kept conjuring images of blooming lilac bushes and Mother in her comical gardening hat, planting vegetables.

Her father's voice broke into her thoughts. "You will have plenty of care, Inez. President McMurrin and the conference presidents will be your shepherds."

"I know. I don't worry about that."

"But?"

"It's the elders. I don't think the other missionaries will be thrilled to have us in the mission field."

Her father brought the rig to a stop at a cross street. "Girls trying to break into the boys-only club?"

"Exactly. Or perhaps they'll consider our feelings too fragile for the mission field or think that we're not doctrinally as smart, or that physically we'll be unable to keep up."

Her father turned to look at her. "Gracious. That is a whole lot of worry for one thimble." He clucked at the horses. "Walk on!" The carriage lurched as the horses moved out. "I actually don't see that happening, Daughter."

"You don't?"

"No. I don't think those young men would have the nerve to scorn you. Most of them have tough pioneer ancestors—grandfathers and grandmothers who walked across this country with wagon train companies or by handcarts."

"Why would that help?"

"Well, they know their grandmothers would take a switch to their backsides if they thought women weren't as good as men."

Inez laughed. "I know Grandma Knight would take a switch to them."

Her father laughed with her. After a time, he sobered and gave her a tender smile. "Well, there you go." He turned the rig onto the road to the train station.

A woman in an oncoming buggy waved her hand in the air, indicating she wanted a chat with the Knight family, and Inez groaned.

"Oh dear," Inez grumbled. "The ill wind of Sister Winslow."

Her father laughed. "Yes, but we still must mind our manners."

"If I must."

The woman pulled her rig alongside the Knights' carriage and smiled broadly, but Inez noticed a hardness in her eyes. "Good morning, Brother and Sister Knight! On your way, I see. I suppose this would be a fine day for traveling under different circumstances . . . " She glanced at Inez. "But this is such an unusual occurrence."

"Good morning, Sister Winslow," Inez's father said.

"Sending off young single girls into the mission field? What a strange notion. What will the Brethren think of next? And you already have two sons over there. . . . I wonder why they don't just send your entire family?"

"Now, that is a splendid idea, Sister Winslow! I wonder why they didn't think of it," Inez's father said with a genial smile.

The acerbic woman narrowed her eyes and continued her observations. "How do they expect young women to keep up with the demands of a mission? Their minds and bodies aren't fit for such pressures."

Inez felt like Sister Winslow might have been telling the truth until she heard her mother's words from behind her.

"Goodness, Marlett, Inez and Jennie are the cream of the crop. You know how faithful they are. They follow the Word of Wisdom, and they know the scriptures inside and out. And *I* know President Woodruff was inspired to call them at this exact time to fulfill this vital calling. So you may want to give some thought and prayer to your disapproval." Sister Winslow sat with her mouth open, unable to utter a sound. Inez turned to look at her mother, who gave her a nod. "And now, Mr. Knight, I think we need to be on our way so Inez does not miss her train," her mother instructed in a confident tone.

"Yes, dear," her father said, working hard to control the laughter Inez could see bubbling up inside him. "Walk on then," he called, tapping the lines on the horses' rumps. "Good day, Sister Winslow." As soon as they were out of Sister Winslow's hearing, her father started chuckling. "Well done, Sister Knight. Well done."

"Most likely I'll regret it come Sunday," her mother said in a remorseful tone.

Mr. Knight burst out laughing. "Well then, you can repent and be forgiven."

Inez laughed too and turned to her mother. "Thank you."

Mrs. Knight smiled and shook her head. "I just don't understand why some Saints feel the need to judge other people's business."

"There will always be pot stirrers, my love."

The smile slid from Inez's face. *And I'm heading to a land where pot stirrers abound,* she thought. A shadow crossed her mood. They were nearing the train station, and she squinted to see if the Brimhall carriage was already at the depot. "I see Jennie! They're unloading her trunk."

A short time later the Knight family arrived at the station. As soon as her father stopped the carriage, Inez scrambled out and raced to Jennie. The two friends embraced.

"How are you feeling?" Inez asked in a rush.

"Scared," Jennie answered.

"Me too, but I'm going to put on a brave face."

Suddenly Jennie tensed. "They're putting my trunk in the baggage car."

Inez turned. "Mine too."

They locked arms and watched the process in silence. Mr. Brimhall came to stand beside them. "Yes, you're actually going," he said quietly. "Into the land of Shakespeare. I'm a bit envious."

"I'll try and find you an early edition of *Hamlet* or *King Lear*," Jennie said.

"I think I'd prefer one of the Bard's comedies—perhaps the *Comedy of Errors*."

"That's probably going to be the title of my mission," Inez said pointedly, and Jennie laughed.

Silence again enfolded the group as the baggage handlers closed and locked the baggage-car door and went about their business as if it were just another day. Mr. Brimhall blew out a breath of air. "And I am doing my best to put on a gallant show of strength."

"That's what *we're* doing," Inez said, glancing at him and forcing a smile.

"Of course—it is what courage demands." The train whistle blew, and

Jennie and Inez started. "Would you two remarkable ladies like some advice?" Mr. Brimhall asked.

"Yes, please, Father," Jennie said, a catch in her voice.

"Pray."

Inez waited for more words of wisdom from the renowned teacher, but none came.

Jennie stepped to him and took his hand. "Please take care of yourself." Suddenly the threesome was surrounded by family and well-wishers, and the precious moment vanished into the noise and bustle.

The last of the passengers were entering their assigned coaches, and the final whistle blasted. Inez and Jennie were unceremoniously ushered to the train, everyone calling out and waving. Inez was grateful for the hasty parting as it gave time only for brief hugs and few words. As she stepped onto the train, her gallant show of strength crumbled, and she hesitated.

"No turning back!" Jennie called to her, planting her hand on Inez's back and pushing her forward.

Just as they found their cabin, the train began to move. Inez lurched to the window and opened it. Jennie joined her to wave their handkerchiefs at those left behind. The sobs and calls from the platform grew fainter and fainter, replaced by the thrum of the moving train.

Inez slumped onto the padded seat, wiping tears away with her gloved hands.

"I will go and do the things which the Lord hath commanded . . . " Jennie quoted. She broke into tears and covered her face.

Inez closed her eyes, leaned her head back against the cushion, and lost herself in the monotonous clack of the wheels on the track.

NOTES

Inez's character: Inez Knight's journal records gems of information concerning her temperament, character, and foibles. Inez writes often of her propensity to stumble, bump into things, and fall down.

Early genealogy work: Since 1894, The Church of Jesus Christ of Latter-day Saints has dedicated time and resources to collecting records of genealogical importance. In the early days of research, Inez would have had to rely on oral family histories, family Bibles, individual journals, written family records, newspapers, Church records at the Historian's Office, and county and town records. Inez's genealogical foray to St. George is mentioned in Orson F. Whitney's *History of Utah*.

Chapter Four

To the Knight Household

Dear beloved parents,

Our company of twenty-six is in Philadelphia awaiting tomorrow's departure of our ship, the Belgenland. *I am faring well, and though I know the coming event will test my mettle, I am not fearful. I must confess to tears from Provo to Springville, but that is just because my mind kept conjuring the image of you two waving from the platform and Mother sobbing. After our cry, Jennie and I made a pact to pretend that we were merely embarking on our originally scheduled journey. That served to calm us and allowed for a bit of excitement to return.*

I have seen a mixture of enthralling and tedious sights as the train crossed this notable country: forests, majestic mountains, and hundreds of miles of flat, monotonous prairie. Father, you were only two when Grandfather Knight died and Grandmother Knight came with nine children to Utah in a wagon train. I cannot imagine it. Such courage. It took you months to cross while it took us only a week by train. We truly live in an age of wonder—trains, light bulbs, steamships, and cameras with the photographic film inside the box. Jennie and I saw a man using one during our brief stop in Chicago.

This will be a short missive as I wish to post it before leaving tomorrow. I will write a long letter while I'm on the ship and include details about our side trip from Buffalo to the Niagara Falls. Oh, Mother, it is the most splendid sight I have ever encountered! Nothing you have seen in pictures can explain the grandeur of this body of water. Indeed, I'm sure I will be unable to paint the picture for you with the meager words in my vocabulary.

Jennie and I are well, though we are tired. We feel the weight of our callings and pray continually for the guidance of the Spirit. We have both been raised to be trustworthy girls, and we will attempt to honor our family through our service.

I must confess, dear ones, that I don't feel very brave of heart at the moment, so I am glad that Jennie is by my side as we embark on this endeavor. She is doing well, but periodic worry for her father's ill health distracts her. I know he is your dear friend, Father, so please continue to watch out for him.

I will close now since the time draws near for my final sleep on American soil (at least for a time). Tomorrow I will rise early, eat my breakfast, and depart for the docks. I try not to think of the distance between us, which grows wider every day. I will dwell instead on thoughts of seeing Ray and Will. I know by now they have received the telegraph of our arrival and the change in our status from traveler to missionary. I wonder what their faces will tell me when I see them in Liverpool.

Tender love to the family.
I remain your devoted daughter,
Amanda Inez

NOTES

Letter: Much of this letter is taken from Inez Knight's journal.

Newel Knight and Lydia Goldthwaite Knight: Inez's grandparents were some of the early stalwart members of The Church of Jesus Christ of Latter-day Saints. Newel Knight was a personal friend of the Prophet Joseph Smith and served in many leadership roles.

George H. Brimhall's health: Brother Brimhall suffered from heart and kidney problems most of his adult life.

Telegraph: The International Telegraph Union was formed in 1865 for worldwide application of the telegraphic system. The following year, the first successful transatlantic cables were completed.

Chapter Five

Inez found Jennie on deck, standing by the railing and staring out into the misty morning. The fog wrapped the ship in an eerie stillness, and though Inez could hear the engines and the hiss of the ship's movement through the water, the sound was muted as though the world was wrapped in cotton. Inez had come searching for her friend when she'd found her absent from breakfast. Her own appetite had been blunted by the excitement of arrival, but she still managed a bowl of porridge, three eggs, and a slice of bread. Inez slipped quietly beside her friend so as not to startle her. Jennie glanced quickly over, then back to the unseen horizon.

"I want to see the shoreline when we approach," Jennie said.

"Well, we're still an hour from docking. Perhaps things will clear."

Jennie rubbed her gloved hands together. "I'm trying not to take it as a bad omen. This trip has been filled with bad omens and difficulties."

"It's not been that bad," Inez said to console.

"Says the one who suffered no seasickness." Jennie shuddered. "The rocking of the ship and the water coming into the dining room? Frightful."

"All in the past," Inez countered. "In an hour or so, we will be on firm ground."

"And what of that German fellow who jumped overboard and drowned?"

"Let's not borrow trouble," Inez said quickly. "I see this morning as a good omen. The wind is still, and the sea is calm."

Jennie took a deep breath. "That's true. My seasickness has finally left me."

"Faces to the future!" Inez said, pointing dramatically toward the hidden shores of England. They stood in silence for a moment, shivering in the moist chill. "Shall we promenade?" Inez asked. "It's cold just standing."

Jennie nodded, and they began walking.

"Oh!" Inez reached into the pocket of her coat. "I brought you a Chelsea bun."

Jennie reached out immediately. "I've grown to like these."

Inez grinned. "I know. If Chelsea buns are any indication, we should like all the English cookery."

Jennie broke off a piece and stuck it in her mouth. "Not quite as good as Flora's cinnamon bread, but still tasty."

"Is anything as good as your stepmother's cinnamon bread?" Inez questioned. "Well, maybe her apple cake or chicken and dumplings or . . . "

"Don't!" Jennie pled on a laugh. "You're going to make me homesick."

"Sorry," Inez said. "Faces to the future, Sister Brimhall." Jennie nodded. "Besides, *your* future will soon include the face of your fiancé."

"Oh my, don't talk about that either. I'm convinced that he will *not* be thrilled to see me."

Inez gave her a skeptical look. "'How do I love thee? Let me count the ways.' Wasn't that the poem my brother gave you the day he left for his mission?" Inez noticed the rise of color in Jennie's face. "Ah! See? You have nothing to worry about, Sister Brimhall. I have a feeling Elder Knight is pacing the Liverpool dock at this very moment."

Jennie took Inez's arm. "I hope you're right."

At that moment a loud, low blast came from the ship's smokestack, and the girls covered their ears.

"That must be the signal that we're getting close to docking!" Inez yelled, and Jennie nodded.

"We should make sure we have everything packed," Jennie called out as another blast sounded.

The two girls turned and headed for their cabin as fast as conditions and propriety warranted. As they were about to leave the top deck, they saw two crewmen attaching a British Union Jack to the ship's flagpole.

"England, we have arrived!" Inez called excitedly.

"He's there between the tall gentleman and another elder," Inez said, handing the binoculars to Jennie.

Jennie quickly put the binoculars to her eyes and scanned the docks. "I can't see!" she said in frustration. "It's blurry."

"Adjust the focus," Inez counseled, showing her friend the knob.

Jennie quickly turned the knob. "Oh! Oh yes! That's better." She continued scanning as Inez waited. "I . . . I can't find him, Inez. Are you sure you saw him? Wait! Wait! There he is!"

"I told you he'd be on the dock."

"There he is!" Jennie called out, waving with her free hand and then dropping it quickly. "Silly. We're still too far away for him to see me." She let out an exasperated breath of air. "Why are we moving so slowly?"

Inez laughed. "I don't think the captain wants to crash full speed into the dock."

Jennie lowered the binoculars and chided herself. "I'm being ridiculous. And here I am being a hog with the glasses."

Inez laughed. "That's very noble of you, but you keep looking."

"I'm glad the fog lifted," Jennie said, returning to her scrutiny of the people on the dock. "Who's that man next to Will?"

"Probably the mission president."

Jennie stared over at Inez. "Goodness, that makes our calling rather real, doesn't it?"

A steward came by calling out a mantra to the passengers: "Levels one and two will depart on the forward gangplank; levels three and four, on the aft gangplank. Docking at oh ten hundred." He passed by, continuing to call out to the eager passengers.

Inez hugged Jennie around the waist. "Come on, Sister Brimhall! Let's go show them our faith and our fortitude."

Jennie stood straighter. "I may have to rely on you for fortitude, my friend."

Inez nodded. "And I will rely on your faith."

NOTE

Death at sea: The incident concerning the German passenger who threw himself overboard is an actual event Inez recorded in her journal. She noted that the occurrence was unsettling for both her and Jennie.

CHAPTER SIX

As Inez descended the aft gangplank, she caught her brother's eye and waved enthusiastically. This action proved disastrous as she lost concentration, tripped over one of the rungs on the gangplank, and plowed into the gentleman in front of her. He turned abruptly, knocking the hat off the man in front of him, who lunged forward to catch it before it tumbled from the gangplank. He was not successful. Inez and Jennie watched in horror as the bowler hat flew through the air and landed with a plop on the murky water, where it floated like a contented duck. Everyone stood transfixed by the scene until the hatless man turned to glare at them.

"That happened to be a gift from my wife," he snarled.

"I'm sorry. I'm so so sorry," Inez moaned. "Please, let me buy you a new one."

"Don't be absurd," the man said, turning with a snort and striding down to the dock, muttering curses.

The man Inez had bumped into smiled at her. "Don't be vexed. I was the one who bumped it off."

"But only because *I* knocked into you."

The man chuckled. "I'm just glad you didn't end up in the drink."

"Hey! Get moving!" someone yelled from behind them.

"I am not making a glowing first impression," Inez grumbled as she, Jennie, and the unknown male casually resumed their journey down the gangplank. "And how embarrassing to be a fool in front of the mission president."

"Everything will be fine, Inez. Perhaps none of them were watching."

Inez thought she heard suppressed laughter behind Jennie's sympathy, but before she could give it another thought, she'd reached the dock and her brother Will was wrapping her in a bear hug.

"Of course! Of course!" he laughed. "Just like you to make such an entrance! I've missed your antics!" Inez growled, and Will laughed again.

She pushed away from him. "Where is Ray?"

"Working in Bradford."

"Well, I believe *he* would have given me a proper greeting."

"Welcome to England, dear sister." Will gave a little bow. "I'm so very glad to see you!" His gaze fixed on Jennie. "So glad to see both of you." He stepped forward and took Jennie's hands in his. "So very glad."

The formidable, bearded man stepped forward. "Elder Knight, I believe introductions are in order."

Will gathered his wits. "Of . . . of course, President McMurrin." He brought Jennie forward. "Jennie, this is President McMurrin of the European Mission. This is President Wells of the Manchester Conference, and these two fine fellows are Elder Rose and Elder Eldridge. Brethren, may I present my . . . um . . . Sister Lucy Jane Brimhall. Who mostly goes by 'Jennie.'" His face flushed with color. "But of course, that's not what we'll be calling her here on the mission—here she'll be Sister Brimhall."

Jennie came to his rescue. "Such a great pleasure, gentlemen."

Inez laid her hand on her brother's arm, and he jumped. "Oh! And this is my dear sister, Amanda Inez Knight."

The men all spoke at once with greetings and handshakes, with no one mentioning the incident on the gangplank. Inez was grateful. As the chatter quieted, President Wells stepped forward.

"Sisters, welcome! Welcome! We are thrilled to have you here; indeed, we are. . . . And two such fitting girls for the task. I know you will be mighty ambassadors for the cause." Inez shifted uncomfortably. She felt that "mighty ambassador" might be a title higher than she could reach. She focused her attention on President Wells as he continued with his accolades. "When the scorners get a look at you two, they will most assuredly have to eat their words. Indeed, they will."

Despite being petrified by what he was saying, Inez liked President

Wells. He was warm and genuine and seemed like someone who would listen to the woes of those under his care. That thought made Inez pray fervently for an absence of woes to report. She took a breath and focused back on what President Wells was saying.

"I don't know where the president is assigning you to labor, Sister Knight and Sister Brimhall, but I hope to keep you in the Manchester area for a few days at least. We surely need you to preach in our part of the vineyard—indeed, we do." He turned expectantly to President McMurrin. "What say we send them out with the elders this afternoon, President? Perhaps a street meeting or singing in the park?"

Inez calculated that the look on Jennie's face prompted President McMurrin to politely take over the conversation. "We may want to give them a day to settle in, right, sisters?"

"We'll do whatever you want us to do, President McMurrin," Jennie said with a conviction that Inez knew was more faith than fact.

President McMurrin smiled at her. "For now, I think it's time we gather your luggage and help you through customs."

President Wells clapped his hands together. "Yes! Luggage, customs, and then on to the mission home!" He clapped his hands again. "I tell you, the disbelievers are not going to know what to make of you two."

Inez glanced over at Jennie. That was exactly what the newest missionaries in the Great Britain Mission feared the most.

Inez and Jennie sat staring out the open windows of the four-person carriage as it rattled along the cobblestone streets of Liverpool. Horses, wagons, carriages, vendors, and people converged in a mass of noise and chaos. Inez craned her neck, trying to take in the formidable buildings, church steeples, and smokestacks. Smoke hung in the chill morning air, obliterating the blue of the sky and the salty tang of the air from the ocean. Inez shook her head. Salt Lake City was a town and Provo a village compared to this bustling metropolis.

"So how do you find the first stop on your British journey?" President McMurrin asked.

"Busy," Inez said as a fire wagon raced by their carriage, so near that she could have reached out and touched it.

Inez and Jennie turned from their windows to focus on their traveling companions. President McMurrin had an inquisitive expression, while Will was grinning.

"Why are you grinning?" Jennie asked.

"Because you have the same look on your face as I did when I first arrived."

Jennie smiled back. "It is a bit to take in."

"Overwhelming," Inez added. "We saw the outskirts of Philadelphia when we passed through, but it was nothing like this."

Jennie looked back out her window. "It needs a good scrubbing," she said simply, as if the observation were obvious. "I feel as though I want to take soap and a scrub brush to every building."

"I agree," Inez said. "I mean . . . the structures are grand, but . . . everything is . . . dirty."

"The Industrial Revolution," President McMurrin said.

"Of course," Jennie said, turning her face to the president. "It's one thing to study it in the classroom; it's another to see it."

"And smell it," Inez added. She suddenly sat straighter. "Oh! That . . . that sounded very superior of me, didn't it?" Will laughed at her. "I promise I don't have a lofty opinion of myself, President, and I don't look down on anyone. I plan to work very hard while I'm here, and . . . and . . . it's just that . . ."

President McMurrin leaned forward. "Sister Knight, there is not one of us who has not voiced the same opinion about the smell of this glorious place."

Inez gave him a half grin and leaned back in her seat. Turning her gaze to the outside, she vowed to keep quiet until they reached the mission home. She was tired, nervous, and disappointed. Tired and nervous she well understood, but disappointed? Why did she feel disappointed? She thought about the once highly anticipated trip to Europe that she and Jennie had talked about for years: sightseeing in London and Paris, eating delicious untried delicacies, walking the enchanting boulevards dressed in their best outfits. They would have visited museums and practiced their French. They would have attended the opera and ridden in fine carriages. They would have . . . Inez felt the press of tears at the back of her throat. She tried to talk herself out of the melancholy, but it assaulted her like the jangle of noise from the street.

"Only a few more blocks and we'll be there," President McMurrin announced. "You two must feel a bit frayed at the edges."

"Not at all, President!" Jennie said with vigor. "Inez and I are excited to get started." Inez looked at her friend as though she had a monkey sitting on her head. "We do not wish to be treated like hothouse flowers, do we, Sister Knight?"

Inez opened her mouth and then shut it, as no words were forthcoming.

"No. We want to be treated just like the elders," Jennie continued.

President McMurrin smiled at her. "I don't know if that's possible, Sister Brimhall. You two are novelties, and I have a feeling you might be pampered by the brethren, at least at first."

Inez thought a few weeks or months of pampering sounded heavenly, but Jennie was having none of it.

"No, President. You must tell the elders that they are to hold us to the same standards. No mollycoddling and no special favors."

"I see."

Will leaned toward her. "At the very least, will you allow us to be gentlemen, Sister Brimhall?"

Inez laughed at that, but Jennie remained stoic. "We would expect nothing less, Elder Knight, but we do not want you to lessen our workload or keep us from difficult challenges."

Where was this coming from? Inez wondered. Just an hour ago Jennie had been unsettled by the prospect of speaking at a street meeting or singing in the park, and now she was talking about not wanting to be kept from difficult challenges?

"You need not fear, Sister Brimhall," President McMurrin stated. "There is plenty of work for everyone and challenges around every corner."

Inez heard the teasing in his voice, but that didn't make the statement any less true.

As the carriage turned and moved down a side street, President McMurrin glanced out the window. "Ah, here we are! Forty-two Islington."

He rapped on the ceiling of the carriage. "This is us, thank you!" He exited the transport as soon as the footman put down the steps and stood waiting as the ladies descended. Inez was first and stumbled slightly when the toe of her shoe caught her hem, but President McMurrin held her hand firmly until she reached the ground. Will followed behind Jennie, gently taking her upper arm and helping her navigate the first step.

The second carriage arrived within moments, and Inez returned the waves being offered by Elders Rose and Eldridge. The two young missionaries jumped from the carriage, standing aside as President Wells exited, and then began removing the trunks and bags from the conveyance. Several elders came out of the building and moved to their comrades, never taking their eyes off the new female arrivals.

Inez leaned toward Jennie and whispered, "I feel like a fish in a bowl."

Jennie looked up at the old three-story brick building and saw male faces peering out from several of the windows. "Well, remember, we're novelties," she whispered back. Inez gave a short laugh, which she stifled when President Wells approached.

"Welcome, sisters, to the mission home. Your temporary lodgings will be in the apartments next door." He turned to the group of elders now assembled around the luggage. "Well, my goodness, how many elders are needed for this job? Ah, well." He called out to them. "You lot take the sisters' belongings up to their flat, and mind you don't break anything." The elders began immediately jockeying for possession of one of the trunks or bags. President Wells shook his head at their chivalrous antics, then turned his attention to Inez and Jennie. "All right then, paperwork, a short meeting, assignment to your field of labor, and dinner. How does that sound?"

"Wonderful," Jennie answered immediately, while Inez only nodded.

"This way then!" President Wells said, moving jauntily toward the mission home. Inez and Jennie followed; Inez tried to understand her friend's newfound certainty while she wrestled with apprehension and a desire to book passage on the first boat home.

NOTES

Conferences: As opposed to the terms used to describe mission areas today, during the period in which this book takes place, the term *conference* was used to describe an area within a mission where missionaries were assigned to labor.

Industrial Revolution: The Industrial Revolution began in England in the mid-eighteenth century when the mechanization of the textile industry transformed the country's rural, agrarian culture into an urban, industrial society.

Forty-two Islington Street: This was the location of the conference home in Liverpool, as noted in Inez's journal.

Chapter Seven

Jennie stood with her back pressed against the apartment door, eyes closed and tears streaming over her cheeks.

Inez rummaged in her trunk and brought out a clean handkerchief. She placed it in Jennie's hand. "Is there anything I can do?"

Jennie shook her head.

Inez went back to her trunk and brought out her scriptures. She sat on the divan, searching the pages for a moment, and then read aloud. "Behold, I send you out to reprove the world of all their unrighteous deeds, and to teach them of a judgment which is to come. And whoso receiveth you, there I will be also, for I will go before your face. I will be on your right hand and on your left, and my Spirit shall be in your hearts, and mine angels round about you, to bear you up." She set down the book and moved to the window, looking out on the unfamiliar street. The afternoon sun was a pale-yellow smudge in the dirty sky, and Inez longed for the blue skies of the Wasatch. She heard Jennie cough and turned to see her wiping her face and blowing her nose.

"Thank you for being my angel and bearing me up," Jennie said quietly.

"Me?" Inez questioned. "*You've* been the brave one."

"That was all show," Jennie said. "I did it so I wouldn't cry in front of Will or the presidents or the missionaries." She wiped away more tears and sat on the arm of the divan. "Just show."

"Well, *I* believed you."

"So now you know the truth." Jennie wiped away the last of her tears. "And you? How are you doing?"

"Disappointed." Inez knew she would never confess this to any other person. "Mostly in myself. I thought I was strong. I thought I was . . . faithful, but now I have all these doubts about myself. I was so eager to say yes to the calling, but now I wonder if I have the spiritual strength to carry it through."

"I feel the same."

"But you've been so determined since we arrived."

"All part of the show, as my tears confess. Just a show."

Inez shook her head. "I don't know how you managed it."

"It's something my father taught me. Believe what you want to become until you become it."

Inez moved over to sit on a small upholstered chair. "I'll try to remember that when we're asked to speak and I can't put two words together."

Jennie took a deep breath. "When did you feel the weight of the calling?"

"When I had to write my name and all my information in the big missionary book."

"That was intimidating."

"And you?"

"When we showed them our certificates from home and President McMurrin handed us our conference assignments."

Inez brought the certificate out of her coat pocket. "Cheltenham. I don't even know where this is."

"I think we'll find out soon enough," Jennie said, moving to sit on the divan. "So many times today, I wanted to turn around and run home."

"Thanks for admitting that. I felt the same." Inez shook her head. "Then I'd picture my mother's and father's faces."

Jennie nodded. "I guess they'd expect us to give the mission more than one day."

Inez grinned. "Or perhaps they'd want us to attend at least one street meeting and hand out a few tracts."

"Or offer our testimonies to a few people." They gave each other a smile. After a few moments of contemplation, Jennie sighed. "Maybe we should unpack a few things."

"I think we should," Inez said, standing and removing her coat. "There's no boat leaving for America today anyway."

Jennie laid her coat over the arm of the divan. "I hope we'll feel better after luncheon."

"I know I will," Inez said, moving to her trunk. "And a bath wouldn't hurt."

Jennie went to find hangers in the room's only armoire. "We have hangers!" she said triumphantly. "And look! We also have books." She stooped over and picked up several books from the stack sitting on the armoire's lower shelf. She perused the spines. "Stevenson, Hardy, Dickens, Wells . . ."

"Wells? I've never heard of him," Inez said, coming over to investigate.

"H. G. Wells," Jennie offered. "*The Time Machine.*"

Inez looked puzzled. "That's an odd title. Maybe it's about a machine that makes clocks?" She picked up another book from the pile. "Bram Stoker? I've never heard of him either." She secured a rather hefty book. "My goodness! Look at this tome! Someone had a lot to say." She read the title. "*Mrs. Beeton's Book of Household Management.*"

Jennie gave her a curious look. "What in the world?"

Inez shrugged. "No idea." She showed the book to Jennie, then randomly opened to a page. "Ah. I believe it's a cookery book," she said, wandering over to sit on the divan.

"I love cookery books," Jennie said with interest, coming to sit beside her.

"There are hundreds of recipes," Inez said flipping through the book. "Look, here are a few offerings on rabbit . . . potted hare, broiled hare, hashed hare, jugged hare—and there's even a drawing of the dear little bunny, still hale and hearty."

Jennie laughed, took the book, and perused more pages. "It also seems to be a book about managing a proper British household. This should be interesting for two naïve American girls." She randomly stopped on a page and read. "In concluding these remarks on the duties of the housekeeper, we will briefly refer to the very great responsibility which attaches to her position. Like 'Caesar's wife,' she should be 'above suspicion,' and her honesty and sobriety unquestionable; for there are many temptations to which she is exposed."

"Temptations?" Inez questioned, suppressing laughter. "I've never considered the temptations that might befall an English housekeeper."

"Obviously, Mrs. Beeton has thought it through and given caution." Jennie ran her finger down the topics on the book's contents page, reading aloud some of the offerings. "The housekeeper, introduction to cookery, general remarks on sauces, observations on the common hog."

Inez chuckled. "Observations on the common hog?"

Jennie glanced up and laughed with her. "Yes, to go along with the natural history of fish, I suppose." She continued reciting from the book. "Recipes for puddings and pastry, invalid cookery, dinners and dining, domestic servants, and disease management."

"It is very British, isn't it?" Inez stated.

Jennie nodded. "You know, Sister Knight, I think this book will give us insight into the English temperament."

"That would be helpful," Inez said. "Is there a chapter on Utah girls managing a new country?"

"Sadly, no," Jennie said, giving her companion an amused smile. "There is a chapter on the management of children and one on the arrangement and economy of the kitchen."

"Check the cupboard again," Inez demanded. "See if there's a book on *missionary* management."

"That would be helpful," Jennie stated.

Inez brightened. "Actually, I think it's a grand idea!"

"What?"

"A book on missionary management. We could write our own book for future sister missionaries called to England."

"Provided we're successful and not sent home before we finish the first chapter."

"Of course we'll be successful," Inez said without hesitation.

Jennie raised her eyebrows.

"Well, we'll have adjustments to make, but we could put that in the book too. We could call it . . . " She frowned in thought. "*The Brimhall/Knight Book of Missionary Management*!"

Jennie smiled at Inez's enthusiasm as her companion continued her imaginings.

"We would be able to share what we learn about the elders, the British people, the food, and preaching in front of large crowds of people." Inez's voice trailed off, and her look became somber.

"I suppose we could add words of encouragement," Jennie offered.

"Words of encouragement would be helpful," Inez said.

Jennie gave a little shrug. "It might be interesting."

A knock came to the door, and both ladies jumped.

Jennie stood. "Oh dear! We haven't accomplished much," she said guiltily. She moved to open the door and found Will standing on the other side.

"I've been sent to escort you to luncheon, which the Brits call 'dinner.'"

"How nice," Jennie said smiling.

Inez approached. "We were just saying we were hungry."

"And afterward President Wells and I are taking you sisters out to buy new shoes. You have to have sturdy shoes for this job."

Jennie pulled her scuffed shoes back under the hem of her skirt.

"What fun!" Inez exclaimed, gathering her and Jennie's coats.

Will stepped into the room to help them with their coats, glancing surreptitiously around the room. He started to say something, but Inez cut him off.

"Don't you dare say anything about our lack of unpacking. We were tired, and then we were distracted by Mrs. Beeton."

"Who?"

"Never mind," Inez said, shrugging into her coat and moving to exit. "We'll tell you all about our new friend at lunch . . . ah, dinner." She stopped in the doorway. "What are we eating, by the way?"

"I think roasted rabbit."

Both Jennie and Inez laughed. Inez turned to Jennie as they moved into the hallway. "Perhaps if we like it, you can send the recipe to Flora."

"Knowing Flora, she'll make roasted jackrabbit." The girls laughed again.

Will followed behind them. "What are you two going on about?"

Inez stopped and took her brother's arm, then continued walking.

"Never mind, dear brother. We are just trying to adjust to our new lives in a new land."

"Believing until we become," Jennie added when he looked over at her.

Will shook his head and smiled. "Women. You're an odd lot, aren't you?"

"Compared with men we are extremely conventional and rational," Inez stated.

Will snorted as they moved out onto the sidewalk. "Back to your sisterly tricks, are you?"

"Yes, so get used to it. Oh! And I've also come with instructions from Mother."

"Instructions?"

"Yes. I'm to report back on your and Ray's behavior and work ethic."

Will sobered. "Oh."

"Yes, oh. And . . . " she elongated the word for dramatic effect. "She wants me to find out why you keep sending home letters filled with half-truths."

"Look! Here we are at the mission home!" Will exclaimed, evading his sister's scrutiny. "We'd better hurry in before the elders eat everything." He ran up the steps and into the building.

Inez laughed. "You've not heard the last of this, Jesse William Knight!" she called after him.

Jennie stood straighter. "Well, I guess we are to escort ourselves in."

"We might as well get accustomed to our independence, Sister Brimhall. Faces to the future!"

The two sister missionaries marched up the steps and into the mission home.

NOTES

Mrs. Beeton's Book of Household Management: This English cookery and household-management book was popular in the mid-1800s. It was first published as a series of guidebooks by her husband, Samuel, and Isabella Beeton later compiled and edited the information into book form, which was published in 1861.

Arriving in England: Upon arriving in England, Jennie admitted in her journal to being "tired in body and spirit."

Chapter Eight

To the Brimhall Household

Dearest Father and Flora,

It is the end of our first day in England, and I find myself exhausted, anxious, a bit muddled, and happy. I know these feelings seem incongruous, but I assure you, as I stepped off the boat, I felt all these emotions. I keep telling myself to be patient and things will settle. I have taken your wise counsel, Father, and am praying many times a day, and I believe Inez is doing the same. I don't know what I would do without my dear friend. She is dedicated to the call and carries on even though she has doubts about her ability to fulfill it. She loves the Lord and the restored gospel, and she makes me laugh.

Will—I mean, Elder Jesse William Knight—met us at the Liverpool docks, along with President McMurrin of the European Mission, President Wells of the Manchester Conference, and two other elders—Rose and Eldridge. President Wells is a positive person, and Inez and I agreed that we would love to have stayed and served in the Manchester Conference, but we have been called to the Cheltenham Conference. We will stay in this area for a time. We don't know how long.

It was wonderful to see Elder Knight again. He is well and asks you to inform his parents that he and Ray are busy in the work of the Lord. As we drove through the streets of Liverpool toward our destination, we received our first look at one of the large cities of Victorian England. And to you in private correspondence, Father, I will admit that it did not impress. Oh, the docks were a wonder of ships and cargo and people, but Liverpool itself seemed dingy and inhospitable. I will give it time, as my addled brain may be conjuring falsehoods.

After dinner, which was roasted rabbit, President Wells and Elder Knight took Inez and me into town to buy new shoes. The streets were crowded with people and sellers of many kinds of wares. There were also shops of every kind. I think Flora would have been interested in the bakeries. The variety of wagons, carts, and carriages was astounding—from small carts where men were sharpening knives to wagons filled with old furniture. There were also women carrying large parcels and goods on their heads. I had no idea this way of carrying things took place in England.

We returned to our apartment near the mission home at forty-two Islington and did a bit of unpacking. Inez said we should just live out of our trunks because she feels we won't be in the Manchester Conference long enough to get settled. I think I agree with her.

This evening we attended our first missionary meeting, and President Wells invited all the new missionaries to share their testimonies. Poor Inez was called on first, and I could see her trembling as she walked to the front of the room. Also, her new shoes made a terrible squeaking, which drew the attention of all. I prayed for her, and I know she prayed for me. I must admit, Father, that Sister Knight and I felt like fish in a fishbowl today. I suppose the novelty of having sister missionaries will wear off with time. This is my hope.

Inez is already in bed, and I will be there shortly. I have been putting on a brave front, but I am tired, body and spirit. How did the early Saints survive their weighty challenges? I know I will feel better in the morning, and by the time you get this letter, I will be passing out tracts and preaching on the street corners.

Tomorrow we travel to Oldham, and on Sunday we have the Manchester Conference general meeting. We hope to see Inez's brother Ray. He has been preaching in Bradford.

I am rambling, so I will stop writing and sign my name.

Flora, at the end of this letter you will find the recipe for roasted hare (rabbit), compliments of our new friend, Mrs. Beeton. She has written an interesting cookery book called Mrs. Beeton's Book of Household Management, *which has not only recipes but also advice on how to run a proper home. I know you will find the notes on the preparation for roasted hare quite interesting and very British. Much of it seems to be in an unfamiliar language, but I figure with your cooking skill, you can "Americanize" it. Inez and I had a good laugh at the gruesome instructions for preparation, but I'm afraid the younger children might find it a vision for nightmares. I hope you will cook it and think of me in faraway England.*

Be well, family!
With love and gratitude,
Your Jennie

ROASTED HARE

INGREDIENTS— Hare, forcemeat (stuffing), a little milk, butter.

CLEANING AND TRUSSING— Choose a young hare; which may be known by its smooth and sharp claws, and by the cleft in the lip not being much spread. To be eaten in perfection, it must hang for some time; and, if properly taken care of, it may be kept for several days. It is better to hang without being paunched (gutted); but should it be previously emptied, wipe the inside every day, and sprinkle over it a little pepper and ginger, to prevent the musty taste which long keeping in the damp occasions, and which also affects the stuffing. After it is skinned, wash it well, and soak for an hour in warm water to draw out the blood; if old, let it lie in vinegar for a short time, but wash it well afterwards in several waters. Make a forcemeat, wipe the hare dry, fill the belly with it, and sew it up. Bring the hind and fore legs close to the body towards the head, run a skewer through each, fix the head between the shoulders by means of another skewer, and be careful to leave the ears on. Put a string round the body from skewer to skewer, and tie it above the back.

MODE— The hare should be kept at a distance from the fire when it is first laid down, or the outside will become dry and hard before the inside is done. Baste it well with milk for a short time, and afterwards with butter; and particular attention must be paid to the basting, so as to preserve the meat on the back juicy and nutritive. When it is almost roasted enough, flour the hare, and baste well with butter. When nicely froathed, dish it, remove the skewers, and send it to table with a little gravy in the dish, and a tureen of the same. Red-current jelly must also not be forgotten, as this is an indispensable accompaniment to roast hare. For economy, good beef drippings may be substituted for the milk and butter to baste with, but the basting, as we have before stated, must be continued without intermission. If the liver is good, it may be parboiled, minced, and mixed with the stuffing; but it should not be used unless quite fresh.

TIME— A middling-sized hare, 1¼ hours; a large hare, 1½ to 2 hours.

NOTE

Letter's details: Many snippets from Inez's journal color Jennie's letter, including comments on the market scene, buying new shoes, and Inez's new shoes squeaking in the testimony meeting.

Chapter Nine

Inez had never seen so much green in her life: rich, vibrant, varied in hue. Hill after hill of rolling green meadowland and trees. Emerald pastures surrounded by dark stone walls to discourage wandering sheep. As the train escaped the dreary gray of Liverpool and rushed into the lush countryside, melancholy fell from Inez's soul like scales, and now she sat with her face close to the window, breathing deeply, trying to suck the verdant color into her body like a tonic. She sighed and sat back.

"I think I might live."

Jennie nodded. "I feel the same. I don't think we're city girls."

The door to the cabin opened, and Will poked in his head. Behind him loitered two other elders. "Mind if we join you?"

Inez sat straighter. "Don't you have your own cabin?"

Will hesitated. "Yes, but there's only you two in this compartment for eight, and . . . " He hesitated. "We . . . we thought you might like company."

"Presumptuous," Inez said flatly. The two elders behind Will stepped back.

Jennie laughed. "Oh goodness! She's just joking."

A smile printed itself onto Inez's face, and she winked at her brother. "Oh, come in then, if you must. I suppose we can put up with elders disrupting our quiet time."

Will and one of the elders immediately sat in seats directly across from Inez and Jennie, but Elder Davis hesitated. "This is Elder Harrison Bailey, and that is Elder Jonathan Davis," Will introduced. "And this is . . . Lucy

Jane Brimhall, but everyone calls her Jennie. And my sister Amanda Inez Knight."

"Whom everyone calls Inez," Inez said. "But, of course, you must call me Sister Knight."

"Of course. How do you do, Sister Knight and Sister Brimhall?" Elder Bailey said, beaming at them.

Elder Davis remained standing and unspeaking.

"Please, have a seat, Elder Davis," Jennie said cordially.

He took a seat, two away from his companions, furthest away from the women, and nearest the doorway. He mumbled a remark, opened a book, and lost himself in the reading.

The other occupants of the cabin stared at him in silence until Inez blurted out. "We don't bite, you know."

"I just prefer reading to mindless gabble," Elder Davis remarked without looking up from his reading.

"Mindless gabble?" Inez spluttered.

"Ah, don't mind him, Sister Knight," Elder Bailey interceded. "I'm afraid Elder Davis isn't much of a joiner."

"I didn't mean to offend you, Sister Knight. I just meant that my time is better spent reading scripture than indulging in idle chatter."

"And why is it, sir, that you think we'd be speaking mindless gabble or idle chatter? Do you believe that Sister Brimhall and I can talk only about fashion and cookery?"

"Inez, leave him be," Will said laughing. "Elder Davis is the most serious of us all."

"Then why on earth did you bring him with you?"

Elder Bailey stared at her for a moment and then began laughing. He turned to Elder Davis. "Well, here's someone who will stand up to you, Jonathan."

Elder Davis stood. "If you'll excuse me, I will find a quieter place to study." He opened the cabin door and turned back. "It will be interesting to hear you speak at the street meeting in Oldham, Sister Knight, . . . without proper preparation."

After a few moments of stunned silence, Elder Bailey sighed. "Really. Why *did* we bring him along with us, Elder Knight?"

Will shook his head. "I thought a fairer company might cheer him. He's such a dour fellow."

"Bad-mannered and foul better suits," Inez stated.

"Inez, we've just met him," Jennie said softly. "Perhaps we should wait to make a comment on his character."

"No, I actually think she has him figured out," Elder Bailey said with a grin. "Elder Davis arrived a few months ago and has offended pretty much everybody."

"So have either of you been to Oldham?" Jennie interrupted just as Inez was about to reply. They all turned to her at the abrupt change of topic. She looked at each innocently. "I was just wondering what Sister Knight and I will be up against. I thought you might be able to give us some help."

Elder Knight gave his fiancée a knowing half grin and settled himself into the seat. "We have both been to Oldham, Sister Brimhall, and it's a fine city with friendly, hardworking people."

"Most work at the cotton mills," Elder Bailey added. "They're a little rough around the edges—"

"Rough?" Inez interrupted.

"But pleasant," Elder Bailey added quickly. "Very pleasant folks."

"We've never had any problems in Oldham," Will assured.

"True," Elder Bailey supported. "We always gather well-mannered crowds."

Jennie smiled. "Friendly, pleasant, well-mannered? I think Oldham must be a city of angels."

Will smiled back. "Well, we've never had any brawls at our street meetings there."

"Oh, that's encouraging."

"Street meetings?" Inez questioned. "Is that what you think we'll be doing today—a street meeting?"

"Most likely several. But don't worry. You probably won't be called on to preach your first day out."

Inez let out the breath she'd been holding. "Well, that's good because I'm sure anything I tried to say would come out as gibberish."

"And I probably wouldn't be able to put two words together," Jennie added.

"Sister Knight and Sister Brimhall!" Will said in a tone of rebuke.

Both women started. "Goodness, Will! You scared me," Inez said.

"Good. I hope I scared you. The Lord has called you to England at this time for a purpose. Do you think He made a mistake?"

"Well . . . "

"No. He did not." He turned to Sister Brimhall. "Jennie?"

"I don't think He made a mistake, but we do have doubts about our ability to stand among strangers and preach."

"We've all felt that way," Elder Bailey interjected. "Well, maybe not Elder Davis."

Inez stifled a laugh but then looked at her brother and sobered. "Sorry, Will." She took a deep breath. "It's just that this has always been a man's world. Going out among strangers—preaching—standing up for the faith—facing hostility."

"That wasn't true for Mother Smith or Eliza R. Snow or a hundred other brave pioneer women, was it?"

"I'm not a hundred other brave pioneer women, Will. I have my strengths in the gospel, but speaking in front of a group is not one of them. This is frightening territory."

"I understand," he said more tenderly. "When Ray and I received the telegram that you two were coming as missionaries, we knew it would be hard for you—for both of you. We knew you'd have to deal with persecution and incivility, and we didn't like the idea. Actually, we wondered if the First Presidency had lost their collective access to revelation."

"Will!" both women exclaimed together.

"But we spent a lot of time praying and fasting about it. We both got a sense of peace about the call. In fact, I think that you two are going to be important to the work here."

The train whistle blew, and the train began to slow.

"Are we in Oldham already?" Inez asked, a note of panic in her voice.

"Not quite, Sister Knight," Elder Bailey assured. "A few more stops, and then the good people of Oldham will hear about the wonder of the Restoration. What do you say to that?"

Inez took a deep breath. "I say it will be a wonder if I don't faint or fall down."

"Sausage rolls! Eel tartlets! Fruit pasties!"

Inez turned to discover the loud voice that so ably touted the baker's wares over the din in the market square. The shouts of the other vendors, the muddled cacophony of a hundred voices, and the clack of clogs on the cobblestone pavement assaulted Inez's ears, and she covered them and shook her head. She admired the clogs with their wooden soles and leather uppers, but they certainly added to the racket.

"I wonder if President McMurrin would approve of our having such footwear," she called out to Jennie.

"I doubt it," Jennie answered. "We'd probably twist an ankle."

"*I* would definitely twist an ankle, without question," Inez said with a laugh as she turned slowly in a circle to take in the scene.

The Tommyfield Market was a wonder of a place, nearly as large as Temple Square and filled, not with gardens and walkways and a newly finished temple, but with stalls, wares, and vendors. Hordes of factory workers thronged the yard, dressed in their best—women in headscarves and shawls, men in suit coats and caps. The collective attitude was one of festive gratitude, glad for a Saturday evening away from the factory.

"I think we should treat the sister missionaries to sausage rolls before we start the next meeting," Elder Bailey announced.

"There's an idea," Will said smiling. "Introduce them to the food of the people." He turned to Inez and Jennie. "What do you say?"

"Yes, I'm starving!" Inez responded immediately. "I think we've walked this entire city. I could eat a horse."

"Probably the main ingredient," came a voice so close behind her that it made her jump. Inez spun around to meet the mocking face of Elder Davis.

"Don't be ridiculous," she said sharply.

"Factual, more to the point," Elder Davis said with a slight lifting of his chin. "If I were you, I wouldn't eat any of the local food."

"But surely they don't eat horsemeat."

Elder Davis grinned. "One never knows. They certainly eat a lot of things that are disgusting: steak and kidney pie, pigeon pie, eels, calves' feet."

"Leave off, Davis," Elder Bailey growled.

"Just because you eat anything that's shoved in front of your face, Bailey, doesn't mean the women have to follow your lead."

Elder Bailey took a menacing step forward. "Just because you're a finicky prude who offends the locals by refusing to try anything new."

Elder Davis, being a head taller than Elder Bailey, looked down at him with contempt. "I'm just trying to keep myself alive till the end of my mission."

"Don't do us any favors."

Will moved to the side of his friend. "Brethren, we need to have the Spirit with us if we wish to preach. What say we leave off?"

"Fine with me," Elder Davis said pompously. "I was just trying to keep the sister missionaries safe."

"As if you care. You've made it perfectly clear you detest them being here," Elder Bailey said.

Jennie had been avoiding looking at the men as they quarreled, but now she looked up in surprise.

Elder Davis shrugged. "It's no secret. I don't think they belong here. It's dangerous, and they're distractions. Nevertheless, I certainly don't want to see them poisoned by the street food."

Just then President McMurrin and President Wells approached the group. Inez caught the exuberant smile of President Wells as he waved at them. She waved back.

"Ah! Here's a few more of our mighty band! Good! Good! We're gathering by the speaker's platform," he said jovially. "We will start preaching in twenty minutes."

"We'll be there, President," Will said. He gave an unnoticed swat to Elder Bailey's arm.

Elder Baily stopped glaring at Elder Davis and looked down at his shoes. "Twenty minutes . . . speaker's platform."

Inez watched as President McMurrin scanned the group and frowned. "Everything all right here?"

Elder Davis stood straighter. "Of course, President. We were just discussing topics for the final street meeting."

"Yes," Elder Bailey said in a heightened voice. "Elder Davis wants to bear his testimony about his kinship with the British people."

President McMurrin studied the two men for a long moment. "Let's keep to the basics, shall we? Restoration of the primitive Church of Christ, the First Vision, charity."

Elder Bailey put a hand on Elder Davis's shoulder. "Charity. Now, that's a topic for you, Elder Davis."

"Good. Good," President Wells said with a little clap. "In the meantime, President McMurrin and I are going over to get some sausage rolls. Anyone care to join us?"

Inez and Jennie laughed—they couldn't help themselves.

"Did I say something funny?" President Wells asked, a look of surprise on his face.

"Not at all, President," Jennie said sobering. "It's just that you spoke of sausage rolls with such delight."

"Ah! That's right—you ladies have not had the joy of the local food!" He took each by an arm and began walking. "Well, we will remedy that immediately."

President McMurrin followed. "Come along, elders. Difficult to preach on an empty stomach."

Inez turned her head to see her brother and Elder Bailey joining the president, a less-than-humble jauntiness in their step.

Elder Davis stood his ground, scowling after them.

Sister Knight and Sister Brimhall stood at the back of the assembled crowd, admiring the elders in their dark suits and tall silk hats as they shared gospel truths with the people of Oldham. Inez rubbed her lower back. Five street meetings on different corners and countless miles of walking on cobblestone streets were taking a toll on her body. Not to mention her new shoes were bringing up blisters on her feet.

Jennie leaned toward her and whispered, "Tired?"

Inez nodded.

"Me too," Jennie said yawning. "Yet look at them," she added, indicating the elders on the platform. "Still firmly and humbly bearing testimony of the truth."

"I don't know how they're doing it," Inez answered. "I'm proud to be numbered with them."

Their whispered conversation was interrupted by a loud male voice calling out to Elder Bailey, who was attempting to talk about the restoration of priesthood power.

"Priesthood power indeed! I've heard about you Mormon men. You come here to entice our young women to join your church and then trap them into going to Utah."

"Where they're treated like slaves!" yelled another.

"Five women to every man!"

Inez and Jennie stared. It was the first time all day they'd heard derogatory comments from the crowd, and now many voices responded to the remarks, until there was a chaos of sound.

President McMurrin stepped onto the platform and moved beside Elder Bailey. He held up his hand. "Gentlemen . . . gentlemen and ladies, please . . . " The crowd quieted. "We are here in Britain to bring you a message of peace and hope. A message for everyone, men and women alike." He looked over the crowd. "Sister Brimhall, Sister Knight, will you please come join me on the platform?"

Inez heard Jennie gasp and felt her own breath catch in her chest. Slowly the two composed themselves enough to take a few steps forward into the crowd. As the people pushed back to allow room, Inez felt every eye on her, and she prayed fervently that she wouldn't trip and fall. After what seemed like an eternity, they reached the platform, and Will helped them up. President McMurrin gave them an encouraging look as he motioned them to his side.

"Here, my friends, are real live Mormon women from Utah! They come as missionaries to tell you the truth about the Restoration of the Lord's gospel, as well as to inform you about their lives in Utah." A surprised murmur rippled through the crowd. "As you can plainly see, they are intelligent, cultured, and content young women."

"Let 'em speak up then!" came a voice from the front of the crowd.

Inez looked down to see the speaker glaring at her, his face skeptical that she was anything more than a deceiver.

"Indeed, you will hear them, friends. Both Sister Knight and Sister

Brimhall will be speaking at our Sunday evening meeting tomorrow, at the Oldham assembly hall."

Inez felt her knees buckle, and Jennie grabbed her arm. "We can do this, Inez," she whispered. "Believe until you become."

Inez nodded and stood straighter. It was all she could manage. She was barely aware of President McMurrin closing the meeting and the elders leaving the platform. As she and Jennie stepped down, they were surrounded by people asking questions and wanting to get a closer look at the peculiar pair. Elder Bailey and Will pushed through the press of people to rescue them.

"Sorry folks," Elder Bailey said in a cheery voice. "No questions tonight! Tomorrow at the meeting. We certainly hope you'll join us!" As Elder Baily was speaking, he and Will nimbly escorted the sisters away from the group to the outskirts of the market square. The party stopped to gather themselves, and Elder Bailey stood straight and clapped Will on the shoulder. "Well, I don't know about you Elder Knight, but I feel it a rare honor to be in the presence of 'real live Mormon women.'"

Jennie started giggling, and Inez growled. "That's enough out of you, Elder Bailey." She turned with an exasperated look at Jennie. "Where in the world did President McMurrin come up with *that* title?"

"Pure inspiration," Will laughed.

Inez glared at her brother. "And that is enough out of you, Jesse William Knight." She growled again. "Real live Mormon women, indeed."

"I don't mind the title," Jennie said sobering. "What I mind is the assignment. Speaking in a conference to who knows how many people?"

"I feel sick," Inez moaned.

President McMurrin's voice hailed them as he and President Wells approached. "Cheers for the sister missionaries!" Inez moaned again, and her brother stifled a laugh.

President Wells came to stand beside Will. "Well, my boy, what do you think of these two remarkable women?"

"Real and remarkable," Will answered.

"And alive," Elder Bailey whispered in an aside to Inez.

"Indeed, they are! Indeed, they are! And they are going to set a lot of things straight about the women of the Church." He turned to Inez and Jennie. "Did you see? Just one look at you, and the crowd was dumbfounded." Jennie started to smile at the man and yawned instead. "Oh my goodness! We have run you two ragged on your first day, haven't we? I am so sorry, my dears."

Jennie patted away the yawn and held up her other hand to calm President Well's flustered apology. "It's all right, President. We're ready for any assignment or any—"

President McMurrin interrupted. "Your assignment is a bit of food and a good night's rest, young woman."

"Thank heavens," Inez grumbled without thinking. Elder Bailey laughed, and Inez gave a startled look. "Did I say that out loud?"

"You did, Sister Knight. And I'm grateful for your honesty," President McMurrin said with a kind smile. He looked at Will. "We've lodged the sisters at the home of Mr. and Mrs. Mills for the next two nights. After they pick up their traveling bags at the mission office, I want you and Elder Bailey to escort them there."

"We're not staying at the mission apartments?" Jennie asked.

"Oh, indeed no!" President Wells exclaimed. "We don't have a separate space for the two of you. You will be much more comfortable with the Mills family. They have two grown daughters who will give you their room—comfortable beds, clean linens. Yes indeed, much more suitable."

"Thank you, President. It sounds wonderful," Inez stated.

"Important Sabbath preaching tomorrow! Must have your rest. Off we go then."

As the group of missionaries moved out of the Tommyfield Market Square, Inez Knight and Jennie Brimhall shared a look of mingled exhaustion and anxiety.

NOTES

Details of Oldham: Many details of the sisters' first encounter with missionary work in Oldham are recorded in Inez's journal, including the description of the Tommyfield Market and the elders preaching in their dark suits and top hats.

"Real live Mormon women": At an Oldham street meeting, President McMurrin did indeed call the sisters "real live Mormon women." Inez referenced this in her journal.

Chapter Ten

To the Knight Household
Monday, April 25, 1898

Dear beloved parents,

I greet you with news that I am safe in England in the company of your faithful son William. I have not as yet seen Ray as he is laboring in Bradford, which is north of where we are. Sister Brimhall and I have been assigned to the Cheltenham Conference and will probably depart for that field of labor within a fortnight. At present we labor in the Manchester area.

I have been on a British train, seen the enchanting English countryside, eaten sausage rolls, and spoken at a conference meeting. I suppose you can guess which one brought fear and trembling.

But I am placing the cart before the horse. We left early Saturday morning from Liverpool on our journey to Oldham, where the Manchester conference was to be held. Oh, Mother! The countryside is so beautiful as to make you weep. How did the British Saints ever leave this paradise to inherit the desolation of Utah? Of course, they did not know what awaited them. It's not that I don't truly love my home, but for them there had to be shock and weeping upon arrival in the arid valley.

Our Saturday in Oldham was spent in street meetings, and Sister Brimhall and I were content to be humble watchers—that is, until President McMurrin called us out as "real live Mormon women" who would be speaking at Sunday's conference. (I suppose Father is chuckling over what the president called us.)

When Sunday evening arrived, Jennie and I felt like Christians in the Colosseum. The hall was crowded with people, and Jennie discerned that a few of the men were anxious to dispute our words. Here's where the fear and trembling come in, dear ones, for when President McMurrin called out my name, I felt as though I could not stand. I prayed a fervent, silent prayer, and suddenly I was on my feet as though someone had lifted me. I thought of the testimony of my grandfather. This gave me strength. I don't remember much of what I said, but I do recall sharing about my wonderful life in Utah and how many noble things my parents had taught me. I suppose I did all right since no one confronted me or threw rotted fruit.

Sister Brimhall spoke next, and she was magnificent! She was calm and articulate as she spoke about the Restoration of the gospel and life in Utah. Everyone who looked at her could see modesty and virtue, and her words were spoken with so much love and sincerity. It was as though pure truth was flowing from her lips.

So with the help of the Spirit we survived our first call to speak, and we certainly slept well Sunday night.

We met President and Sister Noall, who were visiting the conference from Cheltenham. He will be our president, and he and his wife seem like delightful people.

This morning, we attended priesthood meeting, and Jennie and I felt like "female brethren." In the afternoon all the missionaries and leaders gathered in a lovely park and had a group picture taken. Here again, we were surrounded by men. I hope there comes a time when Jennie and I do not feel so conspicuous.

I just tallied the sheets of paper used to write this letter and apologize for my long-winded book, but writing brings you close to me. Also, we are on the train back to Liverpool, it is dark, and Jennie is sleeping, so it is the perfect quiet time to recap my adventures.

Oh! On Saturday I ate sausage rolls when we were in the Tommyfield Market! They are delicious. I will look for the recipe in Mrs.

Beeton's Book of Household Management *and send it to you at the end of this letter. When you eat them, you can feel close to me.*

I will now address my sisters. Dear Jennie Pearl and Addie, mind Father and Mother, eat properly, study your scriptures, and perhaps someday you will have the privilege of being a missionary for the Lord. Please know that I am well.

Love to all.

Your daughter, Amanda Inez

(who did not faint when she had to speak)

SAUSAGE ROLLS

INGREDIENTS— 1 lb. of puff-paste (which we call pastry), sausage meat, the yolk of 1 egg.

MODE— Make 1 lb. of puff paste; roll it out to the thickness of about ½ inch, or rather less, and divide it into 8, 10, or 12 squares, according to the size the rolls are intended to be. Place the sausage meat on one half of each square, wet the edges of the paste, and fold it over the meat; slightly press the edges together, and trim them neatly with a knife. Brush the rolls over with the yolk of an egg, and bake them in a well-heated oven for about ½ hour, or longer should they be very large. The remains of cold chicken and ham, minced and seasoned, as also cold veal or beef, make very good rolls.

NOTES

Oldham: The sisters first began proselyting in this town.

Meeting in Oldham: We learn from Inez's journal the manner in which Jennie spoke at the meeting in Oldham, that they were called "female brethren," and of the photo taken of all the conference missionaries. A copy of the photograph is on file at the Church History Library in Salt Lake City.

Chapter Eleven

Rain—again. Inez rolled over in bed and opened her eyelids a slit to take in the gloomy morning. The room was in shadow except for a pale wash of light from their small apartment window. Jennie, in the opposite bed, groaned and sat partway up.

"I'm not feeling well. My throat is . . . sore."

"I can tell," Inez answered, her own voice gravelly.

"Maybe it's just morning throat," Jennie croaked, sitting up against her pillow.

Inez got out of bed, put a shawl around her shoulders, and padded over to Jennie's bedside. "Mine is morning throat . . . " She put her hand on her companion's head. "Yours is a fever and sickness." Jennie groaned again. "You will not be going anywhere today."

"But we have an appointment in Manchester."

"No, *I* have an appointment in Manchester. You have an appointment with sleep and camphor liniment."

"Nasty stuff," Jennie muttered.

"Perhaps, but effective."

"But I was so looking forward to meeting Will's fishmonger woman."

Inez gave her companion a narrowed look. "I understand, but we leave for Cheltenham the day after tomorrow; don't you want to be well for that adventure?"

"Of course," Jennie whined, "but . . . "

"Sit forward so I can plump your pillow." Jennie followed the order, and Inez gave the pillow several hearty whacks. Jennie started to chuckle at her friend's aggressive manner, but it quickly turned to a whimper as her hand went to her throat. Inez secured a shawl and put it around Jennie's shoulders. "Lie back. I'll see if I can find a lozenge." She lit the gas lamp and went to her trunk. After rummaging for several minutes, she returned to the bedside with a small tin of lozenges. She gave Jennie one and placed the tin on her bedside table. "Rest. I'll dress and go over to the conference house to see if Mrs. Reed can check on you while I'm away."

"You can't go to Manchester by yourself."

"Of course not. With President Wells's permission, I will take Elder Bailey with me."

"And Will?"

Inez smiled at her. "No, I'm sure Elder Knight will want to stay close by to check on you."

The rain clattered harder onto the street.

"I'm such a bother," Jennie croaked.

"You are not a bother," Inez said emphatically. "The rain is a bother, the chill is a bother, but you are not." She went to look out the window. "Now, if we were in Utah, the warm sun would be . . . "

"Ah, don't speak of Utah," Jennie protested. "I don't need a pain in my heart as well as my throat."

"Sorry," Inez said, unlocking the window latch and opening the pane a few inches. "Let's get some clean air in here."

"But it's freezing!"

"Just for a few minutes. We need to get the bad air out."

"Yes, Nurse Florence Nightingale," Jennie said, taking another lozenge from the tin.

Inez placed a lap blanket on top of the bed covers. "When I get to the conference house, I'll send Mrs. Reed over with medicine and some breakfast. Soft eggs maybe."

Jennie nodded. "And Will?"

"I'm sure he will be close on Mrs. Reed's heels. You sleep now."

"Thank you, Inez. Be careful in Manchester."

"I will."

"I'm glad Elder Bailey will be with you."

"Enough talking," Inez reprimanded. "Go to sleep."

Jennie grimaced as she attempted to swallow. She closed her eyes and rolled onto her side.

Inez went to get ready for the day—worry over Jennie and excitement about the Manchester appointment warring for precedence in her mind.

The train whistle blasted, and Inez came abruptly out of her daydreaming. "Have we arrived already?"

Elder Bailey grinned. "We have, Sister Knight. It's only thirty miles. *Tempus fugit*—especially when your mind is on castles and green hills."

"Oh dear! What a dunce I am. You should have pointed me to my duty, Elder Bailey. I should have been considering what to preach."

"Or how to find the obscure address your brother gave us." Elder Bailey chuckled, taking a paper from his suit pocket. "An alleyway off Market Street with a men's haberdashery on one corner."

Inez shook her head. "I don't know how Will expects us to have an appointment when we don't have the name of the shop or the woman he spoke with."

"It's often the way we do things, Sister Knight. Stumble around in the dark until the Spirit shines some light."

Inez gave him a narrowed look. "Stumble around? I do not like the sound of that, Elder Bailey. I've never found that stumbling accomplishes much except a bump on the head."

Elder Bailey suppressed a laugh, then sobered as the train began to slow. "What say we have a prayer, Sister Knight, and ask for some light on our situation?"

"Good idea. And please ask that there be no stumbling . . . tripping . . . or falling down."

Now Elder Bailey laughed heartily, and Inez joined him.

"A miracle," Inez said, staring at the sign above the door of the shop.

"Francom's Fish Shop." She looked over at Elder Bailey. "How did we do this?"

"*We* didn't."

"No, of course not. You're right."

"Now that the Spirit has led us here, we may as well go in," Elder Bailey said, reaching for the doorknob.

Just then the door opened, and a woman exited carrying a market basket and dragging along a crying child. As the twosome passed, Inez smiled but then immediately grimaced as she was hit by the smell coming through the open door.

"Pray for a strong stomach," Elder Bailey whispered to her as he moved into the shop.

Inez nodded, took a brief whiff of her scented handkerchief, and followed him.

A young woman in a shabby dress and headscarf looked over at them. "Mornin'," she said in a cheery voice. "Lookin' for somethin' special?"

"Actually, I think we're looking for you," Elder Bailey said with a smile.

"Me?" She stopped placing salted cod in a stack and turned to take in the brash young man and his lady friend. "Don't know ya. Neva seen ya b'for."

"Yes, that's true. But you have met a friend of ours."

"Oh?"

Inez stepped forward. "Yes, my brother. Actually, you saved him from a gang of ruffians a couple of months ago."

Remembrance softened the woman's features. "The American preacher?"

"That's him! That's my brother Will. Jesse William Knight."

"Where is he then?"

Elder Bailey took off his hat. "He's in Liverpool caring for a sick friend, but he sent us to meet you and see how you're doing. He's very grateful for your help that night."

"Yer American too, are ya?"

Elder Bailey extended his hand. "I'm Harrison Bailey, and this is Inez Knight."

"Addy Francom," the young woman said, cautiously taking Elder Bailey's hand. "Afraid ya might be smellin' of fish after that."

"No harm done. I'm a big fisherman back home in Utah."

"Utah? Where's that?"

"It's in the Western United States."

Addy's eyes widened. "Ah! Cowboys and Indians!"

"How do you know about that?" Inez questioned.

"Me 'usband, Oliver, reads them penny dreadfuls now, don't he? Some of 'em are about the Wild West."

"Well, Salt Lake City is a proper humdrum city, I'm afraid," Inez said with a chuckle. "Not many cowboys, bank robbers, or gun fighters."

"Truly? Well, Oliver would find that boring," Addy said. "He likes a bit of rough and tumble."

"Is he here now?" Inez asked, trying to keep the anxiousness out of her voice.

"Naw. He and his da are off makin' the mornin' deliveries."

"I must say, it's quite a business you have here, Addy," Elder Bailey complimented.

Addy smiled. "Keeps us out of the workhouse."

"Well, Addy, Sister Knight and I are here to keep Will's promise."

"Yuv come back to buy some fish?"

Inez chuckled. "Yes, indeed, we will do that, but we also want to tell you a little about what we believe."

"Yer a preacher too?" Addy asked, staring at Inez. "Never 'eard of a woman preacher."

Inez reached into her satchel. "Would you like to see photographs of Salt Lake City? It's the largest city in Utah." She brought out a small album and held it out to the young woman.

"Photographs? I've not seen many a them," Addy said. She wiped her hands on her apron and reached for the book. "Yeah, I would like to see." She flipped the book open to the first photograph with its view down Main Street. "Well, them's nice buildings. And look at the people's togs. They're dandy then, aren't they?" She flipped to the next photos. "Caw, the streets are wide."

"Wide enough for a wagon with a team of eight to turn around in," Elder Bailey said proudly.

Addy turned another page. "Oh my! You've a castle in Salt Lake City?"

"A castle?" Inez came to stand beside her. She smiled. "That is the Salt Lake Temple."

"Temple?"

"A sacred building. The house of the Lord."

"Who lives there?"

"Well, no one lives there," Elder Bailey said. "It's a place we go to for instruction and to make eternal covenants."

"Wot's that mean?"

"It means promises. The promises we make in the temple can tie a family together forever," Inez said.

Addy looked fiercely into Inez's eyes. "You mean it?" Inez nodded. Addy ran her hand over the photo of the temple. "Tied together forever." Inez watched as the young woman struggled to restrain her emotions. After a time, she cleared her throat and spoke softly. "Our little boy died when he was two. Does this covenant mean I could have 'im back again in heaven?"

Inez felt tears press at the back of her throat. "It does, Addy."

Addy stared at the photo. "Caw, that made me heart jump," she said with hushed reverence.

Elder Bailey handed her a tract. "Would you like to start at the beginning of what we believe?" Addy nodded, never taking her eyes from the photo of the temple.

The shop door opened, and a man entered carrying two large buckets. "Mornin', Addy! Got yer ice then."

"Ah, thanks, Jack. Just take it on down."

"Yes'm," Jack said, giving Elder Bailey and Inez a suspicious glare as he passed into the back room. Inez heard a door open at the rear of the shop and male voices giving Jack a hearty greeting.

"Oh dear!" Addy said, looking startled. "They're back early! It's me 'usband and his da." She shoved the tract at Inez. "Ya better be goin' now."

"But we . . . "

"No. No! I'm tellin' ya, it's no good!"

As Addy hid the tract behind her, a burly man emerged from the back room frowning at the threesome. "What's no good, me girl?" He was soon joined by a younger man of similar look and stature.

Addy tried to calm herself but to no avail. "I . . . we . . . we was . . . "

"Who be these two, Addy?" The younger man demanded.

"Customers, Oliver. Just customers."

"Don't think so." He took a step toward her. "What ya hidin'?" Addy shook her head. "Give it over." Addy brought the tract forward, and he grabbed it from her hand. "*The Voice of Warning*." He glared at the two missionaries. "Wot's this then?"

Inez found her voice. "We were keeping a promise my brother made to your wife."

Elder Bailey groaned.

"Wot's that?" Oliver hissed, rounding on Inez.

"I mean . . . "

"Wot's yer brother got to do with me wife?"

"We're missionaries for The Church of Jesus Christ of Latter-day Saints."

Elder Bailey groaned again.

The older Mr. Francom stepped forward. "It's that American church. I've seen 'em preachin' in the park yonder."

Jack came into the room and joined the fray. "The Mormons? Yeah, they're the ones wot drag our women off to workhouses in Utah."

"Well, that's just nonsense," Inez retorted.

"Inez, be quiet," Elder Bailey urged.

"Nonsense, is it?" Oliver snarled. In one fast motion the big man grabbed the lapels of Elder Bailey's coat and yanked him up.

"Oliver, don't!" Addy pleaded with her husband.

Mr. Francom ignored her and glared at Inez. "'Ow do I know yer not one of his caged females come ta trick me wife ta yer evil ways?"

"Sir! I . . . I assure you . . . "

"I believe I'll give yer mate a voice of warning with me fist." He drew back his arm to land the blow.

"Pike!" Inez yelled so loudly everyone in the shop froze and turned to stare at her.

"Wot's that?" Oliver said in a confused tone.

"Pike. I . . . I want to purchase some pike," Inez answered.

"Not in season," the elder Francom answered automatically.

"Then cod . . . or mackerel."

Oliver gaped at her. "What are ye goin' on about?"

"Or sole. I suppose I could cook up something lovely with sole. I'll have to check with Mrs. Beeton first, but yes, sole might work."

"Saints, bless us," Jack said in a frightened voice. "She's as mad as a March hare."

Oliver let go of Elder Bailey and shoved him away. "Take yer mad female out of my shop!"

"Yes, sir," Elder Bailey said, taking Inez by the arm and heading for the door.

"And don't never come back!"

"That won't be a problem, sir."

They reached the door, and Inez struggled to pull out of Elder Bailey's grip. "But we need to . . . "

"Come along, mad female!" Elder Bailey said in an uplifted, scolding voice. "You promised to behave, and now look at the commotion you've made."

As Elder Bailey dragged her out, Inez called back over her shoulder. "Don't forget the castle, Addy. Remember how you felt about the castle."

Elder Bailey escorted Sister Knight away from Francom's Fish Shop so quickly that she never got to see the secret look of delight on Addy Francom's face.

NOTES

Rules for missionaries: The rules for missionary conduct were much different from today's strict standards. All sister-missionary journals from this period reference times when elders and sisters paired off together to tract, attend cottage meetings, or sightsee.

Florence Nightingale: She is known as the founder of modern nursing, and her writings had a significant impact on English nursing methods of the mid-1800s. She was born in Florence, Italy, on May 12, 1820, and died in London on August 13, 1910. She was considered an icon of Victorian culture and sensibility.

***The Voice of Warning*:** A popular missionary tract written by Parley P. Pratt.

Victorian workhouses: Sometimes referred to as poorhouses, workhouses were facilities provided by the government to house and feed the poor and destitute. They were harsh, dreary places, made such to deter the able-bodied poor from seeking admittance.

Penny dreadfuls: These inexpensive booklets provided escapist reading for the working class.

Chapter Twelve

On the train to Cheltenham, the pike-and-sole story was tossed about by the transferring missionaries many times, with Elder Bailey adding flourishes and jollity at every telling. Inez fled the public area and hid herself in an empty third-class compartment. It was here her brother Ray found her.

"May I come in if I promise not to mention a certain shop in a certain town?"

"You just did."

"Sorry."

"Come in, silly. I'm so glad to see you. I'm prepared to forgive you for talking about anything."

Ray sat across from her and leaned forward, taking her hands. "It was hard not to immediately leave off the preaching at Bradford and venture down to see you."

Inez patted his hand. "But I understand. Will explained how you and your companion were having great success."

Ray sat back. "Yes. An entire family interested—husband, wife, older children. It was . . . Well, it rarely happens."

"And now you have to leave off and venture down to the Cheltenham Conference with your pesky little sister."

Ray winked at her. "Hopefully you've grown out of that." He glanced at the passing landscape. "That's the way of things on a mission, Inez. The work will go on in Bradford, and we will find new adventures in the Cheltenham area."

"I think I've had enough adventures with my escapade in Manchester."

Ray chuckled. "I doubt that. You have a knack for getting into trouble." He hesitated. "Of course, now you have Sister Brimhall's calming influence. Maybe that will keep you under control."

"How can you say such a thing?"

"Because it's true."

Inez started to protest, then closed her mouth and sighed. "It is true."

At that moment Jennie tapped on the glass of the compartment door, and Inez started. "Well, here comes my calming influence!" Inez said with a chuckle. She motioned Jennie in, and she entered, followed by Will.

"We wondered where you went to hide," Will said.

"Yes, so please don't bring the story with you," Inez warned.

"Wouldn't think of it. I just wanted to thank you again for finding Addy Francom."

"Huh! And leaving her without a word of preaching?"

"Sometimes all you have to leave is a feeling."

"That's true, Sister," Ray said. "Sometimes just a word about the gospel is enough, and then we have to have patience with the Lord's timing."

Inez frowned. "You know I've never been very patient."

Jennie smiled at the Knight siblings. "What a joy that the four of us are together," she said. "It will be grand to be missionaries in the same area."

"That's true," Inez said. "I'm just disappointed you have to have Elder Davis as your companion."

Ray gave her a quizzical look. "Jonathan's all right."

"What? Do you know him well?" Will asked.

"I've seen him a couple of times—heard him speak." He looked at Inez. "You seem to have taken a dislike to him. Why?"

"He's sour and standoffish."

"Perhaps he's shy."

Inez raised her eyebrows. "He is not shy. He criticizes everything, he thinks he's better than everyone, and what's more, he's totally against Jennie and me being here."

"How do you know that?"

"Because he said so."

"Inez, I think you may have misunderstood."

Inez crossed her arms in front of her and glared at her brother. "I did not misunderstand, Ray. In front of us and other missionaries, Elder Davis said, and I quote, 'I don't think they belong here. It's dangerous and they're distractions.'"

"Well, it *is* dangerous, and you *are* distractions."

"You can't mean that!"

"I do," Ray affirmed. "The elders get into scuffles all the time, Inez, or we're yelled at or have objects thrown at us. It's dodgy. Must I remind you of the pike-and-sole incident?"

"But we . . . "

"And you *are* distractions. Not that you mean to be—you just are. With women around, the elders feel they need to fuss over you and protect you."

Inez slumped in her seat. "Well then, Jennie and I should just pack our bags for home."

Ray sat forward. "Don't even think about it. Elder Davis is one-hundred-percent wrong on one point, and that is that you two don't belong here. You most certainly do belong here." He looked at Inez straight on. "Do you believe the Church leaders are guided by revelation?"

"Of course," Inez said.

"And you and Jennie are part of that revelation. The Church is continually moving forward, Inez, and we . . . " He motioned to all four in the compartment. "We are part of that movement. Elder Davis and many others may not like it, but the Lord has a great work to do, and He needs us to pick up our burdens and help Him. He needs you and Jennie to do the same."

"Quite a sermon, brother," Will said.

Inez looked over to find Jennie crying. "Now look what you've done. You've made Jennie cry."

"They're good tears," Jennie responded. "Thank you, Elder Knight. I needed those words. I've been letting my burdens weigh me down."

"We all need encouragement," Ray said.

"Encouragement? That sounded more like a lecture from Father," Will said.

"Well, if she's joining our family, she may as well get used to it," Inez put in.

Jennie laughed, and the three Knight siblings joined her. Inez smiled at her friend, took a deep breath, and turned to look out at the passing scenery. The sound of her brothers' voices faded as she lost herself in the beauty of the countryside. She thought of the sun rising over the peaks of the Wasatch Mountains, her father going over ledgers, her mother making a pie, her sisters in school. Were they thinking of her? Did they miss her? *Of course*, she chided herself. *Love is not lessened by distance*. The train passed from open fields into a forested area, and Inez was enchanted by the sunlight flickering through the leaves. She glanced over at Jennie and smiled. Her companion was reading *Mrs. Beeton's Book of Household Management*, and for some reason Inez felt her spirits lift. In less than an hour they'd be in Cheltenham, and the next part of their mission would begin. Perhaps with prayer, the Bible, the Book of Mormon, and Mrs. Beeton's book of household wisdom, she and Jennie just might be able to navigate the meandering paths of proselyting in England.

Chapter Thirteen

Inez and Jennie stood as close to the open doorway as possible so they could dash away at the first sign of a mouse, spider, or rat. Inez looked to the ceiling of the apartment, absolutely sure she would find bats circling there.

"Is this . . ."

"Yes," Jennie said.

"Really?"

"The elders brought us here and dropped off our trunks."

"But . . . look at the . . . "

"I know," Jennie said, taking a step into the room.

"Don't go in there! It smells funny. And what's that on the wall?"

Jennie squinted into the dim interior of the room. "Hmm . . . could be blood."

"Jennie!"

"Or a water stain." Jennie took a breath and walked resolutely to the window. She pushed back the tattered drapes and opened the window a slit. She put her hands on her hips and glared at the pane of glass. "It won't open more than that."

"Jennie, come back! I think the lamp is leaking gas." Sister Brimhall hurried to her companion's side. "How is this possible?" Inez lamented. "I was so pleased with the town when we drove in from the station. Fine residences and fountains and parks."

"And flowers," Jennie added.

"So how did we end up in outer darkness?"

They heard creaking on the stairs and advancing footfalls. Inez peeked around the corner of the doorframe and saw Sister Noall on the landing. Inez stepped out into the hallway. "Sister Noall?"

"I can hardly see you," Sister Noall said, running her hand along the banister. "My goodness. Why is this place so dingy?"

Jennie stepped out of the room to join Inez. "We were wondering that too."

Sister Noall came to stand beside them. She looked into the apartment and advanced slowly inside. She stopped in the middle of the room, took off her gloves, and turned. "Oh no. This will not do. This will not do at all. What was the president thinking—to leave the finding of your apartment to the male missionaries? Most of them could live in a basement with candles." She went to turn on the wall lamp, taking a match from the match holder and preparing to strike it.

Inez rushed to her. "Wait! We thought we smelled a foul smell."

"Indeed, Sister Knight. I smell it too, but I don't think it's the lamp." She struck the match, and Inez flinched. Sister Noall turned on the gas and held the match to it. The shadows disappeared, leaving behind the detritus of neglect and a few sad pieces of furniture that looked forlorn in comparison with the girl's sturdy travel trunks. There was a potbellied stove in the corner so covered in dust that the manufacturer's name could not be seen in the cast iron. A threadbare rug covered half of the wood floor, and Inez thought she could make out a faded oriental design with dragons and flowering trees.

"I think someone in China threw out their old carpet."

"Thank you for attempting levity, Sister Knight, but I'm afraid nothing is going to make this apartment cheery," Sister Noall said, walking to one of the beds and pulling back the coverlet. "Well, at least the bedding seems clean." She turned to the girls. "I'm sure the elders chose this apartment for its proximity to the conference home, but it clearly will not do." She went to the window and ran her finger along the grimy glass. She shook her head and grumbled several unintelligible words. She turned to Inez and Jennie. "I'm afraid you may have to stay here a night or two until we can find another dwelling." Sister Noall moved to the door, giving instructions as she went. "Do not unpack your trunks, sisters. I'm off to find President Noall; we'll get this sorted."

Inez followed her to the door. "Thank you, Sister Noall."

"Don't worry!" Jennie called. "We'll make the best of it till then."

Inez turned from the doorway to stare at her companion. "We'll make the best of it?"

Jennie started giggling. "Well, what else can we do?"

"Run," Inez said, joining Jennie in her laughter. "Cry. Find a bath-house. Scrub the place with lye soap."

Abruptly Jennie stopped laughing and pointed. "What's that?"

Inez spun around. "Where?"

"There—on the wall by the table and chairs."

Inez squinted and moved forward. "Probably just another water mark."

Suddenly the water mark skittered across the wall. The girls screamed, grabbed their satchels, and bolted for the door.

"I told you females weren't suited for the work. Do you think the sons of Mosiah would have run from a spider or worried that their rooms didn't have frilly curtains or silk coverlets?"

"Leave off, Elder Davis," Will warned.

"No one said anything about needing silk coverlets," Inez said. "But I would like cleanliness." She glared at him. "I don't think the Spirit can dwell in unclean spaces, Elder Davis. Wouldn't you agree?"

Elder Bailey laughed. "Well said, Sister Knight!"

"Tell that to Paul or Peter, or Abinadi in prison," Elder Davis argued. "Sometimes missionaries must endure places that are not pristine, Sister Knight."

"And sometimes missionaries have to eat food that's very different from their mother's home cooking," Elder Bailey shot back. His barbed innuendo hit the mark, and Elder Davis's face reddened.

The missionaries of the Cheltenham Conference were sitting at the long table in the common room, which served for studying and eating. Most of the fourteen chairs were occupied, and the majority of those present were far more interested in observing the squabble than studying their scriptures.

Ray Knight stood. "That's enough now, elders. It's not for us to debate whether the sister missionaries should be here. The First Presidency has sent them, and we are to support them all we can."

"Amen," Elder Bailey said.

"What? Run to kill a spider every time they scream?"

Will and Elder Bailey started to stand, but Ray motioned them down. "No, Elder Davis, but encourage them, train them on how to approach people and hand out tracts, suggest which scriptures are most effective in teaching certain doctrines. You could do that, right?"

Elder Davis flipped open his Book of Mormon. "Waste of effort," he mumbled.

The onlookers stared as Sister Brimhall rose to her feet. "Is that because you think us dolts when it comes to the scriptures, Elder Davis?" Her voice was soft, her demeanor calm. "Unable to glean the beauty and doctrine from the psalm of Nephi in 2 Nephi 4, or learn the lessons of repentance and resurrection as taught by Samuel the Lamanite in the book of Helaman, or grasp the doctrine of Christ in 3 Nephi?" The room was still, and Elder Davis did not respond. "Or is it that you think us efficient at only cleaning and cooking?"

"Well, I've seen you wasting time reading that cookery book."

Inez growled, but Jennie went on serenely. "It may be difficult for you to understand, Elder Davis, but women can do many things at the same time. We can cook *and* study the scriptures."

"And teach at the Brigham Young Academy," Will interjected.

Jennie smiled at him. "Thank you, Will."

Elder Davis gave her a patronizing look. "I'm not saying you're unintelligent, Sister Brimhall; I just think your physical weakness and fragile emotions don't lend themselves to the rigor of missionary work."

Now all eyes were on Sister Brimhall as she took a breath and composed herself. "You may be right, Elder Davis." Inez started to protest, but Jennie went on. "But perhaps we should wait and see. This is new territory for all of us. I will tell you honestly that Sister Knight and I were stunned when the call came from the First Presidency." A smirk came to Elder Davis's lips, and Jennie took another breath. "But come it did, and now we're doing our best to figure out where we fit in and where we can best serve. Now, I know you think that means in the kitchen . . . "

"Just so."

Will stood. "You are out of line, Jonathan!"

"It's all right, Elder Knight," Jennie said in a controlled voice. "Elder Davis can think what he likes." She turned to face her opponent, and Inez noted that although her friend's hands were clenched into fists, her voice remained calm. "I would ask a favor, then, Elder Davis."

He turned to frown at her. "What kind of favor?"

"One day, because of our weakness, you may find Sister Knight and me crumpled in heaps by the side of the road. We'd be obliged if you'd scoop us into wheelbarrows and transport us back to the conference home or dump us on the docks where we might find a boat for home." After a moment of stunned silence, the entire room erupted into laughter and clapping. Elder Davis stood, grabbed his scriptures, and left the room.

Inez hurried to hug her companion. "You were wonderful!"

"Actually, I'm feeling quite ashamed of myself."

"Nonsense. He had it coming. And I'm glad you were the one to quote scripture; my brain for it is rubbish."

As several missionaries came to shake Sister Brimhall's hand, a voice rang out from the back of the common room. "What is all this racket?"

The clamor stopped immediately as the missionaries turned to see President and Sister Noall standing at the doorway. Those still sitting, stood, and Elder Bailey stepped forward. "Sorry, President. We . . . we were just . . . "

"It's my fault, President Noall," Jennie said. "I'm afraid Elder Davis and I were having a disagreement."

The couple walked forward. "Well, this is unexpected," President Noall said. "We try and keep disagreements out of the conference home, Sister Brimhall."

"Yes, sir. I'm sorry."

"You and Sister Knight come with us. We have something to discuss."

"Yes, sir," Inez mumbled, feeling as she did whenever Father had "something to discuss," for it usually meant a reprimand or an assignment.

The president looked past them to the elders, who were now talking together in lowered voices. "Elder Abernathy, Elder Cook, please come with me." The two named elders detached themselves from their fellows to join Jennie and Inez in following President Noall.

Inez gave them a puzzled glance, but neither of the elders deigned to look at her. As they moved down the hallway to the president's office, Inez's curiosity got the better of her. "Are we in trouble?" she whispered.

"Well, *we* are," Elder Abernathy confessed, inclining his head to his companion.

"What for?"

"I think you'll be witness to that in a minute."

President and Sister Noall entered the office, and the four missionaries followed. The president went to stand behind his desk. "Please sit, ladies. And, elders, you may stay standing for you will not be here long." He waited until the two young men met his gaze before continuing. "I have just one question for you. Did you truly think that apartment suitable for the sister missionaries?"

"Ah . . . " Elder Cook looked over at his companion and then back to the president. "Ah . . . "

Elder Abernathy waded in. "Well, we realize it's not in the best condition, but . . . "

"Not in the best condition?" Sister Noall broke in. "Would you wish your mother or one of your sisters to live in such conditions?"

"I don't have any sisters," Elder Cook stated.

"No, ma'am," Elder Abernathy said quickly to cover his companion's obtuseness. "No, ma'am, of course we wouldn't, but that was all we could find near the conference home." He turned to the president. "We did try to find something more suitable, President, but there was nothing."

President Noall took a deep breath and sat at his desk. "Then you will just have to make it up to them, elders."

"How, sir?"

"Go find Sister Wilkey and ask for cleaning supplies. Tell her why you need them and get her advice on what to use and how to clean." He hesitated. "Better yet, have her go with you to supervise."

"Supervise what?" Elder Cook asked.

President Noall glanced at the ceiling and shook his head. "Supervise as you and Elder Abernathy scrub the sister's apartment."

Inez noted that Elder Cook seemed baffled by President Noall's directive, and she wondered if he had ever scrubbed anything in his life.

"Off you go, elders," President Noall instructed. "And do not forget to apologize to the sisters on the way out."

"Yes, sir," Elder Abernathy said. "So sorry, Sister Knight and Sister Brimhall. We'll do our best to make it livable." He noticed his companion staring at the girls without speaking. "He's sorry too." Both Inez and Jennie stifled laughter. Elder Abernathy grabbed his companion by the arm and dragged him toward the door. "Come on, Elder Cook, let's get to work."

After the elders' departure, Inez and Jennie turned their attention to the president. He was staring at the doorway where the elders had just departed. He slowly shook his head and mumbled, "Heaven help us." Inez was sure he hadn't meant his statement to be heard by the others in the room, so she feigned inattention when he turned to look at them. "I apologize for not taking a more active part in the apartment hunting, sisters."

"I as well," Sister Noall added. "But we'll get it sorted out."

"We will begin immediately looking for another place, but for now, while Mrs. Wilkey helps the elders clean your apartment, you will stay with us," President Noall said.

"Sister Knight and I do not want special favors," Jennie said firmly.

Sister Noall looked perplexed. "Special favors? Whatever do you mean?"

"We don't want to be treated any differently than the elders."

President Noall grinned at her. "I believe I understand your desire, Sister Brimhall, but the fact is the elders do stay with us from time to time."

"They do?"

"Of course. If they're traveling through or sick or waiting for a companion; it's common for them to stay with us a night or two."

"Oh," Jennie said.

"We'll be grateful to stay with you then!" Inez said in a bright voice. "That will be nice, won't it, Sister Brimhall?"

"Yes, of course," Jennie answered. "But only for a night or two."

Inez was in no hurry to get back to the spider-infested apartment. "How long do you think we'll have to be in that . . . that other place?"

Sister Noall seemed to anticipate the question. "As we said, we'll be looking straightaway for another apartment for you two, but it might be a few weeks."

"In the meantime," Jennie said quickly to cover her companion's moan, "we'd like to help with the cleaning."

"That's not necessary, Sister Brimhall."

"It would make us feel better, President," Jennie insisted.

Inez was sure it would *not* make *her* feel better.

"All right, then, but make sure you let the elders do most of the work," President Noall instructed. "It's part of their penance."

"Yes, sir." Jennie and Inez gathered their coats and satchels and stood. "Is there anything else, President?" Jennie asked.

"Just that I will see you later at priesthood meeting."

Inez stared at him. "Priesthood meeting? You also want us at priesthood meeting like President Wells did?"

"Of course, Sister Knight. It's where training occurs and mission business is discussed. You are now part of the mission, so I need you in attendance. I will probably call on you to tell a bit about yourself, preach a modest sermon, and offer your testimony. Both you and Sister Brimhall."

Jennie nodded. "We can do that, President Noall."

Inez only nodded. Her breath caught near her heart, and she knew that any words out of her mouth would be accompanied by a squeak or a squawk. She followed Jennie from the president's office and then out of the conference home.

"Aren't we going back to study?"

Jennie shook her head. "No. We are going to the baths. I need to wash off travel and bad feelings for Elder Davis."

"And the grime of the apartment," Inez grumbled.

"That too," Jennie affirmed. The two locked arms and set off. "And maybe after our baths we'll find a bakery and eat a dozen Chelsea buns."

NOTE

Living conditions: Though the condition of the Cheltenham apartment was not specifically mentioned in Inez Knight's journal, there are references to dingy living quarters and fleas and bedbugs in the writings of other early sister missionaries in England.

Chapter Fourteen

Inez had had a fitful night's sleep—worries of spiders, the smell of strong soaps, Jennie moaning in the bed across the way, and dreams of riding in a wheelbarrow and being unceremoniously dumped on the dock at Liverpool all combined to keep her tossing and turning. In addition to all those demons, there'd been a sensation of bugs crawling on her skin. She reminded her weary brain that they'd spent the last two days working with Mrs. Wilkey and the elders to scrub the apartment until it emerged quite livable. Mrs. Wilkey had even had the shabby old divan and carpet removed and replaced with things donated by President and Sister Noall. And before climbing into bed last night, hadn't she thanked the Lord for the miraculous transformation? She should have drifted immediately into a grateful and much-needed rest, but that did not come; instead she'd spent hours fretting until exhaustion took her into a few hours of deep sleep. Now awaking, she yawned and scratched her neck. She frowned and scratched her left arm and then her right hand. She bolted from the bed.

"Jennie!"

Jennie sat straight up. "What? What is it?" She scanned the room, trying to focus. "Inez?"

Inez ran to the window and shoved back the new drapes. Morning light spilled into the room, and Inez stared at her arms and hands. Small blobs of red stood out against her pale skin. "I think I've been bitten by something!" She looked over at Jennie and saw her unwittingly scratching her neck. "Oh no! You too?" She rushed to her. "Look at your face!"

Jennie stared at her friend. "Look at *your* face."

"Get out of that bed!" Inez ordered, and Jennie hopped up.

They stood together, shivering and scratching.

"I thought we cleaned everything," Jennie moaned. "Are these spider bites?"

"I don't think so. I don't know what they are, but I don't think spiders."

"But we cleaned everything," Jennie insisted again.

Inez went to her bed and threw back the coverlet and sheet. "We didn't launder our bedding because Sister Noall said it looked clean."

Jennie shuddered. "Can you see anything?"

"Not in this dim light."

"What are we going to do?"

"Dress and go to the conference home."

"Looking like this?"

"We'll sneak downstairs and find Sister Wilkey. Hopefully she'll know what to do."

Jennie went to the window to see her reflection in the glass. She moaned. "I hope Will doesn't see me like this."

"I hope *Elder Davis* doesn't see us like this. He'll consider it just punishment for our arrogance."

"Arrogance?"

"In coming on a mission."

Jennie turned from the window. "Well, that upsets me." She took a deep breath. "I don't think we should let him get away with such bad behavior."

"What do you mean?"

"It means after we talk with Mrs. Wilkey, I'm going to march into the common room for breakfast, not caring what anyone says."

Inez shrugged. "Well, I suppose they stare at us anyway."

"Exactly." Jennie went to open her trunk. "We'll show them we come from tough pioneer stock."

Pioneer stock with the pox, Inez thought as she scratched her neck.

"New mattresses, boiled linens, fresh start!" Mrs. Wilkey said as she supervised the delousing. She sprinkled bicarbonate of soda into the deep, round tub and handed Inez and Jennie wooden paddles. Inez scratched her neck as she reached for the paddle. "Try not to scratch," Mrs. Wilkey instructed, and Inez dropped her hand. Mrs. Wilkey continued with her instructions. "Make sure every surface gets a good soak in the water, and keep the temperature hot hot hot. There are boiling pots of water on the stove." She wiped her hands on her apron. "We'll do your night dresses and undergarments separately."

Elder Abernathy and Elder Cook arrived in the laundry room on the word "undergarments," and both men flushed scarlet. Inez and Jennie abruptly turned to their work, earnestly prodding the sheets as though no work was more important. Inez chanced a peek in the elders' direction and found that, while Elder Abernathy had turned to face Mrs. Wilkey, Elder Cook continued to stare at them. Elder Abernathy swatted him across the chest, which started him coughing.

"President Noall sent us to see you," Elder Abernathy said, shaking his head and patting his coughing companion on the back.

Inez noticed frustration in Elder Abernathy's normally calm and proper British voice.

"Yes. I have work for you," Mrs. Wilkey answered, moving to the other side of the laundry room. "Come with me."

Elder Abernathy grabbed his companion by the sleeve and dragged him along. Inez and Jennie divided their attention between the laundry tub and the threesome at the cupboards.

Mrs. Wilkey removed a small ring of keys from her pocket and unlocked one of the cupboards. She brought out a box of something, a tin pan, and a handful of feathers. She handed the items to the elders. "Now, I want you to—"

"Keating Persian Powder?" Elder Cook interrupted, reading the label on the box. He frowned at Mrs. Wilkey. "What's this, then?"

"Bedbug poison," Mrs. Wilkey shot back, irritated at being cut short.

"Bedbugs?" Elder Cook blurted. He stared over at Inez and Jennie. "Is that what they have? Bedbugs?"

"Good heavens! Be quiet, Mr. Cook. Do you think they ordered them?

You were the ones who secured that dreadful apartment, so if I were you, I'd hush and let me finish my instructions."

"But if they—"

"We're listening, Mrs. Wilkey," Elder Abernathy intervened. "And we're ready to help."

Elder Cook started to protest, and Mrs. Wilkey pointed her finger at him. "One more word out of you, Elder Cook, and I will hang you by your thumbs on my clothesline."

Inez nearly dropped her paddle in the tub as she struggled to keep from laughing out loud.

At that moment, Elder Knight and Elder Bailey appeared at the door. Will went immediately to Jennie. "Sister Noall said you were down here." He stopped short. "Oh goodness! I mean . . . " Jennie's free hand went to cover the side of her face. Will moved closer. "I'm so sorry. That looks painful."

"Painful and itchy," Inez informed.

Will looked over. "Ray reported that you two came into breakfast looking like you had the measles or something."

"Bedbug bites," Inez said, poking at the sheets in the steaming hot water. "And Elder Davis laughed at us and said, 'What's next with you two—the seven plagues?'"

"Sorry I wasn't there," Elder Bailey growled. "Someone needs to teach that boy manners."

"We would have stood up for you," Will agreed, "but President Noall had us running errands all morning."

"It's all right, Elder Knight," Jennie said. "This will just make us stronger."

Elder Bailey brought a small glass jar from his pocket. "Well, you can be strong and not have to suffer." He handed Inez the container.

"What's this?"

"It's a cream of menthol and pulverized chickweed. My mom makes it. Helps with itch."

Inez nodded and put the jar in her skirt pocket. "Smart."

Elder Bailey smiled. "Let me know when you need more."

Just then, Mrs. Wilkey came over with Elder Abernathy and Elder Cook in tow. "Ah, good. Two more helpers." Without waiting for their reply, she handed a stack of tin pans to Elder Knight and a squat ceramic jar of something to Elder Bailey. "I take it you two want to help?"

"Absolutely," Will said.

"So start with the poison. Pour some powder into one tin pan, coat the feather, and run it along and into every crack and crevice of the bedstead and the floorboards. Understand?" Four heads nodded, but Inez thought Elder Cook was merely imitating his fellows. Mrs. Wilkey patted the jar Elder Bailey was holding. "Next, spread a layer of pork grease in the bottom of the other eight tins and place one under each leg of the two beds. Oh! Make sure the beds are away from the walls. Is all that clear?"

"Yes, ma'am," came three replies.

She began to usher them to the door. "Don't breathe in any of the pyrethrum powder."

"The what?" Elder Cook asked.

"The bug-killer powder. It's a natural poison but still a poison—not supposed to hurt humans, but I wouldn't take any chances."

Mrs. Wilkey held Elder Abernathy back. "Keep a close eye on him," she said, inclining her head toward the exiting Elder Cook.

"It is my daily delegation," Elder Abernathy replied, in a tone that mingled mirth, fondness, and frustration.

With that task dispatched, Mrs. Wilkey turned to the girls. "I think it's time for more hot water! Come along girls, and help me fetch it!"

Inez and Jennie propped their paddles against the wall and followed.

Inez leaned in toward Jennie and whispered, "Don't you think Mrs. Beeton would approve of our Mrs. Wilkey?"

"Without question," Jennie said with a smile. "Very efficient. In fact, I'm thinking of popping her in my trunk and taking her home with me."

They both started scratching—Inez, her face, and Jennie, her arms. Each groaned as Inez brought out the jar of anti-itch cream.

NOTE

Remedies of the Victorian Era: Science in the 1800s was making strides in fighting against disease and unclean living conditions, and often Victorian and American householders utilized natural products to clean, disinfect, and heal.

Chapter Fifteen

Folding tracts was not Sister Knight's idea of missionary work, but as the red bumps on her neck and face were still evident, she and Jennie had agreed to one more day of self-imposed quarantine. Inez sighed and folded another tract. The thought of the Prophet Joseph being tarred and feathered hushed her mental complaining. Instead she thought about how Mrs. Wilkey had been victorious in her bedbug battle. Neither she nor Jennie had received any new bothersome bites, and bothersome they were. The memory of the painful itch made Inez wince. *Thank heavens for the anti-itch cream from Elder Bailey's mother.* Absently, Inez ran her fingers across the diminishing bumps on her face.

"Hey ho!" came Will's voice into the common room.

Inez looked to the doorway and saw her brother and Elder Bailey entering, wide smiles on both their faces.

"Well," Jennie said, "those two look like they've won the blue ribbon at the county fair."

Inez chuckled. The two missionaries made their way directly to Jennie and Inez.

"So have you lazy fellows finally come to help us with our boring task?" Inez chided.

"Absolutely not," her brother Will stated with a shake of his head. "You expect successful proselyting missionaries to spend their time on such mundane tasks?"

"Well, that was rude," Jennie said with a frown.

Will winked at her and took the pamphlet from her hand. "I'm just teasing."

"Actually, we've come to release you from your task," Elder Bailey said, taking the pamphlet from Inez's hand. "President Noall has given us permission to take you on a picnic."

Inez looked at her brother. "Really, Will?"

"Yes. We're taking you into the countryside by Bourton-on-the-Water."

Jennie stood. "How delightful! And it's such a beautiful day." She sobered. "But is it appropriate?"

"We all get time off periodically," Will defended.

"I don't mean that. I mean the four of us going off together on such an extended outing."

Elder Bailey's eyes widened, and a red flush crept up his neck.

"Well, Ray's coming along, and President and Sister Noall," Will said. "Might they be acceptable escorts?"

"They will indeed," Jennie said.

Inez groaned, and Will frowned at her. "What's the matter now?"

"If Ray comes with us, his companion comes too."

Will gave her a crooked smile. "Yes, dear sister, but we will have the two of them ride in the carriage with President and Sister Noall."

Inez brightened. "Oh! That's all right then."

Elder Bailey laughed just as Ray and Elder Davis approached the group. "What's all right then?" Ray asked.

Inez turned her smiling face on the twosome. "Everything. Everything is all right, Ray. What could be better than a picnic in the countryside?"

"Doing our jobs," Elder Davis grumbled.

Inez turned, picked up a stack of unfolded tracts, and handed them to him. "Here, Elder Davis. You can take these with you and fold while we're going." She gave him a fake smile. "I so admire your diligence."

Before Elder Davis could respond, Jennie took Inez by the wrist and pulled her away. "Shall we go get our light coats and hats? We'll be back shortly, elders!" They were down the stairs and out onto the street before Jennie released Inez's wrist and spoke again. "Really, Inez. Can you temper your feelings?"

"What?"

"Your feelings for Elder Davis."

"Why should I? He doesn't hide his contempt for the rest of us."

Jennie sighed and began walking to their apartment building. "I'm not talking about his behavior. I'm talking about yours."

"You sound like my mother."

"I'm not your mother, Inez. I'm your sister and your companion." She sighed again. "I just don't want you to have to carry around that burden."

"What burden?"

"The burden of ill feelings," Jennie said, climbing the front steps of the apartment building. "It's making you a little stoop shouldered."

"Wait a minute!" Inez called, and Jennie turned. "Ill feelings? What about your yelling at Elder Davis in front of the other missionaries?"

Jennie's face flushed. "I . . . well . . . well, I repented of that, didn't I? And now I'm trying to take the high ground."

"Oh dear," Inez said, moving up the steps to face her. "Be careful about carrying around *that* burden."

"What burden?"

"The burden of sainthood. It's making your head a little bulbous."

The two glared at each other for a few moments and then burst out laughing.

"Stoop shouldered?" Inez hooted. "Stoop shouldered? Did you really say that?"

"Bulbous head?" Jennie gasped, attempting to catch her breath.

"Good thing you have enough hair to cover it," Inez wheezed, bending over and placing her hands on her knees. A man drove by in a donkey cart and gave the two jovial women a questioning look. Inez, still bent over, offered the man a feeble wave, which sent Jennie into another fit of laughter.

"Stop!" Jennie commanded, holding her sides and trying to calm herself. "We need to get going or the elders will think we deserted them."

"Oh, that's true! That's true!" Inez said, pushing Jennie up the rest of the stairs toward their apartment. "This is going to be a remarkable day! How could we think of spoiling it with a silly spat over Elder Davis?"

"How indeed?" Jennie puffed as she ascended the stairs. "Let's never do that again."

"Agreed," Inez said firmly.

They came to the apartment door, and Jennie fished the keys out of her skirt pocket. "I say we never give another thought to bedbugs, rainy days, or Elder Davis." She held out her hand, and Inez gave it a firm shake.

Somewhere in the distance Inez heard the bleating of sheep and the insistent barking of a dog. Eyes closed, her drowsy senses tried to focus on where she was but found only drifting: a carriage ride, green rolling hills, enchanting villages of stone . . .

"Jennie?" she said lazily. "What would you say is the color of the Cotswold stone?"

There was silence.

Inez opened one eye to see her friend sitting with her back against a tree, looking at Mrs. Beeton's book. "Did you hear me?"

"Yes. I'm thinking." Jennie looked over to a small cottage at the edge of the meadow. "Not yellow, but not beige either. Maybe gold—pale gold."

Inez opened her eyes and sat up. "Yes. Pale gold. That's it. . . . It's like the stone has soaked in the afternoon sunlight so that, even on the dreariest and most overcast day, the Cotswold houses and shops radiate warmth."

"My, Sister Knight, that's a lovely image. When did you become a poet?"

"It's this place then, isn't it? I feel like I've stepped into a fairy tale." Inez stood and stretched her back. "Ugh. I should not have fallen asleep on the ground. It's Mrs. Wilkey's fault."

"Mrs. Wilkey?"

"And the cook's. If they hadn't packed such a wonderful picnic . . ."

"No one said you had to eat three sausage rolls and three slices of lemon cake."

Inez moved over and sat next to Jennie. "Wasn't it the best cake?"

"It was," Jennie agreed. "And look here. I've found a recipe for lemon cake in Mrs. Beeton's book."

"Do you think it's the same one the cook used?"

"I'm going to ask her when we get back. If it is, I'm sending the recipe to Flora."

Inez yawned and looked around. "So, where is everyone?"

"President and Sister Noall took a walk into the village, and the boys are over that hillock kicking a ball around."

"Let's go find them. Maybe they'll let us join in."

"You want to kick a ball around?"

"Why not? I don't know what the game is, but maybe it will be fun."

Jennie looked over at Inez's eager face. "Oh, all right. I'm not much for playing games, though."

Inez stood and extended her hand to help Jennie up. "This I know, but won't it be a grand memory to tell your grandchildren?"

"Wait. Will and I have yet to be married, and you have me with grandchildren?"

"*Tempus fugit*," Inez said grinning. They began walking. "I can picture it; you're standing in your kitchen making a lemon cake and telling your grandchildren . . . " She imitated Jennie's voice. "Now, children, when I was a missionary in England, there was a day unlike any other day, when we had a picnic near a town called Bourton-on-the-Water. We ate sausage rolls and lemon cake and played a game where we kicked a ball around. Your Auntie Inez and I ran the legs off all the elders and won the game twenty to nothing!"

Jennie laughed. "We don't even know how the game is scored. Perhaps the final would be forty to nothing."

"That's the spirit. As long as the fellows get nothing."

As they neared the top of the hill, they began to hear calls and shouts.

"Will! Will! Over here!"

"You've gone outside the boundary, Elder Bailey."

"Not a chance! I was twenty miles away!"

"That would put you in Stratford," Elder Davis scoffed. "Playing football with Shakespeare, are you?" He motioned for the ball. "Come on. Play fair."

Elder Bailey scowled at him, picked up the ball, and threw it to Ray. "We're still ahead, three to two."

Will caught sight of the girls watching from the top of the hill. He waved. "Hello, Sister Brimhall!"

"Seems I'm invisible to him," Inez said to Jennie, making her blush and smile.

Will ran over to them. "Come to watch us play?"

"No such thing," Inez said. "We've come to join."

By this time the other elders were drifting over. Will looked simultaneously surprised and impressed. "Really? You want to play football?"

"What's this?" Elder Davis asked.

Inez didn't like the tone of his voice.

"We've come to play football," Jennie said quickly.

"It's not really a girl's activity, now, is it?"

"Why not?" Inez protested.

Elder Davis pointed at her skirt. "Not very favorable for running and kicking a ball."

Inez hefted her skirt and petticoat to the top of her boot. "Shall we see?"

Elder Bailey laughed. "We'll take Inez on our team."

Will began to protest, but Ray stopped him with good-natured chiding. "Don't worry, Will. We'll take good care of your Jennie." He turned to her. "You don't mind playing on our team, do you, Sister Brimhall?"

"Not at all, Elder Knight. I think I may prove a distraction to a member on the opposite team."

Ray laughed heartily and gave his brother a salute. "So be it. Now, I will tell you ladies the rules of the game."

"There are rules?" Inez questioned.

Ray sobered. "Of course."

"And you know them?"

Ray looked offended. "I'll have you know, Elder Abernathy schooled us expertly in the rules of associated football."

Inez scowled. "Well, all right, but don't get too particular or it won't be any fun."

A half an hour later, President and Sister Noall found their six missionaries engaged in an energetic and chaotic game of football. They watched in amusement for a few minutes before President Noall called the game to a halt.

"Well, that was entertaining," he offered as the group of young people gathered around.

"It's been a lovely afternoon altogether, President," Jennie said catching her breath. "Thank you so much."

The others offered their gratitude also.

"We do need to get back to the conference home, but Sister Noall and I thought we might stop in Bourton first, wander a bit, and have afternoon tea."

There was a general hubbub of excitement as every missionary, even Elder Davis, expressed delight at the prospect. As the group headed back to gather the picnic items, the animated chatter continued until Inez caught her foot on a tree root and fell flat.

Elder Bailey rushed to her prostrate form. "Sister Knight, are you all right?"

"No," she groaned, her voice muffled as her face was addressing the ground. She rolled over slowly, sat up, and spat out a dead leaf. "Brilliant. I don't fall once during our game, and now I fall over a tree root?"

Her brothers stifled their laughter.

"Are you well enough to stand?" Elder Bailey asked solicitously.

She nodded, brushing dirt from her cheek. "I think I've bruised only my dignity."

Elder Bailey caught her under the upper arm, and President Noall assisted on the other side.

"We'll head home immediately so Mrs. Wilkey can take a look at you."

"Oh! I'm fine, President Noall! Don't make everyone else miss out because of my clumsiness."

They managed to pull her up, and Inez stamped her feet and stretched her back. "See?"

Sister Noall came to her and offered a handkerchief. "Are you sure you're all right?"

"Right as a ninepence," Inez answered.

"My word, you're becoming very British, little sister," Ray said.

"Indeed," Elder Davis scoffed. "She looks like one of Dickens's slum characters."

Sister Noall turned to glare at him. "Not necessary, Elder Davis."

"But true," Inez said, looking down at her dirt- and grass-stained blouse. "I'll just stay in the carriage while the rest of you go about."

"You'll do no such thing," Sister Noall countered.

"No indeed," Jennie agreed. "You can wear your light coat, and no one will be the wiser."

"We're off then!" President Noall instructed, ushering the eager group to the carriages.

Elder Bailey hesitated at Inez's side. "See," he whispered. "Everything will work out. I wouldn't want you to miss the lovely adventure."

"Thank you, Elder Bailey."

He moved on to catch up with the other elders as Jennie came to Inez. "I believe someone is a bit charmed."

"Oh, yes, because I'm so charming," Inez deflected. "He's just being a gentleman."

Jennie hooked her friend's arm. "Have it your way."

Inez smiled, and her emotions lifted. She had been devastated to think she would miss touring Bourton-on-the-Water and having afternoon tea, but now she was part of the merriment, and her heart knew it was going to be not only a lovely adventure but a magical memory as well.

NOTES

Inez falling: In an entry in her journal, Inez reports a time when she fell into some mud and Elder Bailey attempted to brush off the dirt on her clothes with some straw.

Cotswold stone: This stone is an oolitic Jurassic limestone, quarried from the hills in the Cotswold area of south-central and southwest England. It is prized for its warm honey color.

Leisure time: Though these early missionaries did not have scheduled preparation days, as present-day missionaries do, Inez's journal mentions theater outings, walks, book reading, bicycling, tea, and dinners with Church members, as well as sightseeing adventures.

Chapter Sixteen

To the Knight Household

Beloved parents,

As I write this letter, my mind and heart are with you in Provo. I hope you have all been well. I miss you, but Sister Brimhall and I stay busy, so I don't have time to dwell on the separation. I know you pray for me, and that helps when things are difficult.

Jennie and I have been in Cheltenham eight days. It is a lovely town with fine buildings, clean skies, green spaces, and flowers. Jennie and I have settled into an apartment not far from the conference home. There were a few problems to start, but everything is in order now, so do not worry.

Jennie had a slight cold, but as of this writing we are both healthy. We are working diligently under the direction of President Noall. He is a good man, and his wife is much like you, Mother; when something needs doing, she gets it done. Will and Ray are here with us, and I'm glad to report they are working hard. They are teaching us the requirements of proselyting and how to hand out tracts to people. It takes courage to knock on the door of a stranger, and sometimes I feel like fainting while we wait for the door to open. The elders seem to have the knack of it, so Jennie and I try to copy them. We figure that soon President Noall will feel confident enough to send us off by ourselves.

The conference missionary choir now has two female voices. We didn't have much choice because every missionary is expected to contribute. Hopefully our voices will be a good addition and not a detraction. We sing at Church meetings and conference meetings. We also sing at street meetings, which always brings a crowd. It's fun to practice together, and it breaks up our time from studying. You must keep up your practice, Jennie Pearl and Addie, and then one day you might sing with your missionary choir.

The other day a group of us went with President and Sister Noall on an outing. It was a picnic near a place called Bourton-on-the-Water. It's in an area called the Cotswolds, and, oh, Father and Mother, it is a wondrous place! Green rolling hills with quaint villages nestled in the hallows. Jennie Pearl and Addie, it is like something from one of your fairy-tale books. Bourton-on-the-Water is a village where all the houses and shops are built from the pale-gold Cotswold stone. The village sits on two sides of a shallow, flowing stream, and there are charming arched stone bridges that cross the clear water connecting one side to the other. There are flower beds and flower boxes everywhere, and newly greening willow trees dipping their long flowing branches into the cool stream. Jennie teases me for trying to be a poet, but I just want to describe it so you can get a small feeling for its beauty. We will just have to come back here, as a family, so you can see it for yourself. Maybe I can get someone with a camera to take a photograph. Of course, then you'd still miss the stunning colors. I will try and paint something.

At the picnic we ate sausage rolls, apples, and lemon cake. Jennie is sending the recipe for the cake to Flora, and I will send it to you also, Mother.

It was a sunny afternoon of diversion with only one dark spot—I tripped on a tree root and fell flat on my face. Now, I imagine you nodding your heads or laughing at my usual clumsy antics. I assure you I'm trying to be less awkward, but I'm afraid my actions go at a faster pace than my thinking. I will practice slowing down and watching my feet.

This letter is getting long, but I must share one more thing. Jennie and I have decided to mimic Mrs. Beeton's Book of Household Management *and write our own book. It will not be about cookery (although we may add a few of her recipes) but a guide for future sister missionaries. We've decided to call it* The Brimhall/Knight Book of Missionary Management. *We will share our experiences and give cautions and encouragement to future sister missionaries. Heaven knows that Jennie and I could have used such a book when we first arrived.*

I must end here as Jennie is calling that it's time for study. I love you all. I am well.

With love,
Your Amanda Inez

LEMON CAKE

INGREDIENTS— 10 eggs, 3 tablespoonfuls of orange-flower water, ¾ lb. of pounded loaf sugar, 1 lemon, ¾ lb. of flour.

MODE— Separate the whites from the yolks of the eggs; whisk the former to a stiff froth; add the orange-flower water, the sugar, grated lemon-rind, and mix these ingredients well together. Then beat the yolks of the eggs, and add them, with the lemon-juice, to the whites, & dredge in the flour gradually; keep beating the mixture well; put it into a buttered mould, and bake the cake about an hour, or rather longer. The addition of a little butter, beaten to a cream, we think would improve this cake.

TIME— About 1 hour.

Seasonable at any time.

NOTE

Missionary choir: In her journal, Inez spoke often of she and Jennie practicing with and participating in the choir.

Chapter Seventeen

"I managed eight tracts on my side of the street," Inez reported as she neared Jennie at the end of Suffolk Road.

"And I did ten on mine," Jennie said, writing down the numbers in a booklet.

"We are doing well for our first time out on our own," Inez praised. "That's nearly sixty tracts for the afternoon, isn't it?"

Jennie checked the book. "Fifty-two."

"Well, that's *nearly* sixty."

Jennie smiled and closed the book, securing it in her satchel. "It's getting late, and we've wandered a ways from Imperial Square. I think we should head back for supper."

"Should we try for a few more?" Inez asked, waving a handful of tracts in the air.

Jennie looked at the sky. "It's threatening rain."

"It won't rain."

"The light is fading."

"There will be enough for twenty minutes or so."

Jennie sighed. "You have your heart set on it?"

Inez nodded. "And my mind."

"Well then, it's no good arguing." Jennie reached into her satchel for more tracts, just as a young servant girl neared them, carrying a basket of bread and eggs.

"Excuse me," Inez said, stepping toward her. The girl slowed, giving Inez a narrowed look.

"Do you read?" Jennie ventured.

The girl stopped, a surprised look on her face. "I do," she said proudly. "Me muver taught me then, didn't she."

"Then we'd like to give you one of these," Inez said, offering her the pamphlet.

"Yer American."

"We are," Inez said. "I'm Miss Knight, and this is Miss Brimhall."

"And I'm Margaret."

"We are pleased to meet you, Margaret," Inez said.

Margaret looked briefly at the pamphlet in her hand. "Wots this then? Ya settin' up a front?"

"A front?" Inez questioned. She was getting accustomed to the quirks of the English speech, but some terms still baffled her.

"Ya know, a front—store front . . . dresses, 'ats, shoes. That sorta thing."

"A shop," Jennie volunteered.

Margaret brightened. "Yeah, that's the ticket."

Inez liked Margaret's unaffected openness and cheery nature. She smiled. "No, we're not opening a shop; we're missionaries for The Church of Jesus Christ of Latter-day Saints."

The only change to Margaret's sunny expression was a slight widening of her eyes. "Missionaries? Yer tellin' me a tale."

"No, it's the truth," Jennie assured. "We *are* missionaries."

"Like th' ones who go to Africa wif their hubbies?"

"Well, something like that," Jennie said. "Although we're not Church of England, and we're not married."

Margaret's eyes widened even more. "Two posh girls come alone ta England to be preachin' the Lord's word?" A broad smile planted itself onto her face. "Well, ain't that an amazin' thing. Yer church must be new thinkin', that's fer sure."

"New thinking about the primitive doctrine of Christ," Jennie said.

"Wot?" Margaret said blankly.

Inez laughed. "She means we preach the gospel as did Jesus and His Apostles."

"Well, that's a square thing."

"So, Margaret, would you like us to tell you more about what we believe?"

Margaret looked closer at the pamphlet in her hand. "Yeah, I would. Yeah." She looked up, and Inez watched as the hopeful expression slid from the young woman's face. Margaret stepped back. "But, ya know . . . now's not a good time." She kept retreating. "I . . . I need to get back ta the 'ouse wif me goods." She leaned toward Inez and whispered, "I'd clear out if I was you." She turned and hurried off.

"Margaret, wait!" Inez called.

"That was odd," Jennie said.

"Not as odd as you two," came a soft, throaty voice behind them.

Inez and Jennie turned quickly and were confronted by two women whose unnaturally pale faces shone out in the murky dusk. Their velvet dresses were low cut and tattered; their hair, dirty and unkempt. One wore limp feathers in her hair, and her face was homely, while her companion's visage was clownish with an abundance of makeup.

The clownish woman sniggered. "Did I 'ear somebody say *missionaries*?" Jennie looked shocked. "Yeah, we was listenin' from over there." The woman jerked her head in the direction of a shadowed alleyway. She put her hands on her hips and leaned forward suggestively. "Well, I be sorta a missionary meself, right Agnus?" She leered at Jennie. "I've always 'ad the gift of turning a man from 'is old ways."

"Ya speak true, Clara. I seen it fer meself." The two women hooted with laughter, and Inez flinched at the harsh sound.

"Ya think yer better than us? Ya think ya can come here from America and lord it over us?" the woman named Agnus growled.

"That is not our intention," Inez said, moving closer to Jennie.

"Ooo! Ain't they fine?" the woman called Clara mocked. "Fancy manners and fancy togs. Thinkin' they can come in and batty-fang the devil outta us."

"Only one problem wif it. . . . We sorta like the devil," Agnus said. The two women broke into another round of harsh laughter.

"Come on, Jennie. Let's go," Inez said gently. She moved to take Jennie by the hand, but Agnus grabbed the strap of her satchel and yanked her back.

"Who said yer goin' anywheres?" Inez wrenched the strap out of the woman's bony fingers, but she immediately snatched it back. "I think this one's the leader."

"An' I think this purdy one's the bait," the clownish woman cooed, reaching out to touch Jennie's hair. "All soft and lovely." Jennie recoiled. "She's a basket of oranges fit for any man's table, she is." The woman moved quickly and seized Jennie's wrist.

"Leave her alone!" Inez yelled, straining against her captor. "I command you to let her go!" Inez's voice seemed to fill the street.

"Hey! You tarts, leave them ladies alone!" a voice called from one of the second-floor apartments. "I'll come down there and bash yer cobb!"

As the women looked up to weigh the threat, Inez and Jennie broke free and ran.

Lord, please help us, Inez prayed. *Help us to run very fast, and help me not to fall.*

The Knights and the Brimhalls would have been shocked to see their daughters racing ungracefully into their Cheltenham apartment and slamming the door behind them; their frenzied looks and disheveled clothing connoted a run from wild dogs or demons. Yet leniency would surely have been granted had they witnessed the scene on Suffolk Road and known their daughters' hearts.

Jennie burst into tears and slumped onto the divan.

Inez stood with her back against the door as if to guard against intruders. She looked mournfully at her friend. "It's all right then, Jennie," she said softly. "We're safe." Jennie nodded, but the tears continued. Inez took a deep breath and sat beside her on the divan. "I'm so sorry. It was my fault for wanting to stay out."

"No."

"It was! I should have listened to you . . . and the Spirit."

Jennie tried to breathe normally, but it was an effort.

"I don't think I'll ever be a proper missionary."

Jennie wiped her eyes on the sleeve of her coat. "And what is a proper missionary, Inez?" She took a ragged breath. "You have the truest testimony of anyone I know."

Inez handed her a handkerchief. "And I nearly faint when I have to stand up and bear it."

"Inez."

"You know it's true." Her stomach growled. "See? How can I concentrate on spiritual things when my body always wants attention?"

Jennie blew her nose. "We're just hungry."

Inez brightened. "You too?"

"Of course. We were out for hours."

"I know the remedy for this," Inez announced.

"Supper?" Jennie said, giving her companion a bemused glance.

"Better than that," Inez said. "I say we go over to the conference kitchen, and I'll cook you a marvelous suet dumpling of which Mrs. Beeton would highly approve." Jennie was still wiping away tears, but Inez noted a slight upturn at the corner of her mouth. "Suet dumpling not to your liking? Hmm, I know! Boar and pigeon pie?" Jenny pressed her lips together and began giggling. "No! No! I have it!" Inez declared with relish. "Savory eel tartlets!" Jennie laughed, and Inez joined her. "No eel then? How about the boar and pigeon pie? I hear boar will strengthen your heart."

"And probably allow me to grow a beard," Jenny answered, blowing her nose and giving Inez a look of feigned reproach.

Inez put an arm around her friend's shoulder. "Stupid fallen world."

Jennie attempted a smile. She took a deep breath and sobered. "I'm trying in my heart to forgive those women, Inez, but they were beastly."

"They were indeed."

"And the law allows their profession."

"So much for proper Victorian society," Inez scoffed.

Jennie became indignant. "Charlatans! How dare they criticize our life in Utah! The decent men of the priesthood would never think of treating a woman with such contempt."

Inez thought of how respectful her father was of her mother. "Mama always said that it's the gospel that teaches women to be modest and men to behave with dignity."

"True," Jennie said in a quiet voice. "My mother is in the asylum, yet Father cherishes her and treats her with the greatest kindness." The tears came again.

Inez took her friend's hand, remembering well the day the newest member of the Brimhall family had died at three days old, and Jennie's elegant and fragile mother had slipped into madness. Her residence now was the Provo Asylum, where Brother Brimhall visited nearly every day, telling her stories of the family's adventures and taking her trinkets and letters from the children.

"They would not comprehend my father's devotion."

"Who?"

"The selfish men of the world."

"No, they wouldn't," Inez said. "Stupid fallen world."

Jennie searched in her coat pocket for another handkerchief and changed the subject. "If those women didn't like what we were preaching, why couldn't they just pass us by?"

"Because they were threatened by us."

Jennie grinned at her friend. "Well, by *you,* maybe."

"At that moment I truly wanted a beard and the knowledge of fisticuffs," Inez said, throwing a few punches into the air. "I thought the elders meant brawling with words, but I suppose if they get shoved around, they have to shove back."

Jennie shook her head. "I don't like to think of it. I don't like to think of Will having to fight about anything, especially the gospel."

"Gives a new perspective to the war in heaven," Inez said, standing. "But I never thought we'd be in a battle our first time out alone, did you?"

Jennie shook her head. "I didn't."

Inez grinned. "But on the sunny side, we did leave a pamphlet with Margaret. Who knows? Something may come of that."

"We'll pray," Jennie said. She took a deep breath. "Let's not tell Ray or Will anything about the incident."

Inez looked at her friend's anxious, tear-stained face. "I think you may be right. Let's not tell anyone, especially Elder Davis. Knowing the way he feels about us even being here, he'd tell us to get on the first ship home."

"Home sounds wonderful," Jennie mused. "I'm sure the fruit trees are in full bloom."

"Ah." Inez reached out her hand, and Jennie took it. "Buck up, dear friend. I'm sure England will have blooming fruit trees any day now."

"If the rain doesn't knock off all the blossoms."

Inez held her friend's hand and pulled her to her feet. "I say we sneak over to the kitchen and have something to eat. I'm sure the elders have left us a crumb or two."

"As long as it's not eel tartlets," Jennie said.

Inez laughed. "Well, we can always wash it down with chamomile tea to soothe our stomachs."

Jennie moved to retrieve the scriptures from her bedside table. "And we can read scriptures to soothe our souls."

As the two companions headed out the door, rain began drumming on the windows. Inez sighed, and Jennie groaned and turned back to grab her umbrella.

NOTES

Tracts: Handing out Church pamphlets was an important duty in early missionary work, especially in Great Britain. In her journal, Inez kept a tally of tracts distributed, houses visited in tracting, houses visited by invitation, gospel conversations (open-air or indoor), and books distributed.

Alsina Elizabeth Wilkins Brimhall: Alsina Wilkins was Jennie Brimhall's mother. With the birth and death of her last child in 1883, Mrs. Brimhall suffered a debilitating brain fever from an infection contracted during the birth. It caused mental incapacity, from which she never recovered. Alsina spent her final years in the newly built mental hospital in Provo, Utah. She passed away in 1926.

Ladies of the night: Prostitution was legal in Victorian England, and every village, town, and city had its share of brothels.

Chapter Eighteen

"Elder Davis, would you please report to the brethren—and female brethren," President Noall said, smiling at Sister Brimhall and Sister Knight, "—the progress being made in the Bristol area?"

Giving a patronizing glance at the assembled missionaries, Elder Davis stood, secured his notebook, and moved to the front of the group. "Of course, President."

Inez leaned over to whisper to Jennie. "Look at the smug look on his face. Pride goeth before the fall, I always say."

"I wouldn't talk about falling if I were you," Jennie whispered back.

"If I could have everyone's attention," Elder Davis said, staring directly at Inez. She narrowed her eyes at him, and he gave her a mocking smile. "That's better." He opened his notebook. "In the past month, the four elders working in Bristol have handed out 900 first tracts and 360 second tracts. We've had conversations with 45 individuals, held 16 street meetings and 12 cottage meetings, and given out 19 Books of Mormon." He smiled at President Noall and handed him the paper from which he'd been reading.

President Noall nodded. "Well done, elders. It seems that Bristol may be a field of white. And has there been much persecution?"

Elder Davis hesitated, glancing over at his companion. Inez also looked at her brother Ray and noted his guarded expression. Inez knew that look. She'd seen it at home when Ray and Will didn't want her to tattle to Mother about a bit of boyish chicanery. He was giving that same look to Elder Davis, who promptly ignored him.

"Yes, President. We've had several run-ins with the Anti-Mormon League."

Ray cleared his throat. "Nothing major, President. Just the usual."

"Well, I need to know the extent as I'm thinking of sending Sister Brimhall and Sister Knight to Bristol for a few weeks."

Inez grabbed Jennie's hand.

"On their own, President?" Elder Davis questioned with a frown at the sisters. "But what of the threats?"

"They will stay with Mrs. Boyers. She is a reputable landlady who has cared for many of the elders. I'll assign them to a safe area where they will be great examples of Utah womanhood." Inez felt as though she'd eaten rocks for breakfast. Going out on their own within the vicinity of the conference home was one thing, but to venture solo into unknown territory was like flying and falling in a nightmare. She expected Jennie to pipe up and declare that they'd be glad to go, lion's den or not, but her companion was uncharacteristically mute. "Let's have the four of you come to my office when we're done here," President Noall continued, and Inez knew that he was oblivious to the fact that she'd been paralyzed by his statement. She tried to focus, but it was no use; the reports from other areas of the mission became nothing but droning.

"Inez?" Jennie pinched her arm, and Inez jumped. "Wake up."

"I'm not sleeping."

"Where are you then? The meeting's over, and we're going to the president's office."

Inez wobbled to her feet and watched as Jennie followed Ray and Elder Davis toward the president's office. Not surprisingly Will stopped her halfway across the hall to have what Inez assumed would be an anxious conversation.

"Are you all right?" Elder Bailey asked, approaching Inez from behind.

Inez jumped. "Ah! Don't sneak up on me like that!"

"Sorry, I didn't mean to . . . "

"Never mind. I was thinking about other things."

"I figured." He glanced at her and then to his shoes. "Bristol's not that far away, you know. I suppose Will and I could take a trip down there. And then, of course, you'll be back for conference."

"What? Oh sorry, Elder Bailey. I'm not paying attention." She moved off. "I have to get to the meeting with the president."

"Of course. We'll . . . we'll talk later."

Inez caught up with her companion in time to hear Will say, "Don't be so set on going."

Jennie looked offended. "And why not?"

"The president may change his mind. You heard Brother Davis. The Anti-Mormon League's persecution is real and extreme, Jennie. President Noall would not put you in danger."

"There's danger everywhere we go, Will."

Will shook his head. "You've personally never experienced persecution."

"Oh, yes, we have!" Inez blundered.

"Hush, Inez," Jennie whispered.

"I . . . I just mean we heard the angry people at that street meeting in Oldham, and . . . and I saw Elder Bailey roughed up a little in that fish shop."

Will did not see Jennie giving Inez frantic gestures to keep her mouth shut. He shook his head and seemed to buy his sister's weak explanation.

"That is nothing compared with an angry mob intent on doing harm, Inez. I'm talking about real danger."

Jennie laid her hand on Will's arm. "Will, we're not naïve to circumstances, and we know President Noall would not willingly put us in harm's way, so why don't you let Inez and me go to our meeting, and we'll see what he says."

Just then, Elder Bailey approached. "We have a cottage meeting across town, Elder Knight. We'd better get going."

Will kept staring at Jennie as though he had more to say. She gave his arm a slight shove. "Go on to your work then, and I'll to mine," she said with a smile. "The Lord will watch over us." She gave a confident smile and turned to discover her and Inez's next assignment.

Chapter Nineteen

NOTES ON MISSIONARY MANAGEMENT

Greetings from Sister Inez Knight and Sister Jennie Brimhall to future sister missionaries in the Great Britain Mission. We have secured this blank-page book and plan to write a few hints that may help you understand and accomplish your special work as female missionaries. We use as our inspiration the English cookery book *Mrs. Beeton's Book of Household Management*, which is why we call our offering *The Brimhall/Knight Book of Missionary Management.*

The first lesson we share is to trust the Lord and be calm.

Mrs. Beeton points out that nothing is foolproof in cooking: the yeast may be scalded, and your bread may not rise; the planned-for cod may be off and need replacing with fowl; the biscuits may burn, and the blanc-mange not set. But even in the midst of seeming insurmountable disaster, the home cook may, with calmness, reclaim the situation.

Sister Brimhall and I have been in the mission field a little over a month, and President Noall is sending us from Cheltenham to Bristol. We are to labor there for an undisclosed amount of time. In truth, we did not think the president would follow through on this assignment after hearing reports of missionaries encountering significant trouble in Bristol. We were mistaken. After solemnly receiving the reports, the president prayed and afterward informed us that Bristol is where the Lord wants us to be.

So we are on our way. Sister Brimhall and I acknowledge the Lord and know He is directing our path. Your mission experience will give you many opportunities to feel the guidance of the Spirit. Be calm, and know that if your missionary efforts go awry, you can, with the Lord's help, reclaim any situation.

Sister Inez Knight and Sister Jennie Brimhall

Chapter Twenty

"I've got your number and your ticket, young lady missionaries!" Mrs. Boyers warbled. "Indeed, I believe you will appreciate the rasher of bacon with poached eggs on toast, muffins with marmalade, veal and ham pie, and cold sliced tongue, though I'm not quite sure about the tongue. Is it something Americans eat at breakfast?"

Inez and Jennie stood at the sideboard in Mrs. Elaine Boyers's breakfast room, unable to utter a word as they stared at the offerings in the silver chafing dishes.

"Oh my. Did I make a mistake altogether? I attempted to make it as American as possible."

Jennie found her voice. "Not at all, Mrs. Boyers. It looks delicious. It's just that Inez and I are not used to so much . . . variety."

"Well, then I'm glad I had the cook leave off the broiled mackerel," she said with a laugh. "Go on then! Eat. Eat. Eat."

Inez and Jennie shared a look of delight as they picked up their plates and began making their selections. Inez attempted to skip the cold tongue, but Jennie gave her a look that indicated she must at least try a small slice so as not to offend.

Inez went to the table, pulled out her chair, and plunked herself into it before a stately older servant could assist. Inez stared at him with chagrin. "Sorry."

"Not to worry, Miss Knight," responded Mrs. Boyers. "I cling to a bit of the bygone era here at Meadowlark Manor. Mr. Kinsey has been with me for twenty-eight years."

"Twenty-nine, ma'am."

Mrs. Boyers laughed. "Oooh dear! He's caught me out, he has. Mind like the royal Lord Nelson!"

"This all looks wonderful, Mrs. Boyers. Thank you," Jennie said, turning from the sideboard with her plate piled high. Mr. Kinsey moved gracefully to pull out Jennie's chair, and Inez gave a little grunt of envy as Jennie sat with ease.

"That's what I like: young women with appetites," Mrs. Boyers said, eying their plates and beaming at them. "Now, I've been around the missionaries long enough to know that you say grace before eating, so on with you. Who's the candidate?"

"My vote's for Sister Brimhall," Inez said. "She'll start the day off right."

"Sterling!" Mrs. Boyers said, turning to Jennie. "We have full confidence in you, Miss Brimhall, to be the pastor of our wandering souls."

Inez bowed her head and concentrated on not chuckling. She was amazed by Jennie's ability to not only keep decorum in her voice but also offer a prayer filled with love for the Lord and simple pleadings for the day. When the "amen" was said, Inez looked up to find Mrs. Boyers staring at her companion.

"My goodness, my dear. Where did you learn to pray like that? I fully expected to look over and find the Lord Himself standing beside you."

Jennie sat wide-eyed, embarrassed by Mrs. Boyers's candid statement. Inez came to her rescue.

"We learn to pray from when we're young."

"And expand on it from that day on, I dare say," Mrs. Boyers asserted. She picked up her knife and fork and sliced into her poached egg. "Eat! Eat, young ladies! You have a busy day ahead."

Inez and Jennie did as they were told, and during the rest of breakfast, Mrs. Boyers questioned them about their travel to England, their family life, and the schools in Utah, as well as begged for stories about what she termed the "Wild West." In turn, she told them tales about the city of Bristol, its landmarks, and her husband, Ned.

"He used to crow like a rooster some mornings to wake the neighbors.

Most thought it a jig, but some kept threatening to call the constable. They never would though because Ned was overall such a decent fellow." She put marmalade on a piece of toast. "There *was* a time Ned was carted off to the jail for punching the town drunkard. He was a mean cuss that killed the McInernys' cat, and everyone knew he deserved a smack in the looker, but everybody was too scared of the brute. Not my Ned. Punched him a good one and ole Sam Higgins hit the ground hard. Didn't puff out his chest much after that."

Inez and Jennie shared a look of delight at Mr. Boyers's antics and her telling of them. "What did Mr. Boyers do for a living?" Inez asked.

"He was an engineer."

"That's impressive," Jennie said.

"Bristol University. Youngest engineer to work on the Clifton Bridge. Did you see it when you came in last night?"

"A glimpse," Jennie said. "It was rather dark when we arrived."

"Well, it is a wonder," she said as Mr. Kinsey entered. "Isn't it, Mr. Kinsey?"

"I beg your pardon, ma'am?"

"The Clifton Bridge. It's quite a wonder."

"It is indeed." He picked up one of the chafing dishes from the sideboard. "Perhaps the young ladies should see it today."

"Oh yes! It's a lovely day for viewing!" She turned to Inez and Jennie. "When you're done with your missionary work, walk through the park to the observatory, and you'll get a marvelous view. It's Bristol's pride and joy."

Mr. Kinsey stopped at the doorway. "Should I see if Mrs. Somers might make them a parcel of sandwiches?"

"What did I tell you? Mind like the royal Lord Nelson! Wonderful idea, Mr. Kinsey. A picnic in the park!" She smiled at Inez and Jennie. "What do you say to that?"

"Delightful," Jennie said.

"Pip, pip!" Inez added, and everyone laughed.

Sister Knight and Sister Brimhall stood on the corner of Harley Place and Clifton Down Road, staring at the stately row homes facing the park. Inez took a deep breath.

"What?" Jennie asked.

"I know why President Noall sent us to this area of Bristol."

"Why?"

"No chance of angry mobs or prostitutes."

"Inez!"

"Well, it's true. Look how . . . clean and fancy everything is. And therefore, no chance of finding anyone to talk with. Easier for a rich man to go through the eye of a needle . . ."

Jennie laughed, then pressed her lips together to contain her emotion. "We've handed out a few tracts along our way here."

"Three."

"Well, three is better than none."

"Optimist."

"I am indeed," Jennie said brightly, hefting her satchel. "And I say we try that row of houses."

"I will go and do!" Inez declared, attempting to match Jennie's enthusiasm. Jennie started across the street, and Inez followed. At the curb, Inez stumbled but caught herself before falling. "Two left feet!" she chided. "And after promising my parents I'd be more careful."

"At least you didn't fall," Jennie encouraged, holding on to Inez's arm as she righted herself and smoothed her skirt. Jennie glanced down the street in the direction they'd just come. "Inez."

"Yes?"

"I . . . I think that woman is following us."

"What woman?" Inez said, moving to turn.

"No! No, don't turn around!" Jennie hissed. "Let's just keep walking." She took Inez by the hand and moved through the gate and up the pathway to the first house in the row.

"What woman are you talking about?" Inez whispered.

"The woman by the fruit market, remember? The one with the basket of walnuts."

"The one who took a tract from us?"

"Yes, that one." They'd made their way to the front stoop, and Jennie raised her hand to take the door knocker.

"Well, maybe she wants to ask us questions. Maybe she read the tract and wants to know more about the Church."

"Maybe," Jennie said, knocking on the door.

After a few moments the door opened, and a slight man in a rust-colored smoking jacket looked out at them.

"Good morning! How may I help you?"

Jennie smiled back and held out the tract. "Good morning. We are missionaries for The Church of Jesus Christ . . . "

"You best slam the door in their faces," a harsh voice called out. Jennie and Inez turned abruptly to find the woman with the basket standing at the gate. "Hear that American accent? They'll be preaching dark doctrine from the land of the Mormons." The door shut with a bang, and the girls jumped. They stood for a moment, then turned away. When they reached the gate, the woman was standing guard. "We don't want your kind here."

Inez pushed past her. "You don't know anything about us."

The woman followed, using a voice far louder than the space between them required. "Oh! I know you all right. Scum from Utah, where women are kept like slaves!"

"Just leave us alone," Inez called back as they made their way to the next doorway. She knocked and watched as Jennie took a deep breath and stood straighter. The door opened to reveal a woman with a toddler by her side. She gave Inez and Jennie a suspicious look as Inez held out a tract. Inez opened her mouth to speak, but before any words could escape, the woman yelled from the pathway.

"Those are wicked Mormon women on your doorstep. I'd shut the door to keep the devil away from that precious child if I were you."

The woman looked alarmed and hurriedly shut the door, crushing the tract in the doorframe.

Inez growled. "What should we do?"

"Carry on," Jennie answered. She moved down the steps and on toward the next house.

The woman dogged them. "So, have you ever watched one of those public executions of wicked Mormon women who want out of polygamy?"

Inez turned and gave her an incredulous look. "You're mad. You don't know what you're talking about."

Jennie grabbed Inez's arm. "Leave her be, Inez. There's no reasoning with someone who won't listen."

"Right you are, little beauty. I won't let you pour your vile filth in my ears." She threw a walnut at Jennie's back. "We don't want you polluting our neighborhood, so get out!" She threw another walnut, hitting Inez in the back of the head.

The two girls raced to the next door, ignoring the knocker and pounding on the door with their fists. Inez glanced back and saw the woman approaching the walkway. "Jennie, she's coming!" At that moment the door opened, and a middle-aged woman with wire-rimmed glasses and copper-colored hair stood smiling at them.

The basket woman stopped her approach, but the vitriol continued. "We don't want you here, you putrid abscesses from America!"

"Goodness!" the woman at the door replied.

"Turn them away!" the woman yelled. "They're degenerates from Utah. Slam the door in their lying faces!"

Inez and Jennie looked steadfastly at the woman, their eyes brimming with tears. Jennie started to speak, but the woman winked at her.

"Would you be interested in a cup of tea?"

Jennie blinked and found her voice. "Yes, ma'am. That would be . . . lovely."

Inez could only nod.

The red-haired woman looked beyond the girls to the intruder on her pathway. "Well, they don't seem like putrid abscesses to me," she declared, moving past Inez and Jennie and advancing on the basket woman. The woman looked startled and stepped back. "Now you, on the other hand, seem dangerously mad, prowling the streets and yelling at the top of your lungs. Such tawdry behavior."

"Don't come near me," the woman croaked, holding her basket in front of her.

"My name is Mrs. Kennison, and this is my home. Need I remind you that you are on my property?"

The woman looked around as though she'd forgotten where she was. "I . . . I . . . "

"Yes, that's what I thought. So kindly vacate, or I shall be forced to get my son's cricket bat and knock you to the outfield."

"You wouldn't dare."

"Oh, wouldn't I?" She called back toward the house. "George, quickly bring me your cricket bat!"

"You're bluffing."

"Am I?" She took a menacing step forward. "Do I look like someone who would bluff?" The intruder's face drained of color. "Off with you now," Mrs. Kennison commanded.

"You've opened the pit of hell, you have," the woman snarled as she turned and hurried away.

"I'm sure you are well acquainted with the pit of hell," the mistress of the house said, more as a joke to herself, but Inez and Jennie overheard it and laughed. Mrs. Kennison moved to them. "Nothing better than a mix of laughter and tears." She held out her hand. "I am Amanda Kennison."

"That's *my* first name!" Inez exclaimed. "Amanda Inez Knight, but I go by Inez."

"Well met," Mrs. Kennison answered with a smile. She turned to Jennie.

"Lucy Jane Brimhall, but everyone calls me Jennie." She took Mrs. Kennison's hand. "Thank you for saving us."

"My pleasure, Miss Brimhall."

The three turned to note the young man hurrying down the stairs with a cricket bat in his hand. He took the final two stairs in a leap and arrived quickly at the front door. He stared at the two young women on his house's front stoop. Dazedly he handed the bat to his mother.

She took it with a knowing grin. "Thank you, George. May I introduce Miss Knight and Miss Brimhall. Ladies, this is my son, George Winston Kennison."

George gave a slight bow. "How do you do?"

"They're from America, and they will be joining us for a spot of tea."

"Jolly!" George smiled at the girls, then frowned at his mother. "Why did you need my bat?"

"I will explain over scones. You *can* take a small break from your grueling university studies, I presume?"

"Yes! Yes, of course," George said heartily.

"In we go then."

Amanda Kennison led the way into the house with George escorting from behind. Inez was feeling euphoric and didn't know if it was because of their escape from the angry woman, the thought of scones, or the feeling that she and Jennie were just where the Lord wanted them to be. She concluded that it was all three combined.

Chapter Twenty-One

"Girls! You've forgotten your umbrellas!"

Inez and Jennie halted at the front door. "Thank you, Mrs. Boyers. I'll get them!" Inez said, sprinting back up the stairs.

"It looks clear now for your picnic, but you never know. I recall Mr. Boyers and myself being caught at the observatory for several hours for the absence of umbrellas. We were young and smitten with each other, so we didn't mind." Jennie smiled at the tenderness in Mrs. Boyers's voice and wondered if she and Will would speak so fondly of each other after forty or fifty years of marriage. "And your fiancé, William, is here in England too?" Mrs. Boyers added as though reading her thoughts.

"Yes, ma'am. He's serving in Cheltenham."

"That's right. That's right. Cheltenham. It must be hard to be apart."

"We keep ourselves busy."

Mrs. Boyers gave her an understanding smile. "I know, but I miss my Ned every day."

"But you'll see him again in heaven."

"Well, I do believe in heaven, but it won't be the same . . . 'until death do you part' and all of that. I did not like that pronouncement on my wedding day." She gave Jennie a wink. "When the minister said those words, I just said in my mind, 'until forever and ever and ever.'"

"I don't like 'until death do you part' either."

"I know. But there it is. You will end up saying those very words on your wedding day."

"Actually, I won't."

Mrs. Boyers gave her an inquisitive look. "Whatever do you mean, Miss Brimhall?"

"I couldn't find my umbrella," Inez interrupted on her descent from the landing. "So we'll just have to share." She missed the last stair and stumbled toward the door. Jennie caught her.

"Oh my goodness, Miss Knight! Steady on!"

"Sorry, Mrs. Boyers," Inez gasped. She gathered herself. "I should not try and do two things at the same time."

Jennie laughed. "What? Walk and talk?"

The threesome laughed together.

"Oh, I'm going to miss you girls. These last few weeks you've brought light into my home. Now, don't misunderstand; the elders who've stayed with me from time to time are very nice, but they can be loud and rather messy. But you young ladies are temperate and kind and filled with . . . well, I don't know quite what to call it."

"Spirit," Inez said openly, causing Mrs. Boyers to chuckle, and Jennie to shake her head. "What? I didn't mean that as boasting. I . . . I just meant that there's a great deal of the Spirit in what we teach—in the gospel."

Mrs. Boyers laid her hand on Inez's arm. "You are absolutely right. Spirit it is. A spirit of peace and hope." She gave each a good-natured shove toward the door. "Now, on with you, or you'll be late for your picnic with the Kennisons."

Inez picked up the hamper. "Please tell Mrs. Somers thank you again for helping us with the pudding and for the other wonderful treats." She headed out the door, but Jennie hesitated.

"Mrs. Boyers?"

"Yes, my dear?"

"When Inez and I get back for tea this evening, I would like to talk more about wedding vows. May we do that?"

Mrs. Boyers nodded. "Of course. Whatever you'd like."

Jennie gave her a broad smile and a hug, then turned abruptly and headed off with her companion.

Elaine Boyers stood at the doorway, tenderly watching the departing sister missionaries.

THE SISTER PREACHERS

"Mother! The sister missionaries have arrived!"

"Mind your manners, George, and bring them back to the kitchen!"

George gave Inez and Jennie a half smile. "Look who's yelling from the kitchen and talking about manners. Come on, then; she must be packing up the last of the picnic." He headed off, and the girls followed. "Oh, by the way, Father's coming with us."

Jennie stopped. "He is?"

George turned with a laugh. "He is. And don't look so frightened." He started walking again. "He might not believe a word you say about Mr. Smith speaking with God or angels flying about, but he finds your dedication intriguing."

"Well, that's comforting," Inez mumbled.

They arrived in the kitchen to find Mr. Kennison in an apron, taking biscuits out of the oven, while Mrs. Kennison placed napkins into a hamper. Inez watched surprise register on Jennie's face, but it seemed as though having her husband in an apron was an uneventful occurrence to Mrs. Kennison. Even George seemed unabashed. Inez thought back to their first meeting the day the mad woman followed them, yelling insults. As soon as they'd been brought into the safety of the Kennison home, the cloistered Utah girls had recognized the unique character of the abode and its inhabitants: the home featured a plethora of statuary from Egypt and India; potted wisteria trees in the parlor; a stuffed mongoose and cobra on the hall table; and chandeliers made of crystal fruits. Then there was Mrs. Kennison herself, with copper hair and vibrant personality to match; George, with his depth of knowledge on topics ranging from horticulture to zoology; and Mr. Kennison, with his full beard, imposing stature, and stories about exotic world escapades. Inez's letters home had been filled with interesting stories of Kennison-family oddities.

Amanda Kennison looked up and brushed her hair from her face. "Good afternoon, girls! We're running a bit behind. Come sit while we finish baking and packing."

"We should put them to work," Mr. Kennison said as he slid the biscuits from the pan onto a dish.

"What would you suggest, Mr. Kennison?"

"Mop floors, dust the parlor, clean the attic."

"Oh, not the attic, Father," George said. He gave the girls a rakish smile. "It's haunted, ya know."

Inez stared at him. "Haunted?"

"Well, that wouldn't bother them, son. I mean, they believe in ghosts and spirits and angels who fly around with golden books, right?"

He said it with a tinge of humor, but it spoke of dismissal. It was the teasing of one approaching the topic from a scientific point of view, and Inez lamented that even after several meetings with the family, they had not made much progress with Mr. Kennison's skepticism. Inez and Jennie shared a look of frustration.

Jennie addressed the family. "We'd be glad to do whatever you'd like," she said in her most sincere voice.

Inez grinned to herself. It was the voice her friend used to melt anger and pride, and it was effective.

"Oh, Edmund, leave the poor girls alone," Mrs. Kennison scolded. "We're ready to go anyway, so take off your apron and store the biscuits." She handed him a napkin, and he wrapped the biscuits and placed them in the hamper with a wink at Jennie and Inez.

"I do like biscuits. 'Cookies' to you Americans, right?"

"You also like puddings and meringues and caramels and Victoria sponge," Mrs. Kennison stated.

"Here now, you red-haired rascal! Don't go telling my secrets!"

Mrs. Kennison pushed the hamper in his direction. "That secret is told in your girth, dear one. Now, pick up the hamper, and let's on with our adventure."

George held out his cricket bat and ball to the girls. "If you'll tote these, I will take your hamper." Inez held it back, and George chuckled. "I promise not to eat everything before we get to our picnic spot."

"I don't know. You might be tempted by the plum pudding we made."

"Pudding?" Mr. Kennison interrupted. "You American girls made a pudding?"

George quickly traded his cricket gear for the hamper.

"With a little help from Mrs. Boyers's cook," Jennie said.

"Here, son. You'd better let me take that basket."

"You already have one."

"But I can carry both."

"No thank you, Da. I can manage," George said, moving quickly down the hallway with Mr. Kennison close on his heels.

Amanda Kennison laughed and snatched up her coat. "Hurry on, sisters, or we may never see those baskets again!"

Inez sat admiring the view over the Avon River Gorge. The warm sun and satisfying meal were making her drowsy, and she was barely able to follow the conversation going on beside her.

"You've been across our bridge, I take it?" Mr. Kennison questioned.

"Yes, many times," Jennie answered. "It's an engineering marvel. I wish my father could see it."

"That's right, your father's a professor—a man of letters and learning."

"Yes, sir."

"And yet, a believer in the odd tales of Mr. Smith."

"Yes, sir, but my father finds them to be neither odd nor tales."

Mr. Kennison grunted. "Doesn't seem compatible to me—science and religion."

"There's a book I need to give you."

Mr. Kennison laughed. "You've already given us that book."

Jennie smiled. "This is another book; one of my father's favorites. The *Key to the Science of Theology.* It talks about science and religion."

"Written by someone in your church?"

"Mr. Parley Pratt. He was one of the first Apostles."

Mr. Kennison chuckled. "Peter, James, and Parley? Never heard of that threesome in the Bible."

Inez thought it a rude statement and turned to make a reply, but before she could blunder, Mrs. Kennison took things in hand.

"Edmund, mind your manners. These girls came all the way from America with a message. The least you could do is hear them out."

Jennie smiled. "Oh, it's all right, Mrs. Kennison. I actually admire how tolerant your husband's been over the weeks with topics out of his depth."

There was a pause, and then Mr. Kennison roared with laughter. George and Mrs. Kennison joined him, while Inez sat wide eyed and open mouthed.

"You're a character, Miss Brimhall," George said between snorts of laughter. "Indeed, a character."

"And brave," Inez said in an aside.

"Only with the Spirit," Jennie whispered back.

Mr. Kennison took a napkin and wiped the tears of laughter from his face. "Ah . . . that was merited," he said, taking a deep breath. He wagged his finger at her. "I think you are your father's daughter."

"A compliment," Jennie answered.

"But now you're in for it, Miss Brimhall. Now that you have my undivided attention, you must make your case for science and religion."

Jennie nodded but took a long time in replying, and Inez knew her companion was offering a fervent, silent prayer for guidance. Inez added one of her own for good measure.

"I think we should take up this topic of science and theology," she announced finally.

"All right, Miss Brimhall. You have the floor."

"Or the grass," George quipped.

"George . . . ," Mrs. Kennison warned.

"Sorry, Mother." He took a biscuit and leaned back against the tree. "This should be interesting."

Jennie pointed at the Clifton Bridge. "We admire that bridge, don't we? It is a work of marvelous craft and ingenuity."

"It is."

"Whose ingenuity?"

"The men who built it."

"Yes. The men who built it. Mr. Boyers, our landlady's husband, was one of the chief engineers. He worked on the project with Mr. Brunel."

"Brunel. Brilliant man."

"Yes, everyone admires Mr. Brunel, the gifted young architect."

Mr. Kennison gave her a crooked smile and answered slowly. "Yes."

"So where did those ideas come from? That brilliant gift?"

"From his imagination—from previous bridge builders."

"Yes, but each bridge idea was expanded and improved by later builders. At first, bridges were wood and stone; now they're made of metal. How did these new ideas arise? And what of the first bridge builder? Where did his idea come from?"

"I suppose you're going to say from God."

"If there is a God, then He made this earth, placed the sun and moon and stars, planted the vegetation, and populated the earth with magnificent creatures . . ." She leaned forward. "If there is a God and He is all knowing, . . . I have just one question."

"And what's that?"

"Would He know how to make that bridge?"

Mr. Kennison glanced over at the bridge, then gave her a knowing look. "He would . . . yes."

"Then all the math, chemistry, and engineering science needed to build that bridge would be at His disposal?"

"Yes."

"Then isn't the key to science . . . " She gave Mr. Kennison a steady look. "Isn't the key to science, in fact, theology, and wouldn't a man of science be wise to know about the source of all science?"

Everyone was still. Inez could hear the chatter and laughter of children at a distance and birdsong in the branches above. She watched Mr. Kennison's features as they shifted from skeptical arrogance to tenderness. He wore an amused smile and glanced over at his wife.

"Well, Mrs. Kennison, what do you think about that?"

"I think you may want to begin reading the book George and I have been reading."

"Hmm. The gold Bible?" He smiled at Jennie and Inez. "Well, perhaps I could be persuaded if they'd offer another slice of the delicious plum pudding."

Inez reached immediately for the knife as Mrs. Kennison reached out for her husband's hand.

NOTES

The Clifton Suspension Bridge: The bridge spans the Avon River Gorge in Bristol, England. It was designed by twenty-four-year-old Isambard Kingdom Brunel and is one of the oldest surviving iron suspension bridges in the world. It took thirty-three years to complete and opened in 1864.

Key to the Science of Theology: This book was written by Apostle Parley P. Pratt and published in 1855. The title page reads: "Designed as an introduction to the first principles of spiritual philosophy, religion, law and government as delivered by the ancients, and as restored in this age for the final development of universal peace, truth and knowledge."

CHAPTER TWENTY-TWO

TO FUTURE SISTER MISSIONARIES OF THE BRITISH MISSION—A NOTE ON MISSIONARY MANAGEMENT

We have won over the heart of Mr. Kennison with words of truth and Mrs. Beeton's plum pudding! He is a man of science, and yet testimony seems to have softened his heart. He has agreed to listen to more lessons, and we will see where that leads.

We have written out the recipe for this dessert, to be used with other educated, glum, or stubborn fellows. This recipe makes a large family pudding, for which Mr. Kennison (who loves sweets) was grateful.

We testify that prayer is essential in missionary work. It brings the direction of the Spirit and the ability to hear, so when you may be thinking an intense lecture on gospel principles is the ticket, you can hear the Lord instead saying, "Plum pudding."

Sister Brimhall and Sister Knight

BAKED PLUM-PUDDING

INGREDIENTS— 2 lbs. of flour, 1 lb. of currants, 1 lb. of raisins, 1 lb. of suet, 2 eggs, 1 pint of milk, a few slices of candied peel.

MODE— Chop the suet finely; mix with it the flour, currants, stoned raisins, and candied peel; moisten with the well-beaten eggs, and add sufficient milk to make the pudding of the consistency of very thick batter. Put it into a buttered dish, and bake in a good steamed oven from 2¼ to 2½ hours; turn it out, strew sifted sugar over, and serve.

Sufficient for 9 or 10 persons.

Chapter Twenty-Three

Sister Inez Knight stood in front of Bristol's imposing Lloyds Bank Building, handing out tracts without comment or enthusiasm. She was in a foul mood. She'd had nightmares in the night of storms and dark water surrounding slave ships departing Bristol harbor. Mrs. Boyers had kept them up late into the night talking about her grandfather who built some of the hated vessels for the British slave trade. Inez yawned and rubbed her eyes. Her tiredness made her surly, and people passing on the sidewalk avoided her like a beggar woman. As one man walked near, she growled out an incoherent complaint, making him sidestep into the street to avoid her. An oncoming carriage horse startled and reared while the driver yelled a few obscenities at the man, who then turned to yell at Inez.

"It wasn't my fault you stepped into the street," Inez countered.

The man came to confront her, and Jennie intervened. "We are so sorry. Are you all right?"

The man stopped. "I . . . I suppose."

"Oh, that's good. Because that carriage driver was terribly surly, wasn't he? Blaming you for his jittery horse. And what terrible language."

The man grunted and started on his way. "Just mind yourselves."

Inez attempted to imitate her companion's diplomacy, but the effort fell terribly short. "Oh, thank you for that good advice." She shouted after him.

"Inez," Jennie said softly.

"I know, you have every right to scold me."

"I'm not going to scold you. You're tired this morning. We're both tired."

"I had bad dreams all night from those horrible slave ship stories," Inez grumbled.

"So did I," Jennie agreed. She offered a tract to a passing woman, who scowled at her and took the offering merely out of courtesy. Jennie sighed and rubbed her neck. "Why don't we find your brother and Elder Davis and see if they won't treat us to an early lunch?"

Inez brightened. "That would be wonderful!" She hurriedly stowed her tracts in her satchel and looked down the street. "Didn't they say they were going to St. Nicholas Market?"

"They did," Jennie said. "Hopefully they're having better luck."

"Better luck then us?" Inez scoffed. "That would not be difficult."

The girls headed east toward the market and Church Park, chatting about light subjects and trying to throw off the melancholy of the morning. After twenty minutes of walking and searching for familiar faces, the elders were proving hard to find.

"They're probably in a café somewhere taking a break and having a beer."

"I doubt they're doing either of those things," Jennie responded in surprise.

"I'm only teasing. They probably wouldn't know how to order beer."

Jennie turned to look down a side street, ignoring Inez's banter. "Let's try down this street, and if we don't see them, we can head to the park. Maybe they went there to find people."

"Good idea."

They moved on, ignoring the stares of the people around them who had obviously heard their American accents and were curious about two unchaperoned American girls traveling in a nontourist area of England.

"You'd think they'd never seen an American," Inez said.

"I'd say some haven't."

Inez glanced back at a few members of the gawking crowd. "Really? Well, that's odd."

Jennie continued her search, and Inez hurried to catch up. They were at the end of their third street and preparing to move on to the park when they noticed the elders talking to a man and woman in front of a bakery. Inez's stomach rumbled in protest for having been deprived of breakfast. As they neared, the man shook his head and hurriedly guided the woman away.

"Ah! I wish you'd been here ten seconds ago!" Ray lamented when Jennie and Inez arrived.

"Well, that's a nice greeting, brother," Inez returned.

"Sorry, it's just that this man and his wife were rebuking us for living in the sin of polygamy, and your input would have been helpful."

"I can run after them if you'd like. They can't be that far away," Inez said.

"Noble of you, Sister, but not necessary. I'm afraid they've made up their minds to dislike us."

"So what are you doing here?" Elder Davis broke in. "I thought you'd be drawing crowds in your area."

There was a mocking tone in his voice that made Inez bristle. "We thought you might need our help," she snapped.

"Or perhaps the work was too difficult, so you abandoned your post."

Inez didn't have a quick response to his charge as his words hit near the truth.

"Be supportive, Elder Davis," Ray instructed.

"I just think it's a waste of their time."

Inez stepped forward. "Preaching?"

"Being missionaries. Be honest. Wouldn't you much rather be home in Utah teaching school or doing genealogy or practicing your craft?"

"Our craft? And what exactly is our craft?"

"Actually, we came to see if we could treat you to lunch," Jennie broke in.

Inez turned to stare at her. "Treat *them*?"

"That's a wonderful idea, Sister Brimhall!" Ray said, joining in to defuse the argument. "But we will definitely be treating *you*. I know a lovely café on the edge of the park." He turned to Elder Davis. "What do you say, Jonathan?"

"I'm not hungry yet."

"He doesn't like English food," Inez stated.

Ray clapped his companion on the back. "Well, he can just come along as company then."

"Oh joy," Inez mumbled. Jennie shot her a warning look, and she countered with a look of innocence. "What?"

"Lead on, Elder Knight," Jennie said. "And after, we can sing hymns in the park. Maybe that will bring a crowd."

Inez felt a sudden tightening in her throat.

"Your bootlace is untied," Elder Davis informed her as he moved off to follow the others.

Inez looked down. "Bother." She noticed that her companions were already crossing the heavily trafficked road, so she decided to worry about her bootlace later. As she stepped off the curb to follow, she felt a tug on her ankle and fell onto her knees in the gutter. She struggled up, hoping to avoid attention—hoping her three companions were not witnesses to her inelegance. She rubbed her hands together to remove the dirt, evaluated the traffic, and walked forward. A heavy hand clamped itself onto her shoulder and pushed her back onto her knees.

"Just stay in the gutter where you belong," said a growling voice.

Inez struggled to free herself from the grip. "What are you . . . "

"Shut it. We don't wanna hear your voice. Pure poison."

Inez heard several other male voices mocking her, and a surge of panic slammed into her chest. *Where are the others? Dear Lord, please help me.*

"We've been watchin' the blokes for some time, and we brought 'em a little present today." This statement was met with suggestive comments and laughter. "An I suppose if yer with 'em, we'll have to give you the same gift."

"Let me go!" Inez yelled.

"Not likely."

"Hey! You there! What are you doing?"

"Mind yer business!" her captor hissed, dragging Inez to her feet. "The little lady had a tumble, and we was helpin' her."

"Doesn't look that way to me."

"Oh no? Well, why don't you just move along like a blind man?"

"And why don't *you* let her go?"

Inez glanced at her deliverer and moaned. The man coming to her rescue was tall and fragile. He wore a stylish suit and carried a thin walking stick and a small brown bag. The brutish man holding her laughed.

"And wot are you goin' to do, fine gentleman? Throw your wee bag at us, or give us all a thrashing?"

The laughter of the gang was cut short as the man landed a stinging blow on the side of the ruffian's head. A scuffle ensued, and as the grip on her released, Inez sprang away. She bolted out into the traffic, narrowly missing impact with a team of horses. Ray met her in the middle of the road, grabbed her wrist, and pulled her out of danger.

"Inez, where were you? We turned around and you were gone!"

The panic in his voice, coupled with her recent escape, made her weep. "I . . . I . . . "

Jennie was by her side. "What happened?"

Inez grabbed Jennie and Ray by the arms and dragged them forward. "We have to go! Walk! Just keep walking!" She heard the shouts of the gang as they crossed the street. "Oh, Ray, they're coming!"

"Who's coming?"

Inez increased her pace. "A gang. They grabbed me, and . . . "

Ray pulled back. "What do you mean, 'grabbed you'?"

"Never mind that now! We have to keep going!"

"There *is* a group of men following us," Elder Davis confirmed. "Anti-Mormon League, I'm guessing."

"What should we do?" Jennie panted.

"You sisters run on, and we'll try and divert them."

"No!" Inez yelled. "We have to stay together!"

"Inez . . . "

"No!"

At that moment, Elder Davis was struck with a heavy projectile, causing him to lunge forward. He righted himself as they all ran on. More objects were thrown as the gang closed the distance. Inez screamed as a bottle crashed near her on the cobblestones. Their pursuers were intent on injury, and Inez tried desperately to figure a way out of the madness. In her terror, prayer was all that came to her thoughts—prayer and a policeman. As they raced into the park, the thugs continued to throw rotted fruit, bottles, and rocks, and many found their mark. Inez's mind flashed on her brother Will. How would he react when he heard of this? She glanced at her friend and saw her struggling to keep up. Just as they neared a ruined church building, and possible protection, Jennie twisted her ankle on a cobble and crumpled onto the grass. Elder Davis turned aside and pulled her up.

"Ow!"

"What is it?"

"My ankle."

"Sorry, but there's nothing for it," he said in a rush, putting his arm around her waist and moving her forward. They quickly met with their companions, who had stopped in the church courtyard.

"No getting away from them," Ray said quickly, attempting to catch his breath.

"Sorry," Jennie cried. "Sorry."

"Not your fault."

"If I hadn't . . . "

"No. Not your fault."

Their pursuers halted their run and advanced slowly, like predators stalking their prey. The leader's face showed smug satisfaction, with narrowed eyes and a mocking grin. His mates jeered and called out insults.

"Shoulda given up at the start," he taunted. "Saved yer legs a bit of running." With a gloved hand, he reached into his gunnysack and pulled out a moldering potato.

Inez saw Jennie lift her chin and stand straighter, though she winced when she put weight on her left foot. Inez tried to imitate her friend's bravado, but she remembered the brute's iron grip on her shoulder, and her stomach clenched. She whimpered and reached for her brother's arm. She could tell he was working hard to control his breathing and his temper.

"We don't want any trouble," Ray said firmly.

"Really? Well, ya shoulda thought about that before comin' here to spread your tripe."

"You've never even heard us preach," Elder Davis challenged.

Inez thought it a bad time to be combative.

The thug gave a grunt and spit on the ground. "Preach? It that what ya call it? More like spewing garbage." The gang shouted their thoughts to this sentiment, and their leader took a step forward. "Oh, we've been told about yer evil ways with women, your worship of gold Bibles and that liar Joe Smith. Yeah, we've heard a lot, and we don't want none of it here. We mean to send you packing."

"Fine," Ray said, stepping in front of Inez. "Fine. We'll leave. We don't want any trouble. We'll just leave."

"Well, I don't rightly know that you've learned your lesson yet, 'cause we've chased your kind off before and you keep coming back."

"Like vermin," another gang member yelled.

The leader grinned. "Yeah, like vermin."

"This time we'll go. Let us get the ladies out."

The leader gave Jennie a vulgar look. "Ladies? Not likely. Mormon whores more like it."

"How dare you!" Elder Davis yelled, lunging toward the group of ruffians.

As the mob surged forward, the thug threw the potato with force. It struck Elder Davis on his neck, and he gave a howl of pain and fell to his knees.

"Elder!" Inez cried, stumbling to kneel beside him. His hand clutched the side of his neck as blood seeped between his fingers. "What have you done?" she screamed at the gang leader. She looked down at the seemingly harmless potato and saw shards of glass imbedded in the pulp. *Please, Lord, don't let us die here.* She put her arm around Elder Davis's back and covered his bloody hand with hers.

"Inez, just leave me."

"I won't."

"Inez . . . "

"No!"

Someone grabbed her coat collar and dragged her across the cobbles, all the while yelling curses and threats. The brute threw her down, and as she waited for the blows, she heard high whistles and shouts at a distance. The chaos of sound around her abruptly stopped, and she chanced a glance in the direction of the whistles. She saw a tall man running to them with a contingent of policemen. The leader of the thugs barked an order, and his gang took off running in different directions.

Inez crawled back to Elder Davis. "It's all right now, Elder. The police are here." She attempted to stand, and a gentle hand took her upper arm and lifted her.

"Easy now, miss."

Inez gave a trembling smile to the large tawny bearded policeman and steadied herself. "My friend is hurt. Can you help him?"

"Doctor's already seeing to him. Don't you worry."

"Doctor?"

"The one that fetched us," he said. His voice was low and soft, and Inez thought of her father. Tears flowed, and the policeman patted her back. "Are you injured, then?"

"I . . . I don't know. My hands hurt." Inez looked at her hands covered in dirt and blood and numbly shook her head. "I don't know." She wiped her eyes on the sleeve of her coat.

Ray came to her at that moment, supporting Jennie who was limping badly. Ray had a cut on his lip and the beginnings of a black eye.

"Inez, are you hurt?" Jennie blurted when she reached her side.

Inez shrugged. "I don't know. But I'm sure the doctor will sort us out." She turned to look closely at the man speaking to Elder Davis in assuring tones and let out a surprised yelp. "It's the man!"

"What man?" Jennie asked.

"The man who helped me." Ray and Jennie gave her uncomprehending stares. "He stood up when the brutes first attacked me."

The man glanced up and smiled. "Glad we arrived when we did."

"And you're a doctor?" Inez questioned moving forward. "But how did you . . . I mean, how did you . . . "

"How did I know you'd need assistance?" He pulled a brown bottle from his leather bag and poured some liquid onto a clean handkerchief. "Sadly, it was evident. When the gang left off with me and followed you into the park, I knew it was trouble." Elder Davis flinched as the doctor gently dabbed the side of his neck with the ointment. "I went for the police. I knew you'd need more help than my puny walking stick."

Inez smiled at him and turned to the policeman. "We're grateful that you're here," she stated, and the others nodded. "Thank you, Doctor . . . Doctor . . . I'm sorry, we don't know your names?"

"Dr. Smith," the man said. "Very easy to remember."

"Sargent Fitzwilliam," the policeman responded. "Not as easy."

"We're very grateful to you both," Ray said soberly. "How's Jonathan?"

"Jonathan is lucky. An inch or two and it might have sliced a main artery."

"Oh dear," Jennie said, squeezing Inez's arm.

Dr. Smith wrapped a bandage around Elder Davis's neck and told him to sit still. He stood and faced his other three patients. "Now, how are the rest of you doing?"

Ray took charge. "This is Miss Jennie Brimhall, and she's damaged her ankle. This is my sister Inez Knight, and . . . I'm not sure of her injuries. Inez?"

"I'm not sure either. Just a few cuts and bruises I think."

Dr. Smith assessed Ray's face. "And you have several wounds and a black eye, Mr. Knight. Anything else?"

Ray shook his head. "I think that's the extent of it, Doctor. It would have been worse if you hadn't shown up."

Dr. Smith moved to Jennie. "Put your arm around my neck, Miss Brimhall, and I will escort you to that stone bench." Sargent Fitzwilliam came to assist, and Jennie did not protest. "I will need to get them to my office for a proper examination, Sargent. Can you get me transport?"

"I can, sir. As soon as one of my men return, I'll send him off to the station for a team and wagon." He turned to Ray. "And then we'll need to get statements on what happened."

"Of course," Ray said, following them.

Inez took a deep breath and turned back to sit on the ground beside Elder Davis. "Statements? Oh, I will definitely be giving the police a statement about those black-hearted louts." Her rant concluded, she turned to take note of Elder Davis's condition. He was covering his face, and his head was on his knees. His breath was ragged, and a moaning came from deep within his chest. Inez put her hand on his back. "Elder Davis, are you all right?" He shook his head. "Should I get the doctor?" Another shake of his head. Inez began to panic. "What can I do?'

He took his hands from his tearstained face and looked directly at the companion beside him. "Forgive me, Sister Knight. Please, forgive me."

NOTE

The British slave trade: Great Britain participated heavily in the slave trade from the seventeenth century into the nineteenth century. Through the transatlantic slave trade, an estimated three million slaves were sent from Africa to the American colonies. Under persistent pressure from William Wilberforce and others, the British Parliament finally passed a bill making the slave trade illegal. The law went into effect on May 1, 1807.

Chapter Twenty-Four

Mrs. Boyers stood in the entry hall, staring at the front door.

"There's nothing for it, madame. The entry bell will shortly ring, and I must answer it."

"I am well aware of that, Mr. Kinsey, but perhaps we can stand here shoulder to shoulder and wish Mr. Noall to lose his way."

"Or perhaps the carriage to lose a wheel."

Some of the strain left Mrs. Boyers's face. "I suppose miracles do occur."

"Well, the young ladies believe they do."

Mrs. Boyers raised a hankie to the corner of her eye. "Just so."

"At least we have had them a few extra weeks while they recuperated."

Mrs. Boyers nodded, but no words were forthcoming.

The sound of footfalls on the stairs made each of the watchers assume a pose more befitting their station; nonetheless, Inez and Jennie gave them surprised looks upon reaching the landing.

Jennie was the first to find her voice. "Is everything all right, Mrs. Boyers?"

"Of course. What would be wrong?"

Inez gave Mrs. Boyers a curious look. "Well, you and Mr. Kinsey don't often stand together in the hallway."

"We . . . were . . . evaluating the floor runner. Whether it needed replacing."

"The floor runner?"

There was a moment of awkward silence, and then Mrs. Boyers spoke. "So, what can we do for you?"

"Nothing," Inez said, moving the rest of the way down the stairs. "We just came to report that we have finished packing."

Mrs. Boyers lifted the hankie to the corner of her eye. "Very well, then. Efficient. Good."

Jennie stepped forward. "Mrs. Boyers."

"Yes, my dear?"

"Don't change the floor runner." She moved quickly to Mrs. Boyers and took her hand. "Don't change the floor runner or the broken cuckoo clock or anything else in your wonderful home. Sister Knight and I want to remember it just this way."

"Oh, my dears." Mrs. Boyers wept, gathering the sisters into her arms. "Let's stand here together and pray for your president to change his mind." The girls hugged her.

"I'm afraid it's not *his* mind that needs changing," Jennie offered gently.

The sound of a carriage stopping in front of the house made the girls step back. Mr. Kinsey straightened his waistcoat, and Mrs. Boyers dried her tears. Suddenly Inez ran forward, put her back to the door, and threw her arms wide.

"I'll block the door to keep them out! You three run for it!"

The others in the company stared at her for a few moments then broke into laughter.

"Oh, Sister Knight, I will miss your pluck."

The front doorbell sounded, and Mr. Kinsey moved to answer. "Sadly, I'm afraid our time for escape has passed, Miss Knight." The doorbell rang again. He gave her a kind smile. "I could always tell them you were sick with malaria and needed several months to recuperate."

Inez brightened for a moment then shook her head. "Thank you for trying, Mr. Kinsey, but I'm afraid they'd catch us out. We try very hard not to lie to our mission leaders." Reluctantly she gave up her post and trudged to her companion.

Jennie was grinning and shaking her head. "What would I do without you, Sister Knight?"

"Probably get into a lot less trouble."

Mrs. Boyers stood straight and took the girls' hands as Mr. Kinsey opened the door.

Hours later the company stood in the sunshine at the front of Mrs. Boyers's house as Elder Knight and Elder Davis loaded the sisters' luggage onto the rental coach. The curving road facing the park was filled with wagons, horses, and carriages as the lovely spring afternoon brought out an excess of eager adventurers.

"Thank you for the wonderful luncheon, Mrs. Boyers, and for taking such good care of our sisters."

"My pleasure, President Noall. Yes, indeed. My pleasure. Please send them back anytime."

"We shall see, Mrs. Boyers. If we do send missionaries back to Bristol, it may be only the lads for a time."

"Coming through!" Ray called out as he and Elder Davis brought Sister Brimhall's trunk from the house. The group moved aside, allowing access to the carriage. The elders secured the trunk at the back of the transport with the other luggage. "I think that's all of it, President," Ray said wiping his brow.

"Vile Anti-Mormon League," Mrs. Boyers declared. "It's sad that a few dunderheads have to block salvation for the rest of us."

Jennie and Inez surrounded her. "Salvation for the rest of us?" Jennie queried. "Does that mean you might be thinking over some of our preaching?"

"Well, how can you mention such things as eternal marriage and not have it speak to my heart?"

"Must be the Spirit," Inez quipped.

"Must be," Mrs. Boyers answered with a half grin. "Besides . . . we have been reading that book."

"We?" Jennie questioned.

"Yes. Mr. Kinsey has been reading it to me, as my girlish eyesight seems to have fled."

The girls turned in unison to stare at Mr. Kinsey, who was standing near the carriage and supervising the work of the elders.

"Mind like the royal Lord Nelson!" Inez pronounced, giving him a salute. He shook his head and, with a half grin, saluted back.

Mrs. Boyers chuckled. "He is going to miss you two."

A stylish carriage pulled from the street onto Mrs. Boyers's drive, and the group turned to determine the occupants. Shock registered on Inez and Jennie's faces as they discovered the Kennison family. As Mr. Kennison secured the reins and went to help Mrs. Kennison from the carriage, George jumped from the back seat and raced to the group, fixing his attention on Inez and Jennie.

"Oh good! We didn't miss seeing you!" he panted. "Your note said you were leaving this afternoon, but we didn't know exactly what time."

"Take a breath, son," Mrs. Kennison instructed as she and Mr. Kennison approached.

"So, you are forsaking us, are you?" Mr. Kennison bellowed at the girls. "What kind of nonsense is that?"

"Edmund, mind your manners; you're intimidating everyone."

"Not us," Jennie said.

Edmund Kennison laughed. "Of course not, you brave girls! You two can stand up to anything."

"Obviously not angry mobs," Inez mumbled.

"Let me make introductions," Jennie said quickly. "President Noall, Mrs. Boyers, these are our friends, Mr. and Mrs. Kennison and their son, George."

"I have heard much about you over the weeks," Mrs. Boyers said with a warm smile. "It is nice to finally meet you."

Inez brought her brother forward. "And this is my brother Elder Ray Knight and his mission companion, Elder Jonathan Davis. And this . . . ," she said turning to Mr. Kinsey, "is our mentor and champion, Mr. Kinsey." Handshakes and greetings followed.

"It's a shame Mrs. Somers isn't here," Jennie said. "I know you'd be happy to meet her, Mr. Kennison. She's the one who's been teaching us how to cook and bake."

"The baker of the plum pudding?"

"The very one."

"You are a lucky woman, Mrs. Boyers. Yes, indeed. Now my Amanda can cook, but baking is not her gift."

"Perhaps I could send you some treats on baking day," Mrs. Boyers responded. "How would that be?" Mr. Kennison's face lit up with delight.

"Oh, don't spoil him, Mrs. Boyers," Mrs. Kennison warned. "Or you will find him constantly on your doorstep begging for treats."

"Please, call me Elaine, and I think it would be wonderful to find you on my doorstep. All of you. I'm afraid life is going to be a bit quiet here at Meadowlark Manor."

"Now that *we* won't be underfoot?" Inez questioned.

"Precisely."

President Noall stepped forward. "Time for goodbyes, sisters, or we shall miss our train."

Inez and Jennie turned to the Kennison family.

"Do you really have to go?" George asked plaintively, twirling his cap in his hands. "I mean you could just stay at Mrs. Boyers's house and we'd bring the people to you. That way you'd be safe from the brainless louts."

Jennie gave him an understanding smile. "That would be lovely, George, but our job is to offer the gospel to as many people as possible, and that means being in the public." George nodded solemnly, and Jennie's heart ached at the loss of the young man's normal exuberance.

Amanda Kennison tucked a stray piece of hair behind her ear and gave her son a clap on the back. "Good gracious, George, buck up! Cheltenham is not that far. We could make a holiday of it. I haven't adventured the Cotswolds for many years."

A broad smile stamped itself onto George's face. "Really, Mum?"

"I don't see what would stop us. Do you, Mr. Kennison?"

"Not in the least. We've been to Egypt, so we can certainly navigate the Cotswolds."

Mrs. Kennison turned to the girls. "Also, *you* would be required to return here if any of us Bristol sinners requested a dip in the pond." As the sisters stood staring, she glanced over at President Noall. "I assume that's the way of it, President Noall?"

"Yes, Mrs. Kennison, absolutely the way of it."

"Then we'd have to come back too!" Elder Davis exclaimed as the girls cried out and ran to embrace the Kennison family.

A timid voice was drowned out by this cacophony of emotional expression. "Excuse me. Ah, beg your pardon." The din lessened as members of the group turned to acknowledge Mrs. Somers standing slightly behind Mr. Kinsey. She had two small baskets draped over her arms and seemed panicked by the attention, but resolute. "I brought some things fer the young ladies." She advanced to the side of Mrs. Boyers. "Might I?"

"Of course, Mrs. Somers. How very kind of you."

"Thank you, ma'am." Inez and Jennie came to her, and she held out the baskets. "Here's some ginger biscuits and a Bakewell tart fer each of ya." The sisters reverently took the offering.

"Thank you, Mrs. Somers. These are our favorites," Inez said.

"I know. I writ the recipe for the tart in the back of yer cookery book."

"Our Mrs. Beeton's book?" Inez asked.

"I hope ya don't mind."

"Mind?" Jennie said, laying her hand on Mrs. Somers's arm. "It will be a treasure."

Mrs. Somers's head bobbed up and down several times as she stepped back to stand beside Mr. Kinsey.

"We really must be off now," President Noall instructed.

The sisters went quickly to Mrs. Boyers, and Inez took her hand. "It seems we will be coming back to pester you, Mrs. Boyers."

"I shall prepare myself."

Jennie looped her arm through Inez's. "Come on, Sister Knight. We need to go. Just keep reminding yourself that we'll be back."

Inez was the last to climb into the rig. She remained standing and turned to the group. "We love you all!" she called in an uplifted voice.

"How very American," Mr. Kinsey said to Mrs. Boyers.

"Just so," Mrs. Boyers replied. "Just so."

When Inez sat, the driver gave the command for the horses to walk on. As the carriage pulled away, peace came over Inez, an assurance that she and Sister Brimhall were leaving behind a gathering of friends—friends united by the spirit of the gospel and ginger biscuits.

Chapter Twenty-Five

To the Knight Household
June 11, 1898

Dear Mother, Father, Jennie Pearl, and Addie,

How is your sheltered life in Provo? Are the fruits coming onto the trees? Is there still snow on the tops of the mountains? Is your garden planted? I thought I always wanted to be a part of the wider world, but now I long for kneeling in the dirt and planting corn.

The months are passing, and Jennie and I have learned much in our mission so far. We have learned that bone tiredness is part of missionary work along with sadness and joy. Who was it that said there must needs be an opposition in all things? We know this is true. I don't like it, but it is true.

Jennie and I were sad to leave Bristol. I have written to you about the Kennison family and Mrs. Boyers. And Mr. Kinsey. And Mrs. Somers. I think about them every day and pray for them. President Noall has decided to close Bristol (temporarily) for missionary work. We hope we have planted the gospel seed in several hearts, and if that is all the Lord called us to Bristol to do, we are content.

Jennie has not been well since our return from Bristol. The weather is pleasant, so we are not concerned that her pneumonia will return, but it seems there is always a toothache or sore throat or headache.

I know her father worries about her weak constitution, and she worries about his bad health. Please don't share her condition with him.

Jennie promises that she has written to the family and has been truthful about her "little" troubles.

Ray and Will are here with us in Cheltenham, and we see them nearly every day. We sing with them in the missionary choir and preach with them at street meetings. It is sad to think of Will finishing his mission the end of this year. I know Jennie pushes it from her thoughts.

Thank you for sending the Walden book. I have been reading it to Jennie during her recent bout with sore throat. We tried the new book by Mr. Stoker but found it frightening, so we set it aside. We still love Mrs. Beeton's book and search it daily for cookery advice and tidbits of wisdom. Speaking of Mrs. Beeton reminds me that I must go and write some words of wisdom in our missionary management book. I will send along Mrs. Somers's recipe for Bakewell tart. I think the family will love it.

Sister Brimhall and I are grateful for your prayers.

As always, your loving daughter,

Amanda Inez

BAKEWELL TART (VERY RICH)

INGREDIENTS— ¼ lb. of puff-paste, 5 eggs, 6 oz. of sugar, ¼ lb. of butter, 1 oz. of almonds, jam.

MODE— Cover a dish with thin paste, and put over this a layer of any kinds of jam, ½ inch thick; put the yolks of 5 eggs into a basin with the white of 1, and beat these well; add the sifted sugar, the butter which should be melted, and the almonds, which should be well pounded; beat all together until well mixed, then pour it into the dish over the jam, and bake for an hour in a moderate oven.

TIME— 1 hour.

Sufficient for 4–5 persons.

NOTES

Walden: A cherished book of the time by American author Henry David Thoreau, *Walden* was published in 1854 and offers a treatise on the essence of Transcendentalism.

Dracula: A gothic horror novel published in 1897 by Irish author Bram Stoker, *Dracula* began a genre of literature based on vampires.

Chapter Twenty-Six

To Future Sister Missionaries— A Word on Missionary Management

Sister Brimhall and I testify that persecution will come. It comes to the elders, it comes to the members, and it comes to us. It comes especially against those searching gospel truths. We testify that there is evil in the world and that the snake of this world craves for the Lord's work to fail.

Following Mrs. Beeton's discussion on the proper care of food both in winter and summer, she writes: "All these things ought to enter into the consideration of every household manager, and great care should be taken that nothing is thrown away, or suffered to be wasted in the kitchen, which might, by proper management, be turned to a good account."

When Sister Brimhall and I returned from Bristol, we spent much time handing out tracts. There was one dreary day we returned to our lodgings discouraged. We attempted to hand out second tracts to people who had eagerly accepted our first tracts. Most were now surly and closed, even malicious. Many yelled unflattering words, and several slammed their doors in our faces. I withstood the rejection, but it is not in Sister Brimhall's nature to be thus treated. In truth, we were ready to dismiss these people as unsavable. Then, Mrs. Beeton spoke up with those words of wisdom that I wish to translate into terms of missionary management:

We, as missionaries, are the managers of the Lord's work, and we should take great care that no son or daughter of God is thrown away or wasted in His kingdom. By proper management we might turn things to a good account.

Sister Brimhall and I prayerfully studied Jacob 5, on the Lord's pruning of His precious olive trees. Also the account of Alma returning to preach to the hard-hearted people in Ammonihah. We were prompted to better manage our spiritual fitness and to not give up on those trees in the garden that need extra pruning. Do not give up! With the Lord's help we can turn things to a good account.

Sister Inez Knight and Sister Jennie Brimhall

Chapter Twenty-Seven

Inez laughed so hard she snorted, which caused the other badminton players to stop playing and laugh with her.

"Very unladylike," Elder Bailey teased.

"She can't help it," her brother Will said, shaking his head. "Our mother snorts just like that."

Inez stood straighter and held her sides. She calmed herself but still giggled through her next words. "Well, how do you expect me to laugh properly when Elder Bailey is making such a goof of himself?"

"Me?"

"Yes. You look like a flamingo trying to bat the . . . the . . . "

"It's called a birdie."

"Trying to bat the birdie with your wing."

"Both wings," Will confirmed, flapping his arms in imitation.

"Be mindful," Elder Bailey retorted. "It's my first time at badminton." He pointed his racket at the others. "First time for all of us, and I daresay none of *you* look very elegant."

"Except for Jennie," Will said.

"Well, of course you're going to play favorites," Elder Bailey said rolling his eyes. He picked up the birdie. "So shall we have another go at it?"

"This may be a good time to stop," Jennie said, moving to Will and handing him her racket. "Sister Knight and I have an appointment with Mrs. Checkly."

"Oh! That's right!" Inez said, running over.

"How's the progress?" Will asked.

"We've only met with her twice, but she's read both tracts we've given her and still seems quite interested."

"Today she might accept a Book of Mormon!" Inez said happily.

"Ever the hopeful," Jennie said, giving her companion an accepting smile.

"Believe in what you want to happen until it happens," Inez quoted.

"Not quite my father's wise saying, but it will do," Jenny said, starting her trek across the park toward the conference house. The others followed quickly. Jennie acknowledged Will when he reached her side. "So what are you gentlemen up to this afternoon?"

"We're going with the president to take Sister Noall to the train station."

"Luggage duty," Elder Bailey said. "And you can see that President Noall chose the two strongest elders, of course."

"Really?" Inez scoffed. "I'd think he would've chosen Elder Abernathy and Elder Green then."

"Ah! I'm wounded!" Elder Bailey lamented, and Inez laughed.

"I wish she didn't have to leave," Jennie said. "She's been a great comfort to me and Sister Knight."

"She has her home in Utah to care for," Will stated.

Jennie stopped walking. "I know that, Will, but she will be sorely missed." Will handed the badminton rackets to Elder Bailey and took Jennie's arm. She pulled back briefly, then accepted the noble gesture with gratitude. "Thank you, Elder Knight." She began walking.

"I know it must be difficult in a world of men," he said, patting her hand. "But you must know how we all admire you."

"Even Elder Davis," Elder Bailey put in.

"I know. He came back from Bristol a changed man," Will said, giving Jennie a quizzical look. "How did *that* happen?"

"I think he found us more capable than he expected," Jennie said with a half smile.

"And brave," Will stated. "He was a fool not to have seen it before. You and Inez have shown great stamina during these past months."

"Stamina?" Inez scoffed. "Of all the words you could choose to describe us, you pick *stamina*? You look at adorable Jennie, and the first thing you think of is stamina?"

"I take it as a compliment," Jennie defended.

"Of course, but he could have said that we've shown great brilliance or spirit. I would even have accepted fortitude—but stamina? It makes us sound like draft horses."

They reached the road facing the conference house, and Jennie unhooked her arm from Will's. "Thank you for the words of encouragement."

"Of course."

Inez took Jennie by the wrist and pulled her away. "Hurry, let's leave him before he gives us any other cherished compliments, like we're hefty or rugged."

Inez and Jennie spent time in their apartment changing clothes, freshening up, and redoing their hair since a visit to the Checkly home required a previsit note and meticulous grooming. The note had been sent in the morning, and with cleanliness achieved, the two missionaries now stood on Mrs. Checkly's doorstep with great expectancy.

Inez rummaged in her satchel.

"You've looked in your bag a dozen times!" Jennie whispered.

"I know. I'm just nervous. Should I give her the book or not?"

"Let the Spirit tell you."

"Sometimes the Spirit whispers so softly that I don't hear Him."

The door opened, and a tall man in servant livery addressed them without a smile. "Good afternoon, Miss Brimhall and Miss Knight." He stepped back. "Please come in, and I will announce your arrival to Mrs. Checkly."

The girls stepped into the receiving vestibule, and Inez gave a slight curtsy to the servant. In return he gave her a look of curious aloofness. Inez read his thoughts. *Silly American, one need not condescend to a servant.* When he turned to ascend the stairs to the private quarters, Inez leaned over and whispered to Jennie. "I know. I didn't need to curtsy."

"It's not a tragedy, Inez," Jennie whispered back.

"It makes me seem like an American know-nothing." She stood

straighter and used her normal voice. "It's just that all this finery makes me nervous."

"Really? With all your family's wealth?"

"Scruffy American wealth. Nothing like this."

"That's true," Jennie said with a half grin. "You don't even have servants."

Inez laughed. "Could you imagine what my mother would do with a servant?"

"Make him sit in a chair while she worked," Jennie stated.

"Exactly," Inez affirmed. "And my father would turn him into an accountant and pay him a good salary." Inez moved to look out one of the tall front windows overlooking the Poseidon Fountain and the Imperial Gardens. She sighed. "Yet, even with all her money, Mrs. Checkly has a very nice nature, not formal or superior." A subdued cough came from behind them, and Inez turned from the window with a start. "Oh! I . . . I didn't hear you. I was . . . we were . . . "

"Mrs. Checkly will see you now in her upstairs reading room," the servant said, without hint of having heard any of the conversation. "Please follow me."

Inez joined Jennie, and the two ascended the curved staircase behind the silent servant. The threesome arrived at the door to the reading room, and the servant preceded them. "Miss Brimhall and Miss Knight, madame."

"Thank you, Mr. Easton." He turned and left as Mrs. Checkly motioned to them. "Come, ladies. Have a seat." Inez and Jennie moved to sit on the settee opposite Mrs. Checkly's high-backed chair. Inez tried not to stare at the elegant woman in her pale-peach morning gown, her dark hair done up in curls and silver clips, her hand resting on a book. Inez self-consciously touched her own hair and thought of her first encounter with Mrs. Checkly.

She and Jennie had walked from the conference house to the Imperial Gardens for an outing. Their plan was to sketch the Poseidon Fountain and send the drawings home in their next letters to family. Inez grimaced as she remembered crossing the road, turning back to see if Jennie was behind her, and walking directly into a huge white horse—a horse attached to Mrs. Checkly's carriage. Inez was knocked on her backside, her hat falling into the muddy street. The carriage driver was immediately by her side, asking her condition and helping her to stand. *God works in mysterious ways,* Inez thought. Because of the incident, Mrs. Checkly invited them to her home for tea and, therefore, conversation.

"We are very glad to see you again," Jennie said.

Inez's meandering thoughts were brought to the present. "Yes, very glad."

"I have been looking forward to your visit. Is there anything I can offer you?"

Inez was just about to ask for some of the puff pastry bites Mrs. Checkly had served them at their first meeting, but Jennie said, "Oh, no thank you, Mrs. Checkly. We had dinner not long ago." Inez sighed and shook her head, vowing later to remind her companion about combining their opinions.

"So what are you reading?" Jennie asked.

Mrs. Checkly lifted the book from her lap and placed it on the side table. "A book by your Mr. Twain. *Huckleberry Finn.*"

"I love that book!" Inez exclaimed.

Mrs. Checkly chuckled. "And why is that, Miss Knight?"

"Other than being a good story, it talks about misunderstanding and injustice."

"The slave issue."

It took a moment for Inez to find her voice. "Well, yes."

"I believe that is something the Mormon people have had to suffer, correct?"

"Slavery?" Inez questioned.

"Misunderstanding and injustice," Jennie offered. "Yes, ma'am. It is definitely part of our history."

"And what do you feel are the main reasons for these misunderstandings?"

Jennie took a breath. "Joseph Smith claiming to have seen God the Father and Jesus Christ, the Book of Mormon . . . "

"The golden Bible," Mrs. Checkly stated.

"Actually, it's a history of the ancient people of America," Inez offered. "And their belief in Jesus Christ." She hurriedly retrieved the book from her satchel, stood, and offered it to Mrs. Checkly, whose look of surprise went unnoticed. "I brought you a copy. We . . . we brought you a copy."

"Very generous," Mrs. Checkly said, accepting the book and looking briefly at the book's spine.

"Make sure you open it," Inez instructed.

"Inez! Don't be so forthright," Jennie exclaimed, as Mrs. Checkly smiled.

"It's perfectly all right, Miss Brimhall," Mrs. Checkly said, looking directly at Inez. "I love reading, Miss Knight, so I will be sure and open it."

Inez felt color rise into her cheeks, and she retreated to her chair.

Jennie spoke up to reclaim the conversation. "But perhaps the harshest persecution is because people think the women of the Church are mistreated."

Mrs. Checkly nodded. "Contempt for a part of your unique history."

"Contempt which comes from a lack of understanding," Jennie said.

"Mistreatment would be news to the women of the Church," Inez said.

"And why is that, Miss Knight?"

"Because most women are treated with respect and kindness."

"Most?"

"Well, there will always be dimwitted men in the group, won't there?" Mrs. Checkly smiled at Inez's candor as she continued. "In our home, my father asks my mother's opinion. She helps him with the business, teaches at church, takes care of us and the house, grows a garden. She even takes part in the suffrage movement in Utah."

"Impressive."

"My father says she's formidable."

"It would seem so," Mrs. Checkly said. She turned to Jennie. "And your mother, Miss Brimhall?"

Jennie stared down at her hands for several moments, then looked at Mrs. Checkly directly. "My mother is not well, ma'am. She has been in a special hospital for many years, yet my dear father visits her nearly every day."

"I am sorry for your mother's condition, Miss Brimhall."

Jennie bit her bottom lip and nodded. "May I be frank, Mrs. Checkly?"

"Of course."

"Sister Knight and I were sent to England by our Church leaders to witness of our life in Utah. We've both grown up in Utah. We know the people and the society. We know the culture and the faith. And we have been raised to live lives of service and decorum."

Mrs. Checkly nodded. "I must agree. You seem proper and well educated."

"Sister Brimhall and I have also both graduated in higher learning," Inez interposed. "And Jennie has been a teacher."

"A teacher?"

"Yes, ma'am," Jennie said. "We are trained in the domestic sciences, but Mormon women are also encouraged in math, the arts, history, government, and medical training."

"Government and medical training?"

"Yes. Even in our town of Provo we have several female doctors."

Mrs. Checkly looked astonished and skeptical together. "And government?"

Jennie gave her a broad smile. "Utah women were the first to vote in America. Our governor gave us the right in 1870."

"But the women of England do not as yet have this right," Mrs. Checkly answered.

"So much for the theory of servile Mormon women," Inez pronounced.

Mrs. Checkly smiled at her. "So much indeed."

"We even have Sister Martha Cannon, the first American woman elected as a state senator."

Mrs. Checkly sat with her mouth slightly opened for several moments. "I . . . I am stunned."

Jennie took up the banner. "Women have a strong voice in our community, Mrs. Checkly. We have our own newspaper and our own women's organization, the Female Relief Society."

"Why does no one know of this?" Mrs. Checkly asked, a tinge of consternation in her voice.

Inez chuckled. "I have a feeling it's one of the reasons Sister Brimhall and I were sent here."

Mrs. Checkly beamed at her. "And I am so very glad you were."

A carriage pulled up to the front of the house, and Mrs. Checkly rose quickly and went to the window.

"Oh dear."

"Is something wrong?" Inez asked.

"Ah. No. No. It's just Mr. Checkly arriving home early." She turned from the window, swept the Book of Mormon from her chair, and placed it on the bookshelf between two books of similar coloring. When she turned back to the sisters, Inez noticed her face was flushed. "Might I request a favor? My husband is a barrister and holds a high position. I have not told him of our meetings. I need to keep this from him—for the time being anyway."

They heard footfalls on the stairs.

"We understand," Inez said resolutely, though her heart was beating against her chest. "What should we . . . "

"I will speak with him. Please, follow what I say."

The library door opened, and Inez took a breath. She saw Jennie do the same. She was amazed to see Mrs. Checkly step forward gracefully with a gentle smile on her face.

Mr. Checkly smiled broadly when he saw her. "I finished the case early, Christine, and I thought . . . " His voice trailed off as he noticed the two young women rising from their chairs.

"Richard, how delightful! You're here in time to meet my new friends."

Inez looked at Mr. Checkly's face and failed to find delight imprinted there. He had a stern jawbone and dark eyes which added to his forbidding demeanor. Inez was glad she would never have to meet him in a court of law. As he removed his hat, Mrs. Checkly commenced introductions.

"Richard, this is Miss Brimhall and Miss Knight." Jennie curtsied, and Inez followed her example. "Ladies, this is my husband, Mr. Richard Checkly."

"How do you do, sir?" Inez said.

Mr. Checkly frowned at her. "American?"

Inez opened her mouth to speak, but Mrs. Checkly preceded her. "Yes. They're visiting my friend, Mrs. Throckmorton."

"The widow Throckmorton?"

"Yes. Second cousins of the New York Throckmortons. They . . . they're here for a tour of Europe."

Mr. Checkly seemed to relax, and Inez was grateful for a softening of his features. She attempted a smile which trembled on her lips for a moment, then slid away.

"So which one of you is related?"

"Ah . . . " Jennie said.

"I am, Mr. Checkly," Inez stated confidently. "We have Throckmortons on my mother's side."

"I see. Well lovely for you young ladies to be on tour. And why did Widow Throckmorton send you to visit my wife?"

"Ah," both Inez and Jennie said.

"She wanted me to take them on a stroll through the Imperial Gardens," Mrs. Checkly intervened. "We live so near, and she does not do as much strolling these days."

"I see," Mr. Checkly said. "And now I've gone and ruined your adventure."

"Not at all, sir," Jennie said. "We really should be going."

"We have work to do," Inez added.

"Work?" Mr. Checkly questioned with a frown.

"Mending, hand-washing. That sort of thing. The sort of thing ladies do."

Mr. Checkly gave her a searching look, and Inez felt her knees go weak. At that moment, Mr. Easton stepped into the room.

"Sorry sir. Mr. Cummins wishes to know if you still want the carriage."

"Oh! Yes, Easton, I do. Mrs. Checkly's guests are leaving, so Mrs. Checkly and I will be going out."

"Very good, sir."

"Please escort the ladies to the door." Mr. Checkly turned his full attention on the girls, and Inez shuddered. She saw her puny self, standing in a dismal courtroom while Barrister Checkly pointed his finger at her and accused her of lying about her lineage. She jumped when he spoke. "Very nice to meet you, ladies. Have a safe time on your travels."

Jennie curtsied. "Thank you, sir. And thank you, Mrs. Checkly, for the delightful visit. Perhaps we will see you again and we can take our stroll together."

Mrs. Checkly nodded. "That would be lovely."

"We're so glad you like to read!" Inez blurted.

Jennie took Inez by the wrist and moved to follow Mr. Easton from the room. Once outside with the front door closed behind them, Jennie turned to give Inez a bemused look. "We're so glad you like to read?"

"Well, I didn't want her to forget about the book."

Jennie shook her head. "What am I going to do with you?"

"We could hunt for sausage rolls. I'm hungry."

Jennie laughed and started off down the street. "You're always hungry."

Inez caught up. "So, what *are* we going to do?"

"I thought we were hunting sausage rolls."

"No, I mean about Mrs. Checkly. I don't feel good lying about our visits."

"Though you were very good at it."

"Jennie!"

Jennie stopped walking. "Sorry." She looked back to Mrs. Checkly's home and shrugged. "I don't know what we're going to do, Sister Knight."

"Well, we have to find some way to teach her. She's going to have a million questions about the Book of Mormon when she reads it."

Jennie grinned and took Inez by the hand. "At least a million."

"Perhaps we should skip sausage rolls and fast and pray about it. I'm sure the Lord knows what we should do."

"I'm sure He does," Jennie answered, linking arms with her companion and striding forward. "In all thy ways acknowledge Him, and He shall direct thy paths."

As Jennie quoted scripture, Inez envisioned Mrs. Checkly laying aside the adventures of Huck and Jim and sojourning with Lehi and his family across the sea to the promised land.

NOTES

The Adventures of Huckleberry Finn: Published in 1876 by Mark Twain, this novel quickly became an American classic. One of its main themes deals with the detriments of slavery.

Universal women's suffrage: Many prominent Utah women were active in the nineteenth-century movement to secure voting rights for women: Martha Cannon, Sarah Kimball, Emmeline Wells, and Zina Young, to name a few.

Chapter Twenty-Eight

"Inez! The soup! The soup!" Jennie yelled as she took the custards from the oven.

Inez dumped the shriveled carrots into the chafing dish and ran for the stove. She searched frantically for a towel to take the hot pot from the flame.

"Just turn it off!" Jennie commanded, setting the pan of custards on the sideboard and turning to survey the kitchen catastrophe. "How's the gravy?"

Inez ignored the curdled soup, stuck a wooden spoon into the gravy pot, and lifted out a thick glob of brown muck.

"A little thick."

Jennie growled. She moved to the cast-iron pan and removed the lid. "And the beefsteaks are burned."

Inez peered in. "Some people like their meat a little more done." She stepped back as Jennie growled again. "The potatoes seem all right," Inez offered. "A little mushy, but butter should fix that."

"Oh, I'm sure mushy potatoes will be plenty of food for six hungry elders," Jennie said tearfully. "So much for our Fourth of July American dinner."

"That's it!" Inez exclaimed. "The Beeton curse!"

"What?"

"We tried to cook an American dinner in an English kitchen, so Mrs. Beeton has cursed us."

Jennie chuckled and wept at the same time. She looked around at the failed dinner. "I'm afraid even the Stars and Stripes won't keep the boys patriotic after this disaster."

"Well, Elder Abernathy's British, so he was never going to cheer this meal."

"That's no consolation, Inez," Jennie said, drying her eyes on her apron and jabbing a fork into the beefsteak. She glared at it. "Well, we may as well plate everything and face the ridicule."

"They're elders," Inez said, draining the potatoes and tipping them into a dish. "They probably won't even notice."

"Huh!" Jennie responded. "Just watch the looks on their faces."

Her words were prophecy because as the plates were placed on the table in the conference hall, the looks of delight on the six male faces diminished with each offering. The elders stood as Inez and Jennie placed the final dishes on the table. There was silence as Elder Bailey stared at the shriveled carrots, Elder Davis looked heavenward, and Ray put his hand over his mouth and bowed his head. Elder Abernathy placed his hand on his heart, and his new companion, Elder Forester, simply frowned at the beefsteak in confusion. Will turned to Jennie and Inez.

"Thank you, Sister Brimhall and Sister Knight. We know this was a lot of work for you, and we appreciate it."

"Maybe, maybe not," Elder Forester mumbled.

"What's that?" Will asked. "Did you say you wanted to offer the blessing, Elder Forester?"

Elder Forester stood tall and looked Will straight in the eye. "Whatever you think best, Elder Knight. You are the senior elder among us."

The newest elder of the Cheltenham group bowed his head and prayed for the mission and America. All was well, until he prayed for a blessing on the *lovely* dinner—that the food would be wholesome and their digestive systems able to handle it.

At his concluding "Amen," Inez was heartened that the other elders were mute, marking their lack of support for his sentiments.

During dinner, Will, Ray, and Elder Bailey did their best to eat without complaint or negative comment. Even Elder Davis ate quietly and had seconds of steak slathered in lumpy gravy.

When Jennie returned from the kitchen with the anticipated dessert custards, the look on her face did not speak of success.

"I'm afraid they're a bit soupy," she said, a tremor in her voice.

"Not to worry!" Elder Abernathy called out. "That's the way my mum cooks custard, and they're delicious! Custard soup!" He saluted, and everyone laughed.

The custards *were* delicious, and Inez's spirits lifted. Her contentment was short lived when she glanced over and saw President Noall striding across the hall toward them.

"It looks like he has the assignments," Jennie said.

"So how was your Fourth of July dinner?" the president asked as he came to the table.

"Wonderful!" Will rushed to answer as Inez noticed Elder Forester ready to make a comment.

"Well, good. Good," the president said smiling around at them. "Now, I have the assignments for the Sabbath evening meeting." He glanced at the paper in his hand. "Elder Bailey and Elder Knight will pray. Elder Abernathy will give the Book of Mormon talk." The other missionaries gave their British compatriot a sympathetic look since his was the topic that drew the most dismissal. "Sister Brimhall will narrate the 'Views of Salt Lake City' slide display, and lastly Sister Knight will talk about a woman's life in Utah."

Inez swallowed hard, the tidbits of undigested dinner warring in her stomach. She tentatively raised her hand. "President Noall, might Jennie and I switch assignments?"

The president gave her a searching look. "I suppose you might, Sister Knight, but I think the Lord would be pleased if you spoke on the subject given." He smiled at her. "Besides, the fliers name both you and Sister Brimhall as speakers at this meeting."

"Fliers?"

"Yes. The elders passed them out while you two were cooking dinner." He addressed the group. "You should clear up here and start setting out chairs. I think we might have a crowd." He turned and moved back toward his office.

Inez swiveled around to stare at her brothers. "You passed out fliers?"

"Just doing what we were told," Will said with a grin. He stood. "Come on, Elder Bailey, we have chairs to set out."

"Sorry," Elder Bailey mumbled to Inez as he moved to follow.

Inez looked at Jennie, who was picking up bowls. "Jennie, they passed out fliers."

"I heard. Now help me clean up."

Ray and Elder Davis began stacking dishes. "Thank you for dinner," Ray said.

Inez scowled at him as she picked up the half-full bowl of shriveled carrots. "Very funny."

"No, really! Parts of it weren't half bad. What do you say, Elder Davis?"

"You both worked very hard. I'm grateful."

"Elder Davis has turned into a diplomat," Jennie said moving toward the kitchen. "Come on, Sister Knight, it's going to take some time to get the kitchen in order."

Inez brightened. "Maybe it will take so long we'll miss the meeting!"

The chairs were set, the large crowd assembled, and the kitchen clean. Inez sat at the back of the hall wondering if any of the attendees could detect the smell of burned steak or hear the sound of her heart thumping against her ribs. She tried to cast her mind to other subjects: the Fourth of July festivities in Provo, her father's renowned barbecue steak, her mother's apricot pie. But she found that these reminiscences only brought tears of homesickness.

Jennie sat down beside her. "You'll do fine."

"That's what we thought about dinner."

"Inez, you've spoken in church before."

"Smaller groups, talks on prayer or scripture, simple testimonies about my family."

"And it's all been wonderful!"

"Wonderful? I've nearly fainted or thrown up every time." Her friend was silent. "And now to defend all the women in Utah to this big crowd? I will probably throw up *and* faint."

Elder Forester stopped as he was passing by. "Who's going to throw up?"

"Never mind, Elder Forester," Jennie said.

"If someone is ill, I'd like to be of assistance."

"Not necessary," Jennie answered.

"You don't look well, Sister Knight. Would you like me to take your spot?"

Inez looked up into the gray eyes of the very handsome Mr. Forester and clenched her teeth. *I have to speak in front of him*? Her mental drifting made it difficult to concentrate on Jennie's next words.

"Though it might be interesting to hear your thoughts on Mormon women in Utah, Elder Forester, I do think Sister Knight will do a much more insightful job."

Elder Forester frowned at them. "I'm not so sure. She doesn't look like such a fair specimen of Utah womanhood at the moment."

Inez flinched.

Jennie rose slowly to her feet, fixing Elder Forester with an icy stare. "This is your first big British Church meeting, isn't it, Elder Forester?"

"Yes," Elder Forester said warily. "Why?"

"Well, I just advise you to watch your back. We often have rowdies attend who are itching to chuck a green elder in the gutter."

Elder Forester's head snapped around to take in the large milling crowd. "I . . . I think I should find Elder Abernathy."

Inez started to giggle. "You can be scary sometimes, Sister Brimhall."

Jennie sat down. "Good. I hope it keeps him quiet for two minutes."

"We just won over Elder Davis, and now we have to deal with Elder Attractive," Inez said with a shake of her head.

Jennie turned to stare at her. "You find him appealing?"

"Well, not his personality, but his face isn't bad."

Jennie jumped to her feet. "Oh, Inez! You will not believe who just came to the meeting!"

"Who?" Inez asked. She stood and looked toward the door. "Who?"

"There!" Jennie pointed. "Mrs. Checkly."

As the sisters hurried to greet their investigator, the others in the conference hall turned to scrutinize the elegant woman joining their assembly. The perusal ranged from awe to envy.

Mrs. Checkly smiled. "I am so glad to see familiar faces. I had no idea there would be this many people."

"It's because we're speaking," Jennie said with openness. "It seems everyone wants to come gawk at the Mormon women."

"I know. I saw the flier, so I came to hear you speak." She smiled again. "Although I have no intention of gawking at either of you."

"That's a relief," Inez said.

President Noall walked to the podium at the front of the hall. "Good evening, ladies and gentlemen. If you will all be seated, we will begin our meeting."

"Would you like to sit at the back with us?" Jennie whispered to Mrs. Checkly. She nodded, and the three took their seats.

As the meeting began, Inez repeated silent prayers for strength, for calm, for the ability to speak with the Spirit, for the blessing of not fainting, for the congregation to be respectful. This hope was short lived for as soon as Elder Abernathy began his talk on the Book of Mormon, an old man stood and shouted at the young missionary.

"Ya dun know what yer talkin' about, young pup! These Mormons a got you hoodwinked! There ain't no more scriptures to be had. We got the Bible, and that's all the Lord intended!"

Several voices in the crowd roared in support as Elder Abernathy vainly attempted to reclaim control. Inez saw President Noall motion to two of the sturdier Church members, who quietly rose, approached the old man, and indicated that it might be a good idea for him to sit down. He did.

President Noall stood at the podium. "Friends! Friends." Things quieted. "We are here among you to preach the gospel of Christ, restored as it was when Jesus walked the earth. We ask you to be respectful of those speaking and for the people who have come seeking wisdom."

There were a few mumbles from the crowd, but it seemed the disruptors were mollified for the moment. Inez was amazed. Those few words from President Noall, and the thugs complied? She took a deep breath. Maybe by the time she spoke, they would be so overcome with the Spirit her words would have them begging for baptism.

Elder Abernathy forged ahead, and the assembly seemed attentive. Inez's thoughts drifted to her talk. She thought about the life she'd seen in Liverpool, Manchester, Cheltenham, and Bristol. Many nights, as she and Jennie had trudged back to their apartment, they saw old men and women asleep on the street, young people drinking and being much too intimate, children crying and begging for food, men fighting—poverty, misery, and wickedness on every side.

She then thought of her dear Provo, and though things were not perfect in her hometown, there was orderliness and industry. There was cleanliness and culture. The Saints who lived the gospel had respect for their fellows. Inez tried to clear her head. What should she tell these people? What did the Lord want her to share? The Spirit cautioned against pointing out the British flaws since that would surely offend; instead, she felt inspired to emphasize the beauty of living in a society created under God's laws. A society that honored life, family, and neighbors. Where men were held to a high standard in caring for their children and cherishing their wives. Where education was encouraged. A calmness settled in her heart. She would talk first about education and the accomplishments of the brilliant women she knew. Then she would talk about the wonderful life she and her sisters enjoyed, and then . . . Jennie touched her hand.

"I've just been called for my presentation," she whispered. "Are you ready?"

"I think I am. Good luck to you."

"Pray nothing goes wrong with the lantern," Jennie said as she stood. "I hate having to work with machines." She moved to the lantern projector set in the middle of the room. After a brief introduction, Jennie inserted the first slide of the Salt Lake Temple. The congregation gasped, and Inez felt a rush of pride. Set in the wilds of the western high desert, it was an impressive structure.

"Stunning," Mrs. Checkly said, a note of awe in her voice. "How ever did they manage it?"

"Faith," Inez said. "Both Sister Brimhall and I have pioneer ancestors, and their whole desire was to build a temple to the Lord when they reached the Salt Lake Valley."

"I had no idea."

"Most people don't."

Mrs. Checkly sat mesmerized as did most of the audience as Sister Brimhall showed photographic slides of Salt Lake City's wide streets, thriving businesses, well-dressed men and women, as well as country scenes of fertile farmland and orchards. To Inez, Utah was a paradise, and she prayed others saw it in the same way. Jennie ended with her testimony of how faith in revelation to a prophet had guided the Saints across the country to a place they could worship God and His son, Jesus Christ.

Inez smiled. Her companion's words swelled her soul and brought peace—that was until she heard harsh grumbling from a group of men standing at the back of the hall.

"A prophet? There's no such thing," one man growled. "They're only men . . . that lying Joe Smith and his devil friend Brigham Young."

"And their lies have poisoned a lot of minds in Utah."

"Yea, and now they're comin' over here to corrupt us."

"Especially our women."

President Noall motioned for Inez to come forward to the podium, and suddenly her calm confidence fled. Jennie came to her side.

"I . . . I don't think I can."

"Inez, you must," Jennie said with a mix of understanding and instruction. "You must."

Mrs. Checkly reached over and took her hand. "I need to hear your words, Miss Knight. Perhaps you can pretend you're speaking only to me."

Inez swallowed hard to keep down the bile that was rising from her stomach. She looked at Mrs. Checkly's encouraging expression and stood. "I'll try." She moved numbly toward the front of the hall.

President Noall stood beside her at the podium. "Our final speaker will be Amanda Inez Knight. Miss Knight has traveled here from Provo, Utah, and will tell you about life in her community." He sat down and Inez felt her legs tremble.

Inez fished in her skirt pocket and brought out a small notebook. She fumbled with the pages as she cleared her throat. "I . . . I want to welcome you . . . "

"We can't hear you!" someone yelled from the back of the hall.

Inez looked up quickly, and her head swam. "Oh! Oh, sorry." She prayed for strength. "I want to welcome you . . . "

"Louder!"

Inez felt as though she were going to cry, throw up, *and* faint. She gritted her teeth, took a deep breath, and began again. "I grew up in the lovely agricultural town of Provo, Utah." This time, no one called out. Inez stood taller and felt a comforting warmth pour into her body. "Hundreds of acres of fruit trees cover the foothills. There are fields of corn, potatoes, soy, and alfalfa. Herds of cattle and sheep wander the pastureland. The rugged Wasatch Mountains rise up on the east side of the valley, providing abundant water for this Eden. And Eden it is to me." Her voice cracked with emotion, and a tear rolled down her cheek. The audience became still. "It is Eden not just because of the beauty, but also because of the faith, the people, and the culture. Also, education plays an important part in The Church of Jesus Christ of Latter-day Saints."

"For the men!" the old rabble-rouser called out.

"And the women," Inez responded confidently. "In my youth I was taught not only the domestic arts but also higher learning. Sister Brimhall and I attended university, where we were encouraged in mathematics, science, history, linguistics, and literature." Inez noted that many women's eyes widened in surprise. She opened her notebook. "A friend of mine, David O. McKay, is now serving in Scotland and sent me his thoughts about education." She read, "True education seeks to make men honest, with virtue, temperance, and brotherly love. It seeks to make men and women who prize truth, justice, wisdom, benevolence, and self-control as the choicest acquisitions of a successful life."

"Look at her, would ya? Spouting the words of the Church brothers," someone yelled.

Inez looked up to see one of the men she'd overheard at the back of the room, standing and looking defiant.

"Let her speak!" a woman's voice rang out.

"And pollute us with her lies? I don't think so." Several of the other toughs stood and supported their friend in the harassment. "She stands there telling us about self-control? How much self-control do Mormon men have with their ten wives?"

"She's just one of them bastard children of polygamy!" The old man shouted, shaking his fist.

"How dare you!" Ray bellowed, jumping to his feet. Will and Elder Bailey stood with him.

"Gentlemen, please!" President Noall pleaded, but his words were lost in the chaos that now filled the hall. Several of the Church men went after the gang of toughs who continued to spew vicious claims, while the Knight brothers went after the old man. When he saw them coming for him, he yelped and ran from the hall. The din increased as more of the assembly joined in the war of words.

Inez stood gripping the podium, unable to move or speak. Elder Bailey raced to her, put his arm around her shoulder, and led her toward the back of the hall and her companion.

"Everything will be fine," he said into her ear. "We've been through this before."

Inez couldn't answer him.

When they reached Jennie and Mrs. Checkly, Jennie took one of her hands, and Mrs. Checkly, the other.

"Are you all right?" Jennie asked.

"I . . . I . . . what did I say to cause this?"

"You did not cause this, Miss Knight. Your words were inspiring," Mrs. Checkly called above the din. "That group of louts spoiled things."

Inez looked shocked as the piercing sound of police whistles cut through the noise in the hall.

"Oh dear!" Mrs. Checkly exclaimed. "Richard will not be pleased if I am sent to jail."

"Let's get you out of here," Elder Bailey directed. "We'll go the back way, through the kitchen."

Jennie took Inez's hand, and the three women followed Elder Bailey. Inez turned to glance at the rush of people heading for the main door.

"Wait."

"What is it, Inez?" Jennie asked.

"I thought I saw . . . "

Police were pushing into the hall, batons in their hands.

"Come on!" Elder Bailey barked. "We have to go!"

Inez couldn't be sure with her tears and the chaos, but she thought she'd seen Mr. Easton scanning the fleeing crowd. He was there for a moment and then—gone.

NOTES

The disastrous dinner: This was an actual dinner recorded in the journal of missionary Josephine Booth.

Fliers: Fliers were often used to announce speaking events. The notice that named Sister Knight and Sister Brimhall as participants in a meeting can be found at the Church History Library.

Lantern slides: The first photographic lantern slides, called hyalotypes, were invented by the German-born brothers Ernst Wilhelm and Friedrich Langenheim in 1848 in Philadelphia and patented in 1850.

Poverty: Several times in her journal, Inez referenced life, as she and Jennie saw it, in the poorer sections of the English cities and towns.

David Oman McKay: He was twenty-three when he was called to serve in the British Mission. He served from August 1897 to August 1899. In her journal, Inez recorded receiving letters from Elder McKay.

Chapter Twenty-Nine

Dear Mother,

I am coming home. I have decided that I am a wretched missionary and that my time would be better spent at home doing genealogy and weeding the garden. I do not have Jennie's grace or confidence, and I certainly do not have her knowledge of the scriptures. I know her father is an educator and taught her well, but you and Father were diligent in teaching us children too. Your instruction seemed to stick with Will and Ray, but I'm afraid my mind was on dresses, shoes, and hats.

Please break the news carefully to Father. I know he will be disappointed in me, but he always says never to waste energy on a failed venture, and I'm afraid my mission is a failed venture. I know you will also be disappointed about my decision, Mother, but I know you will still greet me with a smile.

Be assured that my testimony in the Atonement and gospel principles has never faltered, only faith in myself.

Tomorrow I will check the ship schedules and speak with President Noall. This letter should reach you before I make final plans. I will send you a telegraph concerning my travel.

Your devoted daughter,
Amanda Inez

A knock came to the apartment door, and Inez looked up quickly from her letter.

"I'll get it," Jennie said. She laid her book on the divan and went to open the door. "Will! This is a surprise."

Will and Elder Bailey stood at the entry with bouquets of flowers and boyish smiles. Inez thought they looked overly solicitous. She covered her letter with a book and stood.

"Good day, ladies!" Elder Bailey said, beaming. "Elder Knight and I have come to check on you."

"How nice," Jennie said. "Please, come in."

Will handed his bouquet to Jennie, and Elder Bailey moved to Inez. He held the flowers out to her, but she stepped back. The look on Elder Bailey's face went from excitement to confusion. "I . . . I'm sorry. Do you not care for flowers?"

"I do. It's just that flowers are normally given for a reason." She hesitated. "And I'm not sure of the reason."

"We thought they might cheer you," Elder Bailey ventured.

"Oh, you mean after last night's disaster? After my wretched attempt at public speaking ended in a riot?"

Elder Bailey looked stricken. "Ah . . . no. Nothing of the sort."

"Last night's ruckus was none of your doing," Will asserted.

"Oh really?" Inez scoffed. "Well, Elder Forester seems to think so."

"What do you mean?" Elder Bailey asked.

"To our faces this morning at breakfast, he said we'd done a fine job. Then later we overheard him commenting to Elder Abernathy that he thought the meeting would have been much better if we women had not participated—especially me."

Will came to her. "Inez, when will you learn to stop listening to ill-mannered elders?"

"The man is a fool," Elder Bailey stated. "Trust me, when things settle, people will come back to ask questions."

"Not of us," Inez mumbled. Though she said *us*, she was really thinking, *Not of me*.

"They will," Elder Bailey persisted. "The people were impressed just by the look of you . . . you two . . . the both of you." He cleared his throat. "Most had never seen Mormon women, and they were surprised by your deportment and refined appearance."

"Not to mention good teeth and stamina," Jennie said.

Inez laughed despite the feeling of ineptness that weighed on her spirit.

Elder Bailey again offered the flowers. "Now, are you going to make me hold these all day?"

Inez reached for them. "It would not be courteous of me." She went to their small cupboard and found a ceramic crock. She held it out to Jennie. "What do you think?"

Jennie set down her flowers and took it from her. "As Mrs. Beeton would say, 'Make do with what you have.'" She went to the water closet to fill the jar.

As soon as both bouquets were deposited and the jar set on their dormant pot-bellied stove, Inez felt the gray disappointment return. The colorful flowers should have cheered her, but instead they made her think of home and the confession of failure she would have to report. Inez sighed. She did not have the energy to entertain company but wasn't sure how to get rid of the elders without offending them. She braved on.

"Will, I was wondering . . . "

Her brother cut her off. "Actually, *we* were wondering if we could take you on an outing? It's market day, and we thought you might like to get out into the sunshine and stroll."

Jennie looked over at Inez, her face bright with anticipation. "A stroll would be lovely wouldn't it, Sister Knight? We haven't done anything fun for weeks."

"Yes, but I . . . " Inez sighed. "I'm not in the best of moods, Jennie. Why don't you three go on without me?"

Elder Bailey stepped toward her. "We could do that, Sister Knight, but we thought you might like to examine the new milliner's shop we found."

"Milliner?"

Jennie laughed. "Well, that certainly caught your attention."

"I do love hats. And I need to replace the one that fell in the mud at Mrs. Checkly's place."

"Sounds perfectly reasonable to me," Jennie encouraged.

"It's settled then," Will announced. "You ladies get ready, and we'll meet you out front." He and Elder Bailey put on their hats and headed to the door.

The door closed, and Jennie hurried to find her hat and duster. "Isn't this just what we need, Inez? Even if I don't find something to purchase, I don't care. Just to be out strolling and seeing other people." She glanced over at Inez, who was slowly putting on her hat. "Are you all right? We don't have to go out if you don't want to."

Inez gave her friend a forced smile. "I'm fine, Jennie. Just a bit . . . tired after last night." She put a hat pin in her hat, squared her shoulders, and smiled again. "The thought of looking at hats makes me happy."

Jennie brought Inez's duster from the wardrobe and handed it to her. "Good. So let's spend an afternoon not thinking about tracts or street meetings or churlish men and women who have no notion that we've left our comfortable lives and come halfway around the world to offer them the joy of salvation."

Inez stared at her friend for a moment, then started giggling. "Oh, Jennie. You are a treasure. What would I do without you?"

"You'll never have to know that, will you?" Jennie answered with a crooked smile. She opened the door and stepped out. "We are in this together until the end!"

"Oh, I forgot something!" Inez called to her. "You go ahead. I'm right behind you." As Inez moved to the desk, she glanced out the opened door to make sure Jennie was on her way down the stairs. She slid her letter from under the book, opened the desk drawer, and hid it under a mess of other papers. She pressed her lips together to keep from crying. She hadn't thought about what her leaving the mission would mean to Jennie. She shut the drawer with a snap. She could not think about that right now. Maybe Jennie needed a new companion, one who was not clumsy and who was a better scholar. Maybe she and Jennie would go home together. Maybe the First Presidency sent them to test the waters and other, more capable women would come after. Maybe . . .

"Inez?" Jennie called up the stairs. "Are you coming?"

"Coming!" Inez called back. She turned from the desk, took a deep breath, and commanded herself to think only of strolling and buying a hat.

Two hats! Inez bought two summer straw boater hats: one navy blue with a blue-and-white striped band around the base, and one golden wheat with a spray of delicate bird feathers stuck in the brim. She had been taken with both, so when Jennie suggested that she could certainly use two hats, Inez put money into the hands of the delighted clerk. Inez figured that she and Jennie could share them, as hats were not within Jennie's modest resources.

It had been a carefree and restoring afternoon, and now as the four-some sat in the conference hall discussing the day and waiting for supper, Inez enjoyed the absence of melancholy. Elder Bailey was making them laugh with tales of his antics on his family's farm in Spanish Fork.

"Stop! Stop!" Jennie squealed. "My sides hurt."

"But you haven't heard the one about my old blind dog and the baby pigs."

"No!" Jennie pleaded. "Stop it! Will, tell him to stop!"

"Such inappropriate behavior," came a strident voice from the far end of the long table.

Conversation in the hall quieted as heads turned to find the speaker.

"Elder Forester," Elder Bailey grumbled. "Why doesn't that surprise me?"

"I *was* being rather loud," Jennie said meekly.

"You were just laughing," Inez defended.

Elder Forester's upraised voice came again. "I'm just saying it's rather light-minded behavior for a missionary."

"Laughter is not light-mindedness," came a second voice, and Inez leaned forward to get a view of their defender.

"Elder Davis?"

Elder Forester's next words were combative. "And where were they this afternoon when the rest of us were preaching? Were they handing out tracts? Were they at a cottage meeting? No. They were out buying hats and trinkets."

"You may not be aware of this, Elder Forester, since you are new to the mission, but we all need time off from our labors," Elder Davis defended.

"To buy hats and trinkets?"

"What is your point?"

"I think it speaks to their frivolous natures. Women are not meant for serious thinking and demanding labor."

"Someone ought to inform our mothers of that," Jennie mumbled to her companions.

"You do not know what you're talking about," Elder Davis said.

"Oh, I think I do," Elder Forester persisted. "My father holds a high position in the Church and spoke out against sending single women on missions. He was upset when my call came to serve in the very place they were sent, and he warned me to avoid the confusion."

"What confusion?" Elder Davis questioned.

"The confusion of having females around us. I see that you and many of the other elders are mesmerized by their high-collared, frilly blouses," Elder Forester mocked. "But I am not."

There was a tense pause as Elder Davis stood. When he spoke, his voice was surprisingly calm. "Elder Forester, I caution you to be respectful of your fellow brothers and the sisters. I thought as you do when Sister Knight and Sister Brimhall first entered the mission. I judged them to be spiritually and physically weak. I thought we'd all waste our time pampering and protecting them."

"Just so."

"I was wrong. The Lord had to take me to my knees to realize how wrong I was." His voice filled with emotion. "They are wise and compassionate. They can reach people we cannot, and . . . "

Elder Forester interrupted. "And they can be the reason for distrust and ridicule. At last night's meeting Sister Knight talked about orchards and wandering sheep. Is it any wonder the crowd found it childish and the men found her a pawn?"

Inez felt her face go red with shame as Will and Elder Bailey rose and went to Elder Davis's side.

"You are out of line, Forester!" Will growled.

"Am I? Look at the contention they're causing now."

"They're not causing contention—you are, because you're a witless oaf," Elder Bailey answered, the red rising up his neck.

"Well, of course you'd be her champion," Elder Forester snapped.

Elder Bailey stepped forward. "What do you mean by that?"

"Isn't it obvious? I see the way you look at her."

Elder Abernathy came into the room at that moment, carrying plates for supper. "Blimey! What is going on here? We could hear the brawl from the kitchen." He set down the plates and went to his companion. "Elder Forester?"

Inez leaned over and whispered to Jennie. "I'm going."

"Inez, wait." Jennie took hold of her wrist, but Inez pulled away.

"No, I'm going, and don't come with me." She slid from her chair and moved furtively toward the kitchen and the back exit. She prayed that the others were so focused on the argument, they would not notice her departure. She could feel the heat of embarrassment on her face, and she knew tears would soon follow. She focused her thoughts on something tangible to stop the emotion. *Find an envelope, Inez—find it quickly and send your letter.*

Chapter Thirty

A FEW WORDS ON MISSIONARY MANAGEMENT

There will be times when melancholia will come and sit in your apartment. It will follow you down the street. It will entice you not to pray or read the scriptures. It will happen—either the rain will not stop or people will yell at you during a street meeting or an elder will tell you that missionary work is too difficult for the sisters of the Church.

It is difficult, and gray clouds of doubt may gather. But if our foremothers could stand up to ridicule and hate, if they could remain valiant as mobs burned their homes and killed their husbands, if they could leave everything and walk across a country for the restored gospel, then we can serve missions and preach that gospel to the world.

My companion has the gray clouds about her now, and I will do whatever I can to cheer her. She did the same for me a few weeks ago when I was ill. I know this is the reason the Lord calls us to go two by two—so we can watch out for each other.

I will go to the conference house kitchen and ask Mrs. Wilkey to help me make my companion a chocolate cream. That should cheer her. I will include the recipe from Mrs. Beeton's book in case you have someone to cheer.

Remember John 16:33.

Sister Jennie Brimhall—Cheltenham Conference

CHOCOLATE CREAM

INGREDIENTS— 3 oz. of grated chocolate, ¼ lb. of sugar, 1 pint and ½ pint of cream, ½ oz. of clarified isinglass, the yolks of 6 eggs.

MODE— Beat the yolks of the eggs well; put them into a basin with the grated chocolate, the sugar, and 1 pint of cream; stir these ingredients well together, pour them into a jug, and set this jug in a saucepan of boiling water; stir it one way until the mixture thickens, but do not allow it to boil, or it will curdle. Strain the cream through a sieve into a basin; stir in the isinglass and the other ½ pint of cream, which should be well whipped; mix all well together, and pour it into a mould which has been previously oiled with the purest salad-oil, and, if at hand, set it in ice until wanted for table.

TIME— About 10 minutes to stir the mixture over the fire.

Sufficient to fill a quart mould. Seasonable at any time.

NOTE

Isinglass: A transparent or translucent form of gelatin, isinglass was used in jellies as a clarifying agent and in dessert recipes as a thickening agent.

Chapter Thirty-One

Sister Knight and Sister Brimhall sat on the stone bench at the southwest corner of the Imperial Park. They peered through the bushes and waited.

"Are you sure this is where we're supposed to be?" Jennie asked. "Read the note again."

Inez unfolded the paper and read. "Dear Miss Knight and Miss Brimhall, I would be most grateful if you would meet me at the southwest corner of Imperial Park at noon. If you have other commitments I will understand. I will wait fifteen minutes and then apply for another time. Mrs. Richard Checkly."

Jennie checked her pocket watch. "It's twelve twenty. Something must have happened to delay her."

"I say we continue to wait."

"I think so too," Jennie agreed, standing and stretching her back. "We haven't heard from her since the meeting, and I want to know how she's doing."

"Or if she's still interested in the Church after my disastrous talk . . . well, part of a talk."

"Inez! That riot was none of your doing. It would have happened if President Noall had been speaking. It's been two weeks, so stop dwelling on it!"

Inez scowled. "Someone is in a bad mood."

"No, I'm not!" Jennie snapped. "Sorry. Maybe I am. I'm worried about Mrs. Checkly."

"Worried?"

Jennie shrugged. "It's . . . I don't know. It's just a feeling." She shaded her eyes. "I'm going to stand in the shade. It's too hot today." She moved to stand under a large sycamore, taking a tract from her satchel and fanning her face.

An icy quiet settled between the friends.

See, Inez thought. *It will be good if I go home. Jennie will be better off with a more competent companion.* Instead of dwelling on their unavoidable parting, Inez concentrated on the charming flowers in the nearby flower bed, trying to name as many varieties as she could without mentally wandering off into her mother's garden at home. Horticulture was her mother's delight, and in the summer the plot of land surrounding their home in Provo was always brimming with nourishing vegetables and fragrant flowers. Though she tried to avoid being drawn away to her childhood home, Inez was soon lost in purple and white columbine, pink roses, and tiny blue forget-me-nots. She was grateful when Jennie's voice cut through her mental drifting.

"Inez! I think it's Mrs. Checkly."

"Where?"

Jennie pointed. "There. She's walking at the edge of the park."

Inez went to stand beside her companion. "Hmm. That's funny. Why doesn't she just cut across?"

"I don't know."

"And why is she wearing that big hat in this heat?"

Mrs. Checkly saw them in their partially hidden alcove and gave them a timid wave. She increased her pace until she was by their sides. "Miss Brimhall, Miss Knight. Please forgive my lateness. I . . . I had to go over the supper menu with our cook."

"We were not bothered in the least, Mrs. Checkly. We're just awfully glad to see you," Jennie said.

See her? Inez wondered. Mrs. Checkly's face was so hidden under her hat's heavy veil, she was hardly recognizable.

"And I am delighted that you could meet me," Mrs. Checkly said, looking about. "Shall we find a cab and go for a ride into the country?"

Both Inez and Jennie brightened at the prospect.

"That would be a delight!" Inez said in a rush.

"I love your enthusiasm, Miss Knight," Mrs. Checkly chuckled. "Your exuberance is refreshing. When you live with a barrister, everything tends to earnestness."

As they set off for the edge of the park to find a cab, Inez attempted to imagine Mrs. Checkly's life. She was obviously from an upper-class family and had married into a comfortable situation, though she was many years her husband's junior. She had a fine home, impeccable taste, beauty, and refinement. Besides all that, she had a library filled with books! Inez shook her head in puzzlement. Mrs. Checkly seemed to have everything one would need to be happy, yet there was a sadness about her. Inez was so absorbed in trying to figure out Mrs. Checkly's life, she was oblivious to the low-hanging branch she was approaching until it hit the top of her head, throwing her back and knocking off her boater hat.

"Ow!"

Jennie turned. "What happened?"

"Nothing," Inez said, rubbing her forehead. "Nothing. . . . I just . . . "

"Did you bump into that branch?" Jennie asked, picking up Inez's hat.

"Just slightly," Inez mumbled.

"Are you all right, Miss Knight?" Mrs. Checkly asked as she approached.

"I'm fine," Inez said, smiling and putting on her hat. "Don't worry, I'm used to it."

"It happens all the time," Jennie confirmed, and Inez nodded in agreement.

Mrs. Checkly smiled. "Oh, I needed you girls' companionship today. Thank you for taking the time."

"Our pleasure," Jennie said.

"And I'm ready for our adventure!" Inez said, tapping the top of her boater hat to make sure it was secure.

"Then let's on with it!" Mrs. Checkly said, resuming their trek to find a cab. "And please . . . mind your head, Miss Knight."

Inez laughed, and she and Jennie followed along. As they reached the edge of the park, Mrs. Checkly hailed the driver of a handsome cab who hopped down from his seat and gave her a tip of his hat.

"Yes, ma'am. How may I serve?"

"I'd like you to take us through Pittville Park and then out to Sudeley Castle."

A look of delight registered on the driver's round face. "Out to the castle?"

"Yes. Is it possible?"

"Oh yes! Yes, of course. Of course, it is most assuredly possible!" the man stammered, hurrying to open the cab's door.

Inez hid a smile behind her hand. She liked the cab man's delight in serving, though she figured the eagerness was prompted by the sizable fare he would receive.

"And I suppose you'll wish me to stay while you tour?" the man continued.

"Yes, if you would be so kind," Mrs. Checkly answered.

"Certainly. Of course. Lovely." The cab man smiled broadly as he took Mrs. Checkly's hand and helped her into the carriage. He then helped Jennie and Inez.

As Inez stepped in and seated herself next to Jennie, she had the fleeting feeling of being the daughter of a lord or duke, or the best friend to one of Queen Victoria's granddaughters. *How would it be to live in a castle? An actual castle,* Inez fantasized. She looked down at her plain skirt and scuffed shoes and chuckled. *More likely I'd be the scullery maid.*

The inside of the cab was stuffy, and Mrs. Checkly opened the windows and removed her hat. When she turned back to the girls, they both noticed a purple and yellow bruise marring Mrs. Checkly's cheek near the jawline.

"Oh, Mrs. Checkly! What happened?" Inez blurted out.

Mrs. Checkly's hand went to cover her cheek. "I'm afraid I followed in your footsteps, Miss Knight."

"I beg your pardon?"

"A week or so ago, I tripped on the hallway runner and hit my face on a side table prior to landing on the floor."

"Oh dear!" Jennie gasped.

"Not to fret, my dear. It's healing nicely. Nothing broken."

"Just the same," Inez interjected. "It looks like it was painful."

Mrs. Checkly turned her cheek away from scrutiny and gazed out the window at the passing scenery. "Yes." After a moment of enigmatic silence, she turned back and smiled. "So would you like me to tell you something of English history as we travel?"

"Oh yes!" the girls chorused.

For the next hour, under the tutelage of Mrs. Checkly, the unsophisticated Utah girls lived in the court of Henry the Eighth and his final bride, Catherine Parr. They heard of intrigues, lost loves, and tragic deaths. Mrs. Checkly was a bewitching storyteller, and by the time the carriage reached Sudeley Castle and the girls disembarked, the pale stone walls of the ancient edifice were imbued with life, color, and passion.

The girls stood, staring.

"Are you back in time, ladies?" Mrs. Checkly asked, coming quietly beside them. Having abandoned her heavy hat to the carriage, she opened a lacy white parasol for shade.

"It is like stepping into history," Jennie said.

Inez nodded and found her voice. "And Catherine Parr is actually buried here?"

"She is," Mrs. Checkly said with a smile. "Saint Mary's Chapel."

"And we can visit the place?"

"We can, Miss Knight. It is one of the highlights; therefore I suggest we save it for last."

Inez nodded again.

"Shall we stroll?"

"Yes," Inez said, eagerly stepping forward.

"Oh yes," Jennie said on a sigh. "I've made myself a promise to take strolling home with me to Provo."

"Except the paths there will be dry and dusty," Inez said, looking around at the verdant landscape. "Maybe we could sneak some of this greenery home as well."

"Wouldn't that be lovely," Jennie answered wistfully.

A stooped-shouldered man approached from a nearby garden. He carried a shovel and the look of someone who had spent his life in earnest labor. Inez glanced nervously at Mrs. Checkly, suddenly feeling like a trespasser. The man gave the three women a careful look, then stopped. "Mrs. Checkly?"

"Hello, William! It is good to see you!"

"Well, I'll be! Look a ye. I ain't seen ye fer many a year."

"Several years."

"The last time ye was with that serious gentleman."

Mrs. Checkly nodded. "My husband."

"Not a very friendly sort."

"As you said . . . serious. So, William, these are my friends, Miss Brimhall and Miss Knight. They've come with me to tour."

He gave them a tip of his cap. "Pleased." He turned his attention immediately back to Mrs. Checkly. "The primrose still be bloomin' by the chapel, and I just put in some jack-in-the-pulpit. 'Tis a sight."

"We will look for the glory of your work, William."

William touched the brim of his cap. "Kind of ye."

"How is Mrs. Dent doing?"

"Aer . . . not good, not good," William growled, wagging his head and tapping the shovel tip against the ground. "Winter were hard on her. She be off now to the doctor. Nephew Harry done take her."

"Oh, I'm sorry."

"It be just a check. She's a tough one. Tough as leather . . . "

"And sweet as honeysuckle," Mrs. Checkly finished.

William gave her a teary smile. "Yep. That be her."

Mrs. Checkly stepped forward and laid her hand on William's. "Please tell her I stopped in and was sorry to have missed her. And that I'll be by to visit."

William gave her a measured look. "Soon."

Mrs. Checkly nodded. "Soon."

"She'll be right pleased to hear it." William cleared his throat. "Well, I best be back to work, or Master Harry will send me packin'."

"Never in a million years," Mrs. Checkly stated.

William gave her a wink and started off. "Don't miss the primrose. Pick a posy if ye 'ave a mind."

"Thank you, William!" Mrs. Checkly called. She turned to the girls and found them staring.

"Why . . . how . . . " Inez stammered.

"Mrs. Checkly, how do you know this place . . . well, the mistress of this place?" Jennie asked.

"Shall we walk and talk?" Mrs. Checkly asked, starting off for the back garden; the girls caught up quickly, anxious to hear the story. "I grew up in the near village of Winchcombe. Our family has lived in this area for ten generations."

"Ten generations!" Inez exclaimed. "I can barely get a line to five generations."

"America is a young country, Miss Knight."

"You were saying, Mrs. Checkly?" Jennie intervened. "About your relationship with Mrs. Dent."

"Ah, yes. Well, Mrs. Emma Brocklehurst Dent and my grandmother were friends."

"Friends?"

"Yes. As a young girl I came here often with my grandmother."

"Is your family wealthy, Mrs. Checkly?" Inez asked.

"Inez, that's not something . . . "

"It's all right, Miss Brimhall. I am not bothered talking with you two about personal subjects." She turned to Inez. "Actually, Miss Knight, I come from a long line of merchants—glove makers to be more precise. They were in business with John and William Dent, who purchased Sudeley Castle some seventy years ago."

"Can you actually buy a castle?"

"Well, you can if it's been in ruin for two hundred years. They rescued it and began rebuilding." At that moment, the threesome came around the corner of the main edifice onto a courtyard and a picturesque vison of ruined castle wall. A blanket of green ivy covered one side of the fragile two-story wall, while arches and tall windows in lacy filigree looked down on a tangle of grass and wildflowers at its base. The pale-gold Cotswold stone glowed in the afternoon sun.

"Enchanting," Jennie whispered. "I wish my father could see this."

"Oh my," Inez said slowly. "It must have been brilliant to visit here."

"Magical when I was out of doors; inside there were too many rules."

"Really?"

"Oh yes. Historic English properties must be strictly governed by proper English rules, and I have always found rules . . . oppressive." She reangled her parasol to block the sun. "You see, wealth and position do not always bring freedom."

"I would rather sit on a pumpkin and have it all to myself than be crowded on a velvet cushion," Jennie quoted.

Mrs. Checkly smiled at her. "True words. Who is the source?"

"Henry David Thoreau."

"Of course. I have read his book, *Walden*."

"We're reading it now!" Jennie said with delight. "The freedom to make your way in the world."

"I am afraid I will never know that kind of freedom. It would be marvelous to sit alone by a pond and ponder what one is having for dinner." She began walking behind the ruined wall, toward a large manicured garden. "Such an appropriate place to talk about things that last and things that do not."

Jennie studied her. "Are you troubled, Mrs. Checkly?"

"I am, Miss Brimhall. I am troubled by many things," Mrs. Checkly answered, attempting to put lightness into her tone. She smiled at them. "But at the moment, I am troubled by the antics of Laman and Lemuel."

There was stunned silence as Inez and Jennie stopped short and stared in disbelief. Inez was the first to find her voice.

"You're reading the book?"

Mrs. Checkly turned and gave them a puzzled look. "You instructed me to read it, did you not?"

Inez hurried to her side. "We . . . well, we hoped you would. But, then again, we never know. Have you found it interesting? How far have you read? What did you think of Lehi sending the boys back to retrieve the brass plates?"

Jennie came laughing to join them. "Inez, I think you should take a breath and give her a chance to respond."

"Of course. Sorry. I'm just excited she's read it."

"We can tell."

Mrs. Checkly walked into the garden, the girls beside her on the broad path. "As you know, I have read many books—hundreds—but I find this book unique. A people from Jerusalem coming to the Americas? Communications with God?" She stopped to pluck a rose and place it in her waistband before moving on. "It reads like scripture."

"It is scripture," Jennie confirmed.

"Translated by a prophet?"

"Yes. Joseph Smith."

"Well, I find it fascinating, and I have a hundred questions."

Inez beamed over at Jennie. "I told you she'd have a hundred questions!"

For the next hour the women strolled and talked. Inez offered a tidbit here and there and snatches of testimony, but an underlying sense of incompetence kept her from expressing the doctrine she knew and loved so well. When they reached the small stone chapel at the edge of a garden, the topic of discussion happened to be the doctrine of eternal life.

"So I wonder which of King Henry's six wives will want him for eternity?" Mrs. Checkly commented, a slight edge of mockery in her voice. "Will they be able to choose their eternal fate?"

"God knows the beginning from the end," Jennie offered. "I'm sure He will be able to work everything out for the best."

Mrs. Checkly's eyes widened. "Will He? That might be comforting and terrifying all together." She folded her parasol and motioned towards the entrance to the chapel. "Shall we?"

"Are you sure we're not trespassing?" Inez questioned, holding back.

"Absolutely sure, Miss Knight. As a child I played in this chapel." Mrs. Checkly pushed back the heavy wooden door and stepped in. Jennie followed immediately, but Inez hesitated. She had never been inside an ancient church, especially one where people were buried in its shadowed interior. She only knew outside burials with grass and stone monuments.

Jennie poked her head out the door. "Inez, come on!"

Inez stepped in and gasped. Row upon row of arched stained-glass windows lined the walls and set the chapel ablaze with light. The pale-gold stone glowed with a radiance that even the dark wooden pews could not diminish.

"This is beautiful," Inez whispered.

"I have always found it enchanting," Mrs. Checkly said. "This way to

Queen Catherine's tomb." The threesome moved to the front of the chapel, and when Mrs. Checkly motioned to the left, Inez found yet another reason to gasp.

In an adorned niche sat the polished stone sarcophagus of Catherine Parr. Her white marble effigy showed her in death's sleep, with hands upright over her heart, palms pressed together forever in prayer.

"I've never seen anything so beautiful in all my life," Inez said, her voice filled with awe and tears. She moved slowly to stand beside the monument. "Look at her gown. How did the sculptor capture the softness of the fabric and the ruffles of the cuffs . . . and . . . " Inez brushed tears away and stopped talking.

Jennie came to stand beside her companion, looking over at Mrs. Checkly. "You said she died young."

Mrs. Checkly nodded and laid her hand gently on the queen's embossed stone pillow. "Thirty-six. My age." She paused. "I have an affinity for Lady Catherine."

"Why is that?" Jennie asked gently.

It took a long time for Mrs. Checkly to answer. "We both had daughters named Mary, and we both lost them—Catherine, because she died; I, because my tiny girl . . . left *me* . . . much much too soon."

Jennie laid her hand over Mrs. Checkly's. "I'm sorry. I am so sorry."

Mrs. Checkly stood straighter. "It has been ten years. My heart should have mended."

"I don't believe those kinds of aches will ever mend," Jennie whispered.

"What are we to do then? Spend our whole lives weeping?"

"I believe we can find solace in the doctrine of eternal life."

"The notion of eternal life has never appealed to me, Miss Brimhall. The wicked forever burning in a lake of fire, the righteous floating about on clouds, babies trapped in a netherworld?" She shook her head. "No. Not my idea of happiness."

"Mine either," Inez stated flatly.

"And has your church a different doctrine, Miss Knight?"

"Very different."

Mrs. Checkly stared at Inez's guileless face for a moment, then gave the two missionaries a tenuous smiled. "Well then, I suppose, no matter the consequence, I must continue learning about this odd church with new scripture and unconventional ideas about heaven."

Jennie beamed. "Oh, Mrs. Checkly, we would like that very much."

On the trip back to Cheltenham, Mrs. Checkly devised a plan where they would meet once a week at a place of her choosing. The three women then chatted for a time on various subjects: life in Utah, prophets, fashion, and words of instruction from Mrs. Beeton's book. After a time, the conversation lulled as the warm late-afternoon sun and rhythmic motion of the carriage sent them into their own meandering thoughts. As Mrs. Checkly dozed, Inez and Jennie looked out at the passing scenery. Inez closed her eyes against the never-ending green, and images floated into her imaginings: a ruined castle wall, a Tudor knot garden, a woman of white stone, a posy of primrose in the band of her boater hat, the yellowing bruise on Mrs. Checkly's face, and the letter to her mother hidden in the desk drawer. These last images came uninvited and seemed a mockery of the rest. Inez forced her mind back to the knot garden and slept until they reached Cheltenham.

Chapter Thirty-Two

To the Brimhall Household

Dear Father, Flora, and family,

Today Inez and I embarked on a visit to Sudeley Castle with Mrs. Checkly. It was a royal estate visited by Henry the Eighth. We also visited a church on the castle grounds where the body of his sixth wife, Catherine Parr, is buried. Oh, Father, I would love to teach history over to my students at the academy. I believe I could now make the world come alive for them.

We are teaching Mrs. Checkly the principles of the gospel, and she seems well pleased with the doctrine. She is an exceedingly high-bred lady, and though she is genial and only fourteen years our senior, Inez and I feel like three-legged dogs in her presence. Her husband, Mr. Richard Checkly, is a barrister and rather stern. Mrs. Checkly has made plans to see us again, but it seems she wants to keep our meetings secret. This troubles me. I wish I could have your counsel on this, Father. I will continue to pray about it.

August has been hot and humid. Inez and I go to the baths nearly every day. We try to go tracting in the mornings or early evening between tea and supper. Are you laughing about teatime and how very English I'm becoming? I may come home with an accent. (Do not be concerned as we never drink the English tea.)

The Knight brothers are doing well. I am very proud of Will and his hard work. I try not to think of him going home in three or four months.

I am in good health—no colds or sore throats for a time, although I have a tooth which troubles me. I promise to have it looked at. How is the family faring? Is everyone well? How are you doing, dear Father? You are in my prayers every day.

I am enclosing a recipe from Mrs. Somers. Remember, she is Mrs. Boyers's cook from the time Inez and I were in Bristol. How I miss her ginger biscuits, and how I miss your apple pie, Flora. Food is such a connection to a place and people. I hope these recipes I'm sending from England tie you to me and this place. This pudding was a special treat Mrs. Somers would make for us when she felt we needed cheering. She made it many times.

Love to everyone. Today Inez and I are staying in the apartment, resting, catching up on our mending, reading, folding tracts, and washing our hair. Tonight we will practice with the missionary choir. Oh, don't we lead a jolly life? The gospel is true!

Your devoted daughter,

Jennie

PERSIMMON PUDDING

INGREDIENTS— 1 cup of ripe persimmon pulp (3–4 ripe persimmons), 1 cup of sugar, 1 beaten egg; 1 cup of flour, ¼ teaspoonful of cinnamon, ¼ teaspoonful of salt; (1½ teaspoonfuls of baking soda dissolved in 1 cup of sweet milk); ½ cup of coarsely chopped walnuts.

MODE— Mix in order. Add chopped nuts in with flour mixture, add to persimmon mix, and add milk. Bake in steam oven 1 hour or slightly longer. Test.

Serve with Queen Victoria's Vanilla Custard.

QUEEN VICTORIA'S VANILLA CUSTARD

INGREDIENTS— 1 cup of sugar, ¼ cup of corn starch, 1½ cups of cold water, 3 egg yolks, 1 tablespoonful of butter, 2 teaspoonfuls of vanilla.

MODE— Mix well sugar, corn starch and water; add egg yolks and butter. Stir mixture constantly over medium heat till thickened. Remove from heat, and stir in vanilla.

CHAPTER THIRTY-THREE

The street meeting was over, and Inez breathed a sigh of relief. She had been the only female missionary in attendance since Jennie had been counseled to stay in the apartment because of an oncoming sore throat.

The beginning of September had been marked by cooler temperatures and a scattering of rain, and a few days before the street meeting, a sudden shower had caught the sister missionaries blocks from their apartment without their umbrellas. Inez's constitution could tolerate a soaking, but Jennie's health was fragile. She awoke the morning of the street meeting with chills and a prickly throat. She kept insisting that she could dress warmly and be by her companion's side. It took gentle pleading from Will before she reluctantly changed her mind.

On one hand Inez was glad her friend was caring for herself at home, yet if she were honest, Inez longed for Jennie's wise testimony and calm demeanor. It had been a frustrating meeting. The missionaries had sung a song, and a small crowd gathered. Elder Forester then spoke, but Inez could tell the people were not impressed with his preaching. Will had the missionaries sing again, after which he announced that a Mormon woman would be the next speaker. More people gathered, and Inez pled with the Lord to keep her standing and to fill her mind with words of truth. She preached about the Restoration of the Lord's Church and how the gospel influenced the lives of men and women for good. It seemed to go well, except a woman had kept interrupting with questions and two young women in ragged, revealing dresses had stood at the edge of the crowd, distracting many of the listeners.

Now the meeting was over, and Inez watched as the crowd dispersed. She wondered if her words had touched any heart. She sighed and readjusted her satchel.

"Excuse me, young woman."

Inez turned to find a middle-aged woman staring intently at her. The woman's nearness made Inez step back. "Yes, ma'am?"

"Many of the things you said were true, but this angel business is a pack of rot, and Brigham Young is a vagabond." She gave Inez a toothy smile and patted her arm. "God bless you on your mission." She turned and walked away.

Inez did not have the time or ability to utter a word in reply. She stood staring after the woman with wide eyes and open mouth.

"You'll catch flies if you stand around like that," her brother Will said as he came to her side.

Inez gave her head a little shake and turned to look at him. "Well, I never."

"You never what?"

"I never imagined a mission would offer such peculiar experiences."

"You will have many stories to tell when you get home," Will affirmed. He called to his fellow missionaries. "Come on, elders! Let's catch the trolley back. If we hurry, we'll make it before supper is on the table." He gave Inez a wink. "Can you keep up, Sister Knight?"

"Try me," she said, moving past him in a rush.

As they hurried along, Inez concentrated on not falling. It was difficult as her mind was jumping from subject to subject: her lack of preaching ability, Jennie's illness, the letter in the desk drawer. She began sliding into melancholy, and she scolded herself. *Buck up, Inez. So what if it's September 8th and your birthday? Your birthday that no one remembered—not Will or Ray or even Jennie? No letter from home. Oh, stop! You are twenty-three, not ten. You are on a mission for the Lord, which is much more important than gifts and well-wishes.*

"Penny for your thoughts," Will said as they reached the trolley stop and climbed on board.

"September 8th," Inez said, just as the bell on the trolly clanged.

"What's that?" Will asked. "I didn't hear."

Inez scowled at him. "Never mind. Nothing important." She laid her head against the window and fought back tears. *If I were home, I would be having corn on the cob, roasted chicken, and celebration cake.* Inez was practiced at pushing homesickness aside, but on this occasion, it clung like rust on an old bucket.

"Surprise!"

Inez stood in the conference hall, staring at the paper birthday decorations, Jennie holding Mrs. Beeton's lemon cake, and Mrs. Wilkey placing a roasted chicken on the table. The elders stood around laughing and clapping as Inez tried to regain her composure.

"But, how . . . when?" She gave Jennie a puzzled look. "You should be in bed. You're sick."

Jennie set the cake on the table and came to hug her friend. "I'm not sick," she laughed. "It was all a ruse." She stepped back.

"A ruse?" Inez looked at Will. "So you were in on this?"

"Of course," Will said, with a foxlike grin. "Jennie planned the whole thing, and I helped her carry it out."

"How else was I going to get everything prepared? I couldn't very well go traipsing off with you and bake your cake at the same time."

Inez took her hands. "Oh, dear Jennie, thank you! This has lifted my spirits."

"Did you think we'd forget your special day?" Jennie said, pointing to the end of the table. "Just look there; you have presents and everything."

Mrs. Wilkey arrived from the kitchen with two more roasted chickens. "Happy birthday, Sister Knight."

"Thank you, Mrs. Wilkey. And thank you for my favorite foods."

"Well, the cook is to thank for that, and your brothers, who gave her the marching orders."

Inez smiled over at Will and Ray.

President Noall entered the hall, and everyone quieted. "Please, do not let me dampen the festive mood. I came to join you if it's not an intrusion. I have been smelling those birds roasting all evening."

"We would love you to join us!" Inez said.

"Thank you, Sister Knight. Happy birthday!"

"Now, everyone, sit and eat before it gets cold," Mrs. Wilkey ordered.

After the meal and the cake, President Noall returned to work in his office, and Inez was presented with gifts: Jennie gave her a pudding pan; Will and Ray, a book, *Prince of the House of David*; Elder Davis, a basket of plums; Elder Abernathy, a book of Shakespearean sonnets; and Elder Forester, a small card that read, "Happy Birthday." Inez figured Elder Abernathy had to twist his companion's arm to get that small token out of him.

As the elders dispersed and Jennie went to the kitchen with the last of the dishes, Elder Bailey approached Inez with something hidden behind his back. Inez stopped gathering her gifts and turned to him with a half grin.

"I don't know whether to be angry with you or grateful," Inez snapped.

"Angry . . . at me?" Elder Bailey chocked.

"Yes indeed, Elder Bailey. Keeping that secret meant I went all day feeling forlorn and forsaken."

"I'm sorry, Inez, but I was threatened with my life."

Inez gave him a full smile. "I'm aware how persuasive my brothers can be. It was a lovely surprise. Thank you for keeping the secret."

Elder Bailey nodded and shifted his weight. "You're welcome."

"What's that behind your back, Elder Bailey?"

"Hopefully it's something you'll like."

"Well, I won't know until you give it to me."

"Oh, true!" He brought the gift around and held it out.

"Hmm . . . " Inez said, taking it from him. "A mysterious little wooden box tied with a ribbon." She untied the bow and read the label on the lid. "Seeds of the English Spring." She looked up. "Are these flower seeds?"

"They are. I thought you might like to plant them in Provo. Then you can always remember this place."

Inez's voice came out in a whisper. "Oh, Harrison, this is such a thoughtful gift." She took one of his hands. "Thank you."

"You are welcome. There's something more to . . . "

Jennie walked into the room at that moment, and Elder Bailey snatched his hand away. She came to them stretching her back and yawning. "Are you ready to end this day? I'm exhausted." She came near and gave Elder Bailey a focused look. "Are you all right, Elder Bailey?"

"I . . . yes, I'm fine. Why do you ask?"

"Your face is rather flushed."

"Is it, really? Well, I find it a bit hot. Don't you think it's hot in this room? Stuffy?"

"Not really," Jennie answered.

"Oh . . . well then . . . I'd better be off for study time. Elder Knight has us studying the book of Revelation after supper."

"Sounds like something my brother would do. I'm afraid I'd be asleep after three minutes."

"It takes me only two," Elder Bailey confessed. He took a couple of steps back. "Happy birthday, Sister Knight. I hope your party was a good surprise."

As soon as he'd left the room, Inez held out the box to Jennie. "Look what he gave me. These are seeds for an English flower garden."

"What a tender gift," Jennie said. "I can see them sprinkled in your flower beds. What do they look like? Open it. Maybe there's a guide inside to tell you the varieties."

Inez carefully pried off the wooden lid, and the two peered inside. Tiny seeds of various sizes, colors, and shapes greeted their eyes.

"What's that?" Jennie asked, pointing at a glint of gold.

"No idea," Inez said as she carefully caught the edge of a gold chain and unearthed it from the seeds. On the end of the chain was a finely worked oval locket. "Oh dear," Inez said as she rested the locket in her hand. She turned it over.

"Is it engraved?" Jennie asked.

"It is," Inez said. She swallowed and read. "Brother Bailey to Inez."

Jennie worked at keeping her face composed. "Oh, Inez. I think Elder Bailey wants you to remember more than English flowers."

NOTES

The street meeting: The street meeting in this chapter is mentioned in Inez's journal. She talks of a woman with many questions, slovenly clad "tarts" (ladies of the evening) causing distraction, and being addressed after the meeting by a woman who spoke of Brigham Young as a vagabond and of "the angel business" as "a pack of rot."

Inez's birthday celebration: Inez recorded this event in her journal. She noted gifts she received, which included the gold locket hidden in the box of seeds from Elder Bailey.

Chapter Thirty-Four

Inez stood in the conference hall, staring at the black-draped podium. Three days before, the hall had been filled with birthday festivities, but it now felt cheerless and cold. Her gaze slid over to the two elders arranging chairs for the Sunday service. Elder Davis worked methodically, while Elder Abernathy often stopped to wipe tears from his face. *Dear Elder Wilford Abernathy*. Whenever he was asked about his and President Woodruff's shared given name, he always responded with affection and deference. The Apostle had come to Herefordshire in 1839 and converted Elder Abernathy's grandparents James and MaryAnn. As such, the family Abernathy's love for Wilford Woodruff ran deep.

Jennie came to Inez's side with a large vase of flowers. "Mrs. Wilkey just finished arranging these. Where do you want them?"

Inez assessed the black-draped table, on which sat a picture of President Woodruff, a Book of Mormon, a picture of the Salt Lake Temple, and a folded American flag. She rearranged her work to allow space for the flowers near President Woodruff's picture.

"I think he would like these English flowers near."

Jennie sniffed as she tenderly touched the Book of Mormon and the flag. "All these things were precious to him. The dedication of the Salt Lake Temple and Utah becoming a state."

"Now don't make me cry again," Inez demanded. "I've just gotten ahold of myself."

The girls looked over at Elder Abernathy, who stood and mournfully continued his work.

"How's Elder Abernathy doing?" Jennie asked.

"He's been weeping all morning."

"Mrs. Wilkey too," Jennie stated. "And she has so much work with all the elders in the area being gathered for the memorial."

Inez took one final look at the table. "Well, I'm finished here, so we can go and help her."

The sisters headed for the kitchen but were intercepted on the way by President Noall. "Sister Brimhall, Sister Knight, I have an assignment for each of you. I would like both of you to participate in the evening's memorial service." He handed each a paper. "I will be telling of President Woodruff's life, and I would like you, Sister Brimhall, to weave in the story of his miraculous conversion. And when I get to the part of his final meeting with the Prophet Joseph Smith, if you would be so kind as to read your contribution, Sister Knight?"

"We would be honored," Jennie added.

"Thank you for your willingness," President Noall said as he scanned the room and trailed off to talk to the elders without waiting for their response.

"He seems distracted," Inez observed.

"I would imagine," Jennie said. "He's grieving and yet he must carry on with the work of the mission." She took a quick breath and squared her shoulders. "Should we go to the apartment and study our parts?"

"That is a good idea. I want to merit the president's trust."

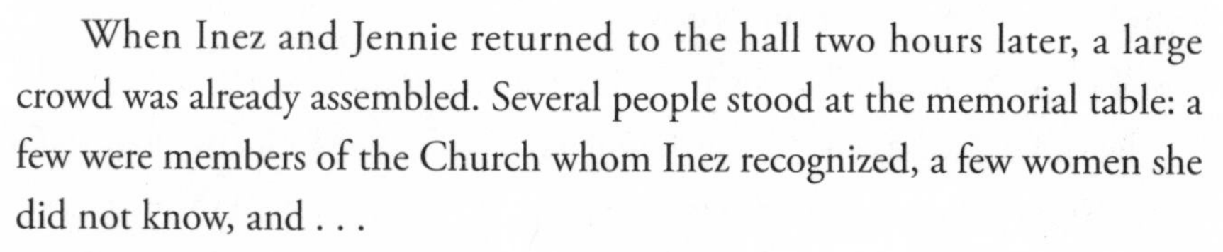

When Inez and Jennie returned to the hall two hours later, a large crowd was already assembled. Several people stood at the memorial table: a few were members of the Church whom Inez recognized, a few women she did not know, and . . .

"Mrs. Checkly?"

Jennie turned. "What?"

"Mrs. Checkly is there by the table."

"Where?" Jennie asked squinting.

"She's hard to recognize. She looks like a schoolmarm."

At that moment Mrs. Checkly saw the girls and came quickly to them, taking each by a hand. "Oh, dear Miss Brimhall and Miss Knight, I am sorry for the loss of your prophet."

"Thank you, Mrs. Checkly," Inez returned.

"What a dreadful shock, and you two so far from home." She glanced around at the gathering crowd. "So I imagine they will be searching for your next prophet?"

Jennie gave her a tender smile. "There's no searching, Mrs. Checkly. We already know who the next prophet will be."

"You do?"

"Yes, ma'am. His name is Lorenzo Snow."

"How was that decided so quickly?"

"Whoever is the senior member of the Quorum of the Twelve Apostles becomes the next prophet."

Mrs. Checkly stood, staring at Jennie's guileless face. "I am surprised at every turn, Sister Brimhall."

"How did you know about the service?" Inez asked.

"My friend Mrs. Fletcher is newly investigating your church, and she shared the news at tea yesterday."

"Mrs. Fletcher?" Jennie questioned.

"Yes, Mrs. Eleanor Fletcher. She is just there by the table."

"Do you know she is being taught by Elder Knight and Elder Bailey?" Jennie asked with a smile.

"Really?"

"Yes. Will . . . Elder Knight, told me about Mrs. Fletcher just last week."

"Well, isn't that a coincidence?" Mrs. Checkly said, glancing over at her friend.

Jennie and Inez shared a knowing look.

Mrs. Checkly turned her attention to the sisters. "I hope you don't mind me attending the service."

"Of course not," Inez answered.

"When Eleanor said she was attending and invited me, I thought it would be a grand chance to see you."

"We are so pleased," Jennie said, beaming at her.

Mrs. Fletcher approached. She also looked the part of a schoolmarm, and Inez wondered if the long black skirts and simple black tailored jackets were mourning wear or disguises for the elegant women.

"Eleanor, these are my friends, Sister Brimhall and Sister Knight."

Mrs. Fletcher's gaze went directly to Inez. "Sister Knight? Does Elder Knight happen to be . . . "

"My brother," Inez said with a grin. "Yes."

"Well, it is very nice to meet you. My word, two siblings out being missionaries at the same time."

"Three," Inez corrected.

"Three?"

"Yes. My brother Ray is also in England."

"Well, I am astonished. Your family must be well rooted in your church, Miss Knight."

"Yes, ma'am. Both Sister Brimhall and I have solid pioneer heritage."

Mrs. Fletcher smiled at Jennie. "A pleasure to meet you, Miss Brimhall."

"Likewise, Mrs. Fletcher," Jennie acknowledged with a slight curtsy.

"We probably should find you seats," Jennie announced after perusing the gathering crowd.

"Will you not be joining us?" Mrs. Checky asked.

"We have to sit up front with the other speakers," Inez explained. "But we'll come find you when the service is over."

President Noall stood at the podium as Inez and Jennie slipped into their seats next to Will. He announced the program and began telling of President Wilford Woodruff's history. When he came to Brother Woodruff's introduction to the Church, President Noall invited Sister Brimhall to the stand.

Inez watched as Jennie composed herself, laid the paper on the podium, and looked directly into the faces of the congregants.

"We are a people who believe in miracles. Members of The Church of Jesus Christ of Latter-day Saints believe in promptings, inspiration, divine interventions, and ongoing revelation. I will now read for you, from

President Woodruff's journal, the account of his conversion miracle. I quote:

"For the first time in my life, I saw an elder in The Church of Jesus Christ of Latter-day Saints. That was Zera Pulsipher. He told me that he was inspired of the Lord. He was threshing grain in his barn when the voice of the Lord came to him and told him to arise and go to the north. The Lord had business for him there. He called upon Brother Elijah Cheney, his neighbor, and a member of the Church. They traveled sixty miles on foot . . . in deep snow, and the first place they felt impressed to call upon was the house of my brother and myself."

Inez looked out over the congregation and saw many faces imprinted with astonishment. They anxiously waited for Jennie's next words.

"They went into the house and talked with my brother's wife, and they told her who they were and what their business was. They told her that they were moved upon to go to the north, and they'd never felt impressed to stop anywhere until they came to that house. When they told her their principles, she said her husband and her brother-in-law both were men who believed those principles, and they had prayed for them for years. They appointed a meeting in the schoolhouse upon our farm."

Inez looked at Will, whose rapt attention spoke to not only the verity of the subject matter but also an adoration for the speaker.

"I came home in the evening, and my sister-in-law told me of this meeting. I had been drawing logs from the shores of Lake Ontario (I was in the lumber business), and I turned out my horses, did not stop to eat anything, and went to the meeting. I found the house and the dooryard filled with people. I listened for the first time in my life to a gospel sermon as taught by the elders of this Church. It was what I had sought for from my boyhood up. I invited the men home with me. I borrowed the Book of Mormon and sat up all that night and read. In the morning I told Brother Pulsipher I wanted to be baptized. I had a testimony for myself that those principles were true. Myself and my brother . . . went forth and were baptized—the two first in that county."

Jennie folded the paper and took a deep breath. "I testify that the same gospel truths that converted Wilford Woodruff are here in the hearts and mouths of every missionary you see in this meeting today. Like Zera

Pulsipher and Elijah Cheney, we have followed the voice of the Lord and have symbolically trudged our way through deep snow to be here in England for you. I so testify in the name of Jesus Christ. Amen."

When Jennie sat down, her body was trembling, and Will modestly reached over and laid his hand on hers. Inez reached for her handkerchief. For several minutes she was so busy trying to calm her emotions that she nearly missed President Noall calling her to the pulpit.

Do not cry. Do not cry. Do not cry, she chided herself silently. *Please Lord, let me honor thy prophet. Give my body strength.* She laid the paper on the pulpit and gripped its edges. When she spoke, she was surprised to hear her words come out strong and clear.

"Early in 1844 the Prophet Joseph was sending out the Apostles on their missions. Elder Woodruff was being sent for a second time to England; this time as the European Mission president. This journal entry tells of the Prophet Joseph's last instructions to his friends and fellow servants of the Lord before they departed. These are words from Brother Woodruff as recorded in his journal. I quote:

"The Prophet Joseph, I am now satisfied, had a thorough presentiment that that was the last meeting we would hold together here in the flesh. We had had our endowments; we had had all the blessings sealed upon our heads that were ever given to the apostles or prophets on the face of the earth. On that occasion the Prophet Joseph rose up and said to us, 'Brethren, I have desired to live to see this temple built.'"

Inez's voice caught.

"'I . . . I shall never live to see it, but you will. I have sealed upon your heads all the keys of the kingdom of God. I have sealed upon you every key, power, principle that the God of heaven has revealed to me. Now no matter where I may go or what I may do, the kingdom rests upon you.'"

Inez gulped as a band of pain tightened around her chest. Tears poured from her eyes, and she stepped back. President Noall was by her side whispering to her.

"Courage, Sister Knight. Courage. All is well. The two faithful prophets are shaking hands in paradise." She nodded. "Can you go on?"

"Yes, President," she said with a slight nod. She took out her hankie, wiped her eyes, and blew her nose. She stepped forward. "I'm sorry," she said to the congregation. But on examination she noted that apologies were not necessary since most members of the congregation were weeping or wiping their eyes as well. "I will continue," Inez said. "I quote:

"Now don't you wonder why we, as Apostles, could not have understood that the Prophet of God was going to be taken away from us? But we did not understand it. The Apostles in the days of Jesus Christ could not understand what the Savior meant when He told them 'I am going away; if I do not go away the Comforter will not come.' Neither did we understand what Joseph meant. 'But,' he said, after having done this, 'ye Apostles of the Lamb of God, my brethren, upon your shoulders this kingdom rests; now you have got to round up your shoulders and bear off the kingdom.' And he also made this very strange remark. 'If you do not do it you will be damned.' I am the last man living who heard that declaration."

Inez looked up. "I know that all the apostles and prophets have kept the promise to bear off the kingdom. I know that President Wilford Woodruff kept this promise. I know that on June 27, 1844, the Prophet Joseph Smith and his brother Hyrum were cruelly murdered by a mob and that they sealed their testimonies of the work with their blood. I humbly bear my testimony of these things in the name of Jesus Christ. Amen."

Inez remained standing and joined the missionary choir to sing one of President Woodruff's favorite hymns, "O My Father." Inez had worked diligently to avoid tears, but when they sang the words, "When I leave this frail existence, when I lay this mortal by, Father, Mother, may I meet you in your royal courts on high," a rush of emotion nearly took her voice. She noticed the other missionaries were struggling as well. Poor Elder Abernathy. When he stood forward to address the congregation, as his fellows took their seats, his eyes were red from crying, and his voice was husky. Nevertheless, he stood tall and preached with certainty.

"My family has been associated with President Wilford Woodruff for fifty-eight years. In 1840 he knocked on the door of my grandfather's farmhouse outside Bishops Frome. Brother Woodruff was thirty-two years old and a newly ordained Apostle of the Church. He came preaching the gospel of Jesus Christ, and my grandfather James and grandmother MaryAnn listened. They listened, they studied, and they accepted. My father, John, was six months old at the time and had his name firmly attached, but my grandparents were so moved by the message and messenger of the restored gospel that they changed over his middle name to Wilford. And, when I came along thirty-five years later, I was honored with the great man's name as well.

"Some two thousand souls were converted in the regions of Herefordshire during the years Elder Woodruff walked these hills and valleys as a missionary. At one time there were thirty thousand members of the Church in this country. Though many of those converts immigrated to the Utah territory, the Abernathys stayed. And we are still here to witness of the truth of Joseph Smith's prophetic calling, the Book of Mormon, and the ongoing priesthood authority held by apostles and prophets. Elder Woodruff was a prophet of God. I so testify in the name of Jesus Christ. Amen."

On his way to the pulpit, Elder Knight shook Elder Abernathy's hand, and the two shared a smile. Inez thought that bearing his testimony must have been a tonic for the English missionary's sorrowing soul. She turned her attention to Will as he began reading. He had a captivating voice, and Inez knew that was the reason he'd been given the honor of speaking the words of President Woodruff's final conference address.

Words flowed of Elder Woodruff's early years in the Church and his defense of the Prophet Joseph Smith; of his admiration for Hyrum Smith's son Joseph F. Smith; and of Joseph's last speech to the quorum of the Apostles and his last charge to them to rise up and bear off the kingdom.

Will's voice took on strength, and Jennie reached over and took Inez's hand as he read out the words of President Woodruff:

"I am going to bear my testimony to this assembly, if I never do it again in my life, that those men who laid the foundation of this American government and signed the Declaration of Independence were the best spirits the God of heaven could find on the face of the earth. . . . Every one of those men that signed the Declaration of Independence, with General Washington, called upon me, as an Apostle of the Lord Jesus Christ, in the Temple at St. George, two consecutive nights, and demanded at my hands that I should go forth and attend to the ordinances of the House of God for them. . . . Would those spirits have called upon me, as an Elder in Israel, to perform that work if they had not been noble spirits before God? They would not. I bear this testimony, because it is true. The Spirit of God bore record to myself and the brethren while we were laboring in that way."

The congregation was collectively stunned by this pronouncement, and not a sound was heard as Will continued to share President Woodruff's admonitions to the Saints to consider their commitment to their covenants and loyalty to the oracles of God and gospel of Christ.

Will's voice colored with emotion as he read the Prophet's final warnings about the nearness of the last days and the Saints' duties. The talk ended with instruction on each person's responsibility to attend to temple work for their ancestors.

Jennie turned to stare at Inez. "That was powerful."

Inez nodded.

The closing prayer was said, and within moments Mrs. Checkly and Mrs. Fletcher were at their sides. Will and Elder Bailey joined too.

"So how does one apply for baptism, Elder Knight?" Mrs. Fletcher asked without fanfare.

Inez turned to see Will's reaction, which mimicked someone who had just suffered a blow to the chin.

"I . . . I. Are you serious, Mrs. Fletcher?"

She gave him a curious look. "I most certainly am, young man. When I make up my mind about something, it is made up. I just do not see any way around it."

"It would be better if you trust her word, Elder Knight," Mrs. Checkly said. "When Eleanor Fletcher makes up her mind about something, it is with reason."

"There are too many spiritual coincidences to unravel with logic," Mrs. Fletcher stated.

Elder Bailey shook her hand impulsively. "Welcome to the fold, Mrs. Fletcher!"

Inez chuckled as she watched her brother compose himself and take on the demeanor of a senior missionary. "We are delighted, Mrs. Fletcher, but we will need a few more meetings and an interview with the mission president."

"I understand. So shall we meet here tomorrow?"

"I . . . I . . . think that should work."

"Wonderful, should we say ten in the morning? And I will bring along Mrs. Checkly as my companion." She turned to look at her friend. "Yes?"

Mrs. Checkly hesitated. "Yes, of course. If you can invent a plausible story to tell Mr. Checkly."

"Done!" Mrs. Fletcher said. She looked at Inez and Jennie. "And you two will be in attendance?"

"Of course," Jennie answered.

"Wonderful!"

Inez liked Mrs. Fletcher. She reminded her of her father—a person of decision and candor.

"And now we will be on our way," Mrs. Fletcher said, pausing to give the missionaries an unaffected smile. "Remarkable. Prophets in our day." She looked at her friend and sighed. "Well, I suppose we must leave you for a time." She waved to the missionaries. "Tomorrow then."

Mrs. Checkly took the sister missionaries' hands. "It seems we will be seeing each other sooner than anticipated. It was an inspiring service." She turned and exited with her friend.

"Well, what do you think of that?" Inez asked to no one in particular.

Jennie was silent. She thought of Mrs. Fletcher concocting a story to tell Mr. Checkly. She was not sure *what* to think of that, but it did not sit well.

NOTES

Wilford Woodruff: Wilford Woodruff served as the fourth President of The Church of Jesus Christ of Latter-day Saints, from 1887–1898. He issued the manifesto that ended plural marriage in 1890; dedicated the Salt Lake Temple on April 6, 1893; and was the Prophet when Utah became a state on January 4, 1896. He gave his final talk in the April 1898 general conference.

Memorial service for President Woodruff: Details of the memorial service held in the Cheltenham conference home were included in Sister Knight's journal. She recorded the singing and the reading of President Woodruff's last general conference talk. She also noted that she and Sister Brimhall had been asked to speak. Wilford Woodruff's journal, which is quoted in this chapter, can be found at the Church History Library. Historical information about the Prophet's life was taken from the Church manual *Presidents of the Church: Teacher Manual* (2005).

Mrs. Fletcher: She is an actual person mentioned in Inez's journal as an investigator. Little is written about her life and background. Inez wrote in her journal that she and Jennie attended her baptism.

Chapter Thirty-Five

The four missionaries sat at the conference hall table with the two elegant English ladies, answering question after question. The room had been partially straightened from the previous night's service for President Woodruff, but there was still black bunting on the podium, and the memorial table retained its honored place. Inez had decided to leave it up until the cut flowers began to wilt. She stretched her back and smiled at Mrs. Checkly. Nearly an hour had gone by, and still the inquiries continued—questions about visions, angels, polygamy, tithing, priesthood, and the characteristics of the Father and the Son. The conversation was now on the translation of the Book of Mormon.

"And Joseph Smith was how old at this time?" Mrs. Fletcher asked.

"Twenty-five," Will answered.

"Approximately your age."

"Yes, ma'am. And . . . his was a rustic education."

"Then it seems implausible that he could have written such a book."

"Impossible," Inez stated firmly before Will could respond.

Both English women smiled at her. "And why is that, Miss Knight?" Mrs. Checkly asked.

"Because . . . " Inez took a breath, but before she could utter a word of explanation, the front door to the conference house slammed open and Mr. Easton came bolting into the room. Everyone at the table stood in alarm, and Inez's chair clattered to the ground.

"What in the world?" Mrs. Fletcher exclaimed. "Why is your man here, Christine?"

Mr. Easton rushed to Mrs. Checkly's side and took her arm. "Madam, I need to get you away."

"Explain yourself," Mrs. Checkly insisted, attempting unsuccessfully to release his grip.

"There is no time."

Will was by his side. "Tell us."

"Under the barrister's orders I have been following his wife." He turned a remorseful face to Mrs. Checkly. "But after he beat you, I have not been telling him about your meetings. Today, when I was elsewhere, he sent another servant to spy on you."

Mrs. Checkly's face drained of color. "Oh no."

Mr. Easton turned to Will. "Mr. Checkly has paid a gang to threaten you with violence."

"Reprehensible!" Mrs. Fletcher growled.

Will laid his hand on Mrs. Fletcher's back and moved the three toward the back of the conference hall. "Leave the back way, through the kitchen. We'll stall them until you're away."

"What about the girls?" Mrs. Checkly called back as Mr. Easton ushered her and Mrs. Fletcher along.

"We'll get them to their apartment!" Elder Bailey called after.

"I don't think there's time," Jennie said quietly. She moved beside Will and took his arm. "I hear them coming."

The company of missionaries stood silently as a cacophony of rumbling voices, jeers, and shouts approached from down the street. Inez turned to affirm that Mrs. Checkly was away.

"They made it out," Inez announced.

"Good. Now you two hide in the kitchen," Will ordered.

Jennie tightened her grip on his arm. "I won't."

"I won't either," Inez concurred, stepping next to Elder Bailey.

"Jennie . . . "

"No."

The noise intensified as the gang reached the front of the conference house. A stone exploded through one of the front windows, and the missionaries scrambled back. A roar of approval issued from the mob, and suddenly a barrage of projectiles was launched, shattering window after window.

"I say we try and get out through the kitchen!" Elder Bailey yelled, dragging Inez in that direction, but the sound of breaking glass on that side of the building stopped them short. "What should we do?"

"We have to make it to the police station!" Will yelled back.

"You mean go *through* them?"

"There's no other choice." Will took off his suit coat. "Take off your coat, Elder Bailey. When we go out, put it over Inez's head."

A brick careened through one of the already broken windows and smashed into the memorial table. The vase of flowers shattered, and the picture of Wilford Woodruff toppled to the ground. Inez involuntarily cried out.

"Let's go!" Will commanded, and the four ran for the front door.

As they rushed down the steps, the mob pelted them with rocks, mud, and sticks. A wet mass of foul-smelling mud caught Inez on the side of the face before Elder Bailey could cover her with his coat. The growls, hisses, and yells from the mob as they fled past sounded to Inez like demons from the pit. She concentrated on the small space of sidewalk in front of her, keeping her head down and fingers clutching the coat. Several times a rock or clump of mud hit her back or head, causing intense pain. She agonized that without any shielding, Elder Bailey would suffer terrible injury. They kept moving.

"Leave off!" a voice yelled, and Inez thought it sounded very much like her brother Ray. "Leave off!"

Bodies slammed into her from behind, and Inez fell to her knees. Elder Bailey was no longer beside her, and she tore the coat from her head and struggled to make sense of the chaos around her. One of the hired thugs tripped over her sprawled legs, and she caught a glimpse of Elder Davis swinging a large stick to bash him. She yelped and crawled quickly for a small alcove in the side of a building. She looked frantically for Jennie and caught sight of her huddled under a vegetable cart. Will and a red-haired fellow were in a wrestling match. Ray was pushing a scrawny man to the ground while his fellow tried to land a punch on Ray's head. Elder Davis and Elder Bailey were standing back-to-back, one holding a stick and the other a brick. The lackeys seemed terrified of the tall Americans, and Inez imagined they were thinking about the bounty and wondering if it was worth a cracked skull. Indeed, several of the gang had already made the decision to jump ship, and when the police whistles sounded, the rest abandoned their prey and flew for cover.

"Inez! Are you all right?" Elder Bailey panted, as he crouched down beside her.

She rubbed away the last of the mud, but there was still a stain of it on her cheek. "I'm fine, but what about you? You took some nasty blows."

He helped her to stand. "I was so mad I didn't feel a thing."

The missionaries gathered to their location as the police arrived.

"What's going on with you lads . . . and ladies?" the head policeman questioned.

"We were attacked, sir," Will answered. "As was our building—all the windows broken out."

"Attacked?"

"Yes, sir. By that band of ruffians."

"This is serious business, then. I think we need to get you to the station." He scrutinized Inez and Jennie. "Are the ladies capable?"

Elder Davis looked at the two sister missionaries with tender approval. "Oh yes, Officer. They are more capable than you can imagine."

Inez Knight and Jennie Brimhall sat in their beds as the light from a full moon poured in through their apartment window. Each was considering the events of the day, and though they were exhausted, sleep did not seem the remedy. Inez had unsettled thoughts bumping around in her head and figured Jennie was experiencing the same.

"I'm angry that we broke down and cried in front of that pompous police chief at the station," Inez grumbled.

"Hmm . . . ," Jennie said, laying her hairbrush on the side table. "He certainly was not on our side."

"The police who came to our aid were helpful, but when we arrived at the station, it was different. I think the chief of police detests us."

"Well, certainly our church."

"Without knowing anything about what we believe?"

"Hmm . . . "

"Or I bet he's in the barrister's pocket."

"It's possible."

"I wonder why Will wouldn't let us mention Mr. Checkly's name?"

"It may have caused Mrs. Checkly trouble."

"Oh, that's probably true," Inez answered, plumping her pillow with a little too much enthusiasm. "It makes me feel like crying all over again." She punched her pillow. "I don't understand how we can be so horribly treated in a civilized country."

Jennie tied her hair back with a ribbon. "You are pushing against the waves, Inez."

"What?"

"It's something Father taught me. A problem you cannot solve is like pushing against the waves of the ocean. You will uselessly wear yourself out." Jennie laid back against her pillow and closed her eyes. "Go to sleep."

"The elders were brave, weren't they? Willing to take blows for what they believe—fighting to protect us. I've never seen Will fight like that."

"I know," Jennie answered softly. Inez did not see the tears that leaked from the corner of her eyes.

"It was fortunate that Ray and Elder Davis arrived when they did."

"Hmm . . . "

"Good Elder Davis. He is truly on our side now."

Jennie got out of bed and moved to her trunk. "It's colder tonight. Do you want an extra quilt?"

"I suppose," Inez answered, knowing that Jennie was using the fetching of the quilts to change the subject. Inez chided herself. She knew she could be tiring when she was trying to unravel a puzzle. And tonight, she was puzzling out bigotry, dear Mrs. Checkly's life with a husband who could wield so much power, and her own inadequacies. Inez felt tears press against the back of her throat. She wanted to be brave, like Will and Ray. She wanted to be more faithful, like Jennie. She wanted to serve the Lord, like her parents—but there always seemed to be a chasm between her desires and her abilities.

"Don't think too much on things tonight," Jennie said, spreading the quilt over her friend.

"I won't," Inez answered, and Jennie gave her a disbelieving look. "I'll try. I promise."

"We've said our prayers, so we should just leave it in the Lord's hands," Jennie instructed as she snuggled back down in her own bed.

"Yes, Mother."

"Go to sleep."

Inez lay down with her back to her companion. "Bossy."

"I heard that."

Inez growled. "And ears like a donkey."

The room grew still as the sounds from the street faded into the night and the occupants of the apartments put away their petty miseries and escaped into sleep. Inez turned from side to side, adjusted her pillow, and repeated several scriptures to herself. Suddenly she slid out of bed and onto her knees. Her silent prayer was one of pleading and promise—of longing and tears. After a time, she rose and went to the desk.

Jennie groaned. "Inez, what are you doing?"

"I'm sorry. I didn't mean to wake you. I need to find something. Go back to sleep." Inez quietly opened the desk drawer and rummaged inside.

Jennie let out an exasperated breath of air and turned over.

Inez found the letter to her mother and padded back to bed. She sat for a long while looking out at the full moon, the letter pressed against her chest. Then, she held the missive in front of her and gently tore it in half.

NOTE

Mob violence: The incident of mob violence and the shattering of all the windows in the conference home are two separate events, both recorded in Inez Knight's journal. They occurred later, when Sister Liza Chipman was Inez's companion, but I combined the two events and presented them here for impact and continuity.

Chapter Thirty-Six

Inez swept glass into the dustpan, carried it carefully to the barrel, and dumped it. She glanced over to the window and stared at Elder Abernathy as he stood on a ladder, cautiously removing shards of glass from the windowpane.

"Be careful, Elder Abernathy!" Inez called over.

"I will, Sister Knight. Mind yourself as well."

"I will." She trudged back to her appointed place and began sweeping. Instead of thinking of the damaged windows or the chilling English drizzle moving in, Inez thought about the glorious days of autumn soon to arrive in Provo. She thought of her mother harvesting the garden and putting up stores of vegetables and fruit for the winter. She thought of apple trees and berry vines heavy with their offerings, and her father coming home from the mining office to eat apple pie or berry cobbler. Her heart began to ache with thoughts of home, and she stopped sweeping and chided herself. "Be still, Inez. You've made a commitment—now stick to it. The Lord can't help you if you go moping around."

"Sister Knight?"

Inez started.

"I'm sorry, I didn't mean to scare you," Elder Davis said.

"Not at all, Elder Davis." She took a deep breath. "I am perfectly calm." She gave him a half smile, and he grinned back.

"President Noall sent me to help you clean up the memorial table."

Her smile vanished. "Oh."

"Are you all right?"

"I was trying to avoid that area. It breaks my heart."

"You did a wonderful job with the display. The people enjoyed it."

"Did they?"

"I think the entire congregation stopped to admire it at some point."

"Well, that is very nice of you to say, Elder Davis."

"So shall we go see what we can save?"

"Yes." Inez looked around and found Elder Forester loitering at the bottom of the ladder. She called to him. "Elder Forester!" He looked at her and shrugged. She motioned for him to come over, and he shrugged again. "Oh! That man is infuriating!"

Elder Davis took two strides forward, and Elder Forester, looking startled, came immediately to them.

"What do you want?"

"It's what Sister Knight wants."

Elder Forester turned a sour face to her. "What is it?"

She held out the broom and dustpan. "I need you to clean this area. President Noall has given us a different assignment."

"Sorry, I can't. I have to watch out for Elder Abernathy on the ladder."

"My brother Ray is already working with him." Inez shoved the broom forward again. "Here, be useful."

Elder Forester started to protest, but after a furtive look at the scowling Elder Davis, he took the cleaning items and turned away.

"He is so disagreeable," Elder Davis growled. "I apologize if I was ever that bad."

Inez raised her eyebrows and then broke into a laugh. "Well, you were bad, but not as bad as *that*." She tilted her head in the direction of Elder Forester.

"That's good to know." As they walked together to the ruined memorial table, Elder Davis continued his confession. "I had a lot of repenting to do."

"Jennie and I are glad to have you on our side now," Inez stated. She gave him a lopsided grin. "Especially when we saw how handy you are in the fight." They reached the table, and Inez grew quiet as she surveyed the damage. "Oh dear." She reached for the American flag.

"Careful!" Elder Davis warned. He handed her a pair of gloves. "Put these on first."

Inez complied. She picked up the flag and gave it a gentle shake. Shattered bits of glass fell onto the table along with a cascade of destroyed flower petals. Inez set her jaw to keep from crying. *It is not as though I'm the first person in my family to suffer persecution.* She thought of her grandfather Newel Knight, who had been threatened and tormented by mobs for years. Finally expelled from Nauvoo in the winter of 1846, he died in the wilderness, leaving his second wife, Lydia, and seven children alone. Inez's father had been five years old. *Years of senseless persecution.* She glanced over at the broken window, and her mind conjured the image of the Prophet Joseph being shot by the mob and falling through the window at Carthage Jail. She took a deep breath and began carefully folding the flag.

Elder Davis retrieved President Woodruff's picture from the floor. The picture frame was damaged, and the broken glass had gouged a hole through the Prophet's suit coat. "Well, this is ruined." He went to throw the remains in the barrel.

"Wait!" Inez said, laying the flag on a nearby chair and reaching for the picture. "Here, give it to me," she said gently. "I think I'll keep it in my journal to remember." She spent time removing the picture from the ruined frame and smoothing the paper.

"You know what really makes me angry?" Elder Davis said, snatching up the Book of Mormon.

"What?"

"Mrs. Checkly's husband knows nothing about what we believe, and he does not care to know. He has contempt for something he has not even investigated. You would think a barrister would weigh the evidence."

"You would think."

Elder Davis gave an uncharacteristic growl and laid the Book of Mormon on the flag. "I feel sorry for his wife."

Inez was surprised by his invective but agreed with the sentiment. "I do too." She felt the sting of tears and busied herself with placing President Woodruff's picture between the pages of the Book of Mormon.

Jennie came from the kitchen area, removing her apron and moving purposefully toward her companion. "President Noall wants to see us."

"What about?"

"I don't know. Morning, Elder Davis."

"Morning, Sister Brimhall."

"He said it was important. So we best not make him wait."

Inez handed Elder Davis her gloves. "I'm sorry. I guess you are on your own."

"I think I can manage."

As they moved toward President Noall's office, Inez tried to think of what she might have done or not done to warrant a meeting with the president. Before she could summon an answer, Jennie was knocking on his office door.

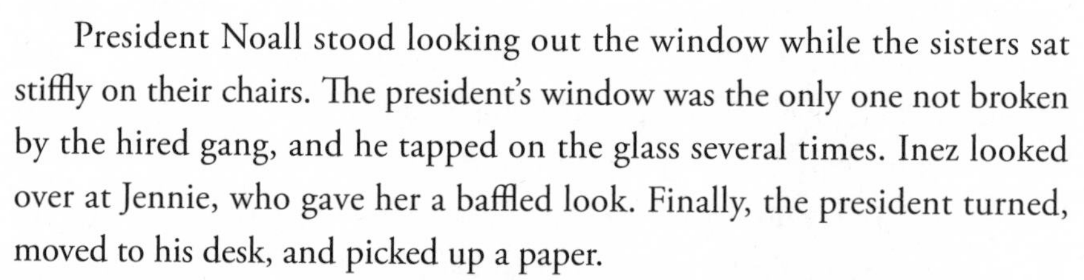

President Noall stood looking out the window while the sisters sat stiffly on their chairs. The president's window was the only one not broken by the hired gang, and he tapped on the glass several times. Inez looked over at Jennie, who gave her a baffled look. Finally, the president turned, moved to his desk, and picked up a paper.

"I had a man come to my office this morning with this missive." He held up the paper to them. "Do you two know a Mr. Easton?"

Inez was so dumbfounded she could not utter a word. Jennie, on the other hand, spoke up immediately. "Yes, President. He's a servant of the Checkly family."

"And you have been teaching the gospel lessons to Mrs. Checkly."

"Yes, President."

"My records show for several months."

"Yes."

"And you have been doing this in secret?"

Inez found her voice. "No! Not in secret. I mean, we didn't know she was keeping it secret from her husband. We only found out last night when Mr. Easton told us."

The president nodded. "Sister Brimhall?"

"I had a feeling she was meeting us secretly."

Inez turned to her. "You did?"

"Yes. The day we went to Sudeley Castle. Her bruised face spoke of a beating, not a fall. And when she said she would contact us with meeting places and times, I figured it was because she had decided not to tell her husband. She did not want Mr. Checkly to know."

President Noall shook his head and sat down. "Why did you not come to me with this?"

Jennie hung her head. "I . . . we . . . we wanted to teach her. She found the gospel message true and comforting."

President Noall's voice took on a softer tone. "I understand this, sisters, but your actions have put the Church in a difficult place."

"How?" Inez asked.

"Mr. Checkly is threatening legal action against us."

"What!" Inez shouted, standing up. "He dares to threaten action against *us* after hiring thugs to smash up the conference home and do us harm?"

"Please sit down, Sister Knight. We cannot prove that he hired anyone."

"Mr. Easton told us . . . a group of us heard him when he came to warn us."

"Mr. Easton is a servant. He is not going to speak against his employer in court. And Mr. Checkly is a barrister, a high official in Queen Victoria's government." The president took a deep breath. "Please, sit down, Sister Knight." She did. President Noall folded the letter and placed it in his desk drawer. "We must just pray that this blows over."

"I am so sorry, President," Jennie said. "Are you going to send us home?"

Inez stared at her companion.

"Do you wish to go home?" he asked with a concerned look. "You have been through much since arriving, and I would understand a longing for home."

"No, sir," Jennie answered fervently. "With all my heart, I wish to stay."

"Sister Knight?"

"Even though I am not the best missionary, President, I want to stay. I've made a commitment to stay. I'm going to work hard and try to come up to a better standard."

"Good. Good," President Noall responded, working hard to keep his emotions in check. After a pause he looked steadily into Inez's face. "A better standard? Goodness, Sister Knight. Your and Sister Brimhall's testimonies of the restored gospel are powerful. I would like to see a dozen sister missionaries working in the field." He cleared his throat and picked up another letter. "I am certainly glad you both have chosen to stay because I have something else to share with you."

Inez sobered. *Oh dear. What now?*

"I think I will read this one to you."

Dear President Noall of the Cheltenham Conference,

We have read the Book of Mormon cover to cover, met with the Saints, and read every Church pamphlet available to us. We have pondered the teachings of Sister Brimhall and Sister Knight and have prayed for guidance. The long and short of it is that we wish to apply for baptism into The Church of Jesus Christ of Latter-day Saints at your earliest convenience. Please return word as soon as possible on the next steps.

Yours with the very kindest regards,
Mr. and Mrs. Kennison & George

Jennie and Inez were in each other's arms weeping and laughing at the same time. Forgetting decorum, they raced to give President Noall a hug.

"Is this true, President?" Inez cried. "It is really true?"

"It is indeed true," he said, chuckling. "Here is the letter to prove it."

Jennie took the letter, and she and Inez poured over each word. Jennie fixed her gaze on President Noall. "So what *is* the next step?" she asked excitedly.

"I think perhaps a trip to Bristol for all of us? What say you?"

"Yes!" the sisters chorused. "Yes, yes, yes!"

Chapter Thirty-Seven

"Inez Knight! So this is where you've hidden yourself," Elder Bailey said, sitting down next to her in the third-class compartment and giving her a sunny smile. She did not return the offering. The exuberance slid from Elder Bailey's face. "I'm sorry. I'm interrupting you." He started to stand.

"No, you're not . . . well, yes . . . yes, you are interrupting me, but perhaps you can help."

Elder Bailey sat warily in his seat and spoke with caution. "I'd be glad to help you with *anything*." Inez gave him a look, and he flinched. "If I can. I'll help if I can."

"I need to find a scripture."

Elder Bailey waited as she flipped through pages of her scriptures. He cleared his throat. "Is it New Testament? Doctrine and Covenants? Book of M—"

"I don't know! That's the problem."

Inez thought back to her solitude prior to Elder Bailey's arrival. She had sought out a place to be alone and apart from the other "smart" missionaries who were blissfully joyous on the train ride to Bristol. President Noall was in their midst, sharing stories of his missionary adventures and instructing them in scripture and Church doctrine. He was also giving assignments for the baptismal service. Inez had panicked when he assigned her "dedication to gospel principles." She felt inadequate to give counsel on the subject matter—inadequate and dimwitted—and the more she tried to talk herself out of such feelings, the more they persisted. Finally, she had stolen away, finding an empty compartment where she could read and pray.

"So what is the topic?"

"What?" Inez asked, coming out of her musing, and giving Elder Bailey a confused look.

"What's the topic of the scripture you're looking for?"

"Oh! Oh, the topic. Well, it's something about trusting the Lord."

"Proverbs 3:5 and 6?"

She glared at him.

"What?" he squeaked. "Isn't that it? 'Trust in the Lord with all thine heart; and . . . '"

"Yes, that's it," she said curtly. She picked up her Old Testament and began intensely flipping the pages.

"Are you angry with me?"

"No."

"Then why are you so . . . "

"I am not angry with you, Elder Bailey. I am angry with myself."

"Why in the world would you be angry with yourself? As far as I can see, you haven't a fault."

"Well, you need glasses then, Elder Bailey."

"Inez . . . "

"No, Elder. I gave only a portion of the gospel topic, and you came up with the scripture like that." She snapped her fingers. "I earnestly study and study and still fumble around with where to find things."

Elder Bailey laid his hand on hers. "Inez, people have different strengths."

She stared at his hand. "Elder Bailey," she said slowly. "I find that inappropriate." He slid his hand away, and Inez noticed color come to his face. "Not that it wasn't comforting; it was very comforting. It is just that we must remember our callings as missionaries."

"Of course, you're right," he said, standing and swaying a bit with the motion of the train. "I . . . I will leave you to your study." He moved to the compartment door.

"Elder Baily," Inez called after him. He turned. "I do appreciate your help."

"Of course. Anytime." He hesitated. "Sister Knight, I want you to know how much I admire you, as a missionary. You and Sister Brimhall are such perfect examples of the women of the Church. You are smart and tailored and faithful. And though you may think Sister Brimhall outshines you with her gospel knowledge, you complement her with your insight and tremendous testimony. When you speak with the Spirit about your love of the Savior and His restored gospel, the message goes straight into the heart of the listener." Inez opened her mouth to reply, but no words were forthcoming. Elder Bailey gave her a gentle smile. "Just focus on that strength, and I'm sure the Lord with be pleased." He turned and moved out of the compartment.

Inez sat for several moments with her hand on the Bible and her mouth open. She took a deep breath and looked down at Proverbs 3. She whispered the words of verses 5 and 6: "Trust in the Lord with all thine heart; and lean not unto thine own understanding. In all thy ways acknowledge Him, and He shall direct thy paths."

Inez repeated the words several times, and her worry began to subside. *Lean not unto thine own understanding.* How often had she relied on her own meager intelligence to figure out a problem? How often had she turned a problem over to her Savior only to snatch it back again when the resolution was long in coming? If she was going to be a better missionary, she had to do her part and let the Lord take care of the rest. She had to trust Him.

Inez stood to gather her belongs, ideas flowing into her mind about how to approach her assigned message—dedication to gospel principles. Another seed of testimony settled itself into her heart as the once elusive talk now came to her in ordered fashion. Her spirits lifted as she hurried out of the compartment to find her companion. Together she and Jennie would celebrate the anticipated reunion with the Kennison family.

"And then the impertinent young woman starts talking about bridges, and scientific knowledge, and God being the great scientist. What was I to do with that approach? She made God sound as though we could be chums in the International League of Scholarship."

Everyone at Mrs. Boyers's dining table laughed, including Sister Brimhall.

"Well, Sister Knight and I couldn't decide between using logic or Mrs. Somers's baked goods to soften your heart."

"I think you triumphed with both," Mrs. Boyers said.

"Indeed," George concurred, giving his father a friendly clap on the back.

"I wonder if I can put that on your baptismal papers?" President Noall questioned with a smile. "Reason for joining The Church of Jesus Christ of Latter-day Saints—logic and baked goods."

Inez and Jennie could not stop laughing.

"I would say, President Noall, you could absolutely write down on your papers—gobsmacked by the Book of Mormon," Mrs. Kennison stated, giving her husband a wink.

"Ah . . . well, yes. There's that of course," Mr. Kennison answered, scooping up the last of his plum pudding. "And what about you, you red-haired devil? What converted you? Wasn't it something about getting your clutches into me for eternity?"

The elders laughed heartily at this charge.

"What are you talking about?" Mrs. Kennison countered. "That was one of the doctrines I had to ponder long and hard."

"It's true, Father. She wondered if she could put up with you for eternity," George chuckled. "Many a night I heard her pacing the floor."

"I'll give you pacing the floor," Mr. Kennison warned, nicking his son's plate of unfinished plum pudding.

"Not cricket, sir!" George protested.

"And it is obvious what set my son on the path to conversion," Mr. Kennison said, nonchalantly waving his spoon in the sisters' direction. "Well, can you blame him? Just look at those angel faces."

The elders hooted, and Inez and Jennie's faces flushed scarlet.

"Wait! Wait!" Jennie called out, gaining control of her embarrassment. "I thought you didn't believe in angels."

Mr. Kennison shook his head and chuckled. "There she goes again. Using her intellect to catch me out."

"I suppose he must believe in angels now, mustn't he?" Mrs. Kennison said, patting her husband's arm.

"And gold Bibles," Mr. Kennison mused. "My word. What in the world has gotten into me?"

"The spirit of truth," Inez said.

The room quieted as Mr. Kennison sat back in his chair, crossed his arms, and considered the sister missionaries. "There is something to that now, isn't there? When I read the Book of Mormon, my expertise in linguistic anthropology told me this was no book of 1850 America, and my knowledge of social anthropology made me ask how the upstart Joseph Smith was able to conjure such a vast story of people, places, and culture with his limited education. It was not conceivable." He winked at Sister Brimhall. "So it was science that convinced me of the truth of it, after all."

"And the Spirit that confirmed it," Jennie said softly.

Mr. Kennison nodded, and Mrs. Kennison laid her hand on his.

"The plum pudding didn't hurt either," George said with a grin.

Mr. Kinsey came into the room, and Mrs. Boyers turned to him. "Mrs. Somers wishes to know if anything else is required from the kitchen."

Mrs. Boyers surveyed her guests and smiled when Mr. Kennison raised his hand.

"I was wondering if I could . . . "

"Oh no, Edmund," Mrs. Kennison said, pulling down his arm. "If you indulge another bite, you may just sink to the bottom of the pond tomorrow."

Mr. Kennison laughed and addressed the elders. "It might take two or three of you to dunk me under and bring me forth!"

"We will be at the ready," President Noall said.

Inez was surprised by the president's droll response and wondered if some of the Kennisons' jollity had rubbed off on him during supper.

The company stood from the table, and the Kennisons went to Mrs. Boyers to thank her for the evening's festivities and to pass along their praise to Mrs. Somers for the scrumptious celebratory supper. After their departure, the elders moved to speak with President Noall, and Inez and Jennie went to the kitchen with Mr. Kinsey, where they hugged Mrs. Somers and caught up on all the market gossip.

Later that night, the two sister missionaries lay in their beds in Meadowlark Manor, reading scriptures, going over their talks for the next day, and chatting about the miracle of meeting the Kennison family.

"If it hadn't been for that poor woman tormenting us, Mrs. Kennison might not have taken us under her wing and invited us in," Inez said on a yawn.

"Very true. And then we would not have met George and Mr. Kennison."

"Or been invited on the picnic where you made the case for science."

Jennie giggled. "And where we offered the plum pudding as a bribe."

Inez laid her scriptures on the side table. "It is going to be a glorious day tomorrow."

"It may rain."

"Even if it rains buckets, it will still be a glorious day."

"Our first baptism," Jennie said, snuggling down into her pillow. "Good night, Inez."

"Good night, Jennie," Inez whispered, standing and moving over to turn off the gas lamp. She went to the window and pushed back the drapery so she could gaze at the night sky. She heard the leaves rustling on the trees and sighed. Thoughts of love and gratitude came into her mind as a prayer. *Thank you, Father, for my blessing. For promising me that when I am cast down and everything becomes dark, you will raise up before me a great light that shall expel the darkness. This has been the light of the Kennison family. Thank you for the blessing of meeting them and seeing them now at the gate of baptism. Thank you for my sister Jennie and for all the things we have experienced together. Thank you for the blessing of spiritual strength. Thank you for helping with my talk.* A slight smile touched her lips. *And . . . thank you for being patient with me.*

Inez Knight was oblivious of the passing minutes. She stood at the bedroom window, contemplating the endless velvet of space.

Chapter Thirty-Eight

It did not rain. In fact, the Bristol natives debated for a time whether it was the warmest or second-warmest end of September they could remember. Inez was content for any weather. Her heart was concentrated in the spirit of the day and in the assembled congregation, which included the elders, President Noall, and members from the Bristol Ward who had come in support of the Kennison family. Also in attendance was an unexpected soul: President McMurrin. He had arrived from Scotland on the early-morning train, and Inez smiled as she watched him converse and laugh with Mr. Kennison. The two had a similar stature and bravado, and Inez could easily imagine them as mates on a trek through Egypt.

"Do you think that pond's deep enough?"

Inez jumped. "What? Oh, George, it's you!"

"Sorry, didn't mean to scare you," George said with a chuckle.

Inez gathered her wits. "The pond?"

"Yes. I mean, I think it will be sufficient for me and Mum, but my father is . . . Well, the volume of water may not cover him."

Inez giggled. "Young Mr. Kennison, you are a rascal." She sobered. "I think it will be fine." She pointed to the far side of the pond. "See there? Brother Worthen owns this land, and he came early with the elders to dam up the outlet. That's increased the water's depth."

"Seems like you lot have done this before."

Inez smiled. "Immersion requires a bit of planning."

As Jennie and Mrs. Kennison came to join them, Inez admired Amanda

Kennison's dress and demeanor. Her brilliant-red hair was pulled into an intricate plait, her feet were shod with Egyptian sandals, and her long gauze dress of cream and yellow looked as though the sun had touched the fabric with its warmth. Her face seemed to shine with that same warmth, and Inez felt a thrill of enlightenment. Amanda Kennison would be a mighty force in the Lord's Church.

Mrs. Kennison stood beside her son and laid a hand on his shoulder. "So, George, are you still sure of your decision?"

"I am. I will be staying true, even if you and Da back out."

Mrs. Kennison gave him a half grin. "Oh, there will be no backing out."

"What is it about the gospel that makes you so sure, George?" Jennie asked.

George looked down at the ground. He took a deep breath and looked up. "Many things, Sister Brimhall, but I think it's the martyrdom of Joseph and Hyrum that put the truth of the Church into my soul. If Joseph was a charlatan, he might have put his own life at risk, but not his brother's." He shook his head. "No, he would not have sacrificed Hyrum's life."

"I agree," Jennie said, her voice thick with emotion.

President Noall approached. "We are ready to begin. We're gathering under those trees for the service, and after we'll attend to the baptisms."

George took his mother's hand. "Come on, Mum. Shall we go change our lives?" The two followed President Noall.

"I told you it was going to be a glorious day," Inez whispered to her companion.

"In every way," Jennie answered.

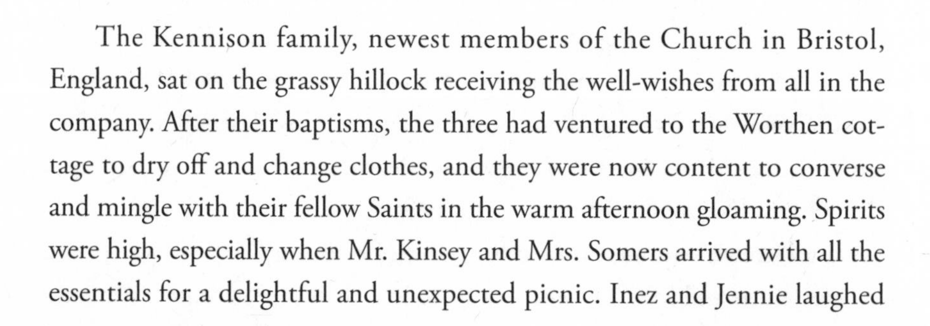

The Kennison family, newest members of the Church in Bristol, England, sat on the grassy hillock receiving the well-wishes from all in the company. After their baptisms, the three had ventured to the Worthen cottage to dry off and change clothes, and they were now content to converse and mingle with their fellow Saints in the warm afternoon gloaming. Spirits were high, especially when Mr. Kinsey and Mrs. Somers arrived with all the essentials for a delightful and unexpected picnic. Inez and Jennie laughed at how quickly the elders helped unload the wagon and set up the makeshift tables. Mrs. Boyers supervised the laying of linen tablecloths and the placement of food: hand-raised mutton pies, pigeon pie, pickled salmon, a joint of cold roast beef, potato cakes, crocks of pickles, Stilton cheese, round loaves of bread, a basket of salad, and pints of lemonade. Many of the dessert items Inez and Jennie recognized: ginger biscuits, lemon cake, and fresh plums and apples, but they had to ask George about a few of the offerings.

"Those are tea cakes, treacle scones, baked apple dumplings, and I believe a barberry tart," George said joyfully as he looked over the plethora of food. "That barberry tart is delicious. I won't be surprised if my father tries to make off with that."

"I think he may have to wrestle one of my brothers for it," Inez suggested.

George laughed. "I suppose we have to feed the body as well as the spirit."

"Very true," Jennie said. "But I truly feel as though I could live for days on spirit alone. What an outpouring of faith."

"My mother looked like an angel standing out in the water, didn't she?"

"She did," Inez concurred. "There was a glow about her."

"Made my father cry. Cry, mind you! I have never seen him cry."

"A softened heart," Jennie said. "Another one of the gifts of the Spirit."

George looked at the horizon, and Inez could tell he was trying to govern his emotions. "I can't tell you what this day means to our family."

Both sisters reached out and laid a hand on his arm.

Jennie was the first to find her voice. "Oh, George. Sister Knight and I cannot tell you what your family's friendship means to us. When we're back home in Utah, we will think of our times together: the first day we met, you running down the stairs with that cricket bat while your mother defended us, or the time you and your father attempted to steal our picnic basket."

"Or coming to Mrs. Boyers's to see us off when we had to leave Bristol," Inez added.

Jennie shaded her eyes and looked around at the joyful gathering. "And now, we will add this glorious day to our memories."

Inez started sniffling.

Amanda Kennison came up behind Inez and Jennie, put her arms around their shoulders, and gave them a squeeze. "Thank you, women, for this grand day!" She looked sideways at Inez. "Goodness, Sister Knight, are you well?"

"I am well, Sister Kennison. Happy." She wiped a tear from her cheek.

"Exactly how I feel—happy. Happy, joyous, light. It's how I felt as a child."

"Today we *are* children, Mum. Newly born."

"Even your father?" Inez questioned.

Sister Kennison gave her a crooked grin. "Well, the transformation there will be slight as he's always been a child."

The foursome laughed at this pronouncement.

"And you would know," George said. "You have lived with him the longest."

"Oh, look! Here he comes now," Sister Kennison said. "His ears must have been burning."

Mr. Kennison joined the group, accompanied by Will and Elder Bailey. "Come along, women!" he bellowed. "They won't let us men tuck in until all the women have been served!" He gave his wife a mock scornful look. "You were sent to fetch them, Sister Kennison. What happened?"

"Oh, stop growling. I left your side three minutes ago."

"Which can seem like an eternity to a starving man."

"Starving man?" George questioned. "You could hibernate through the winter."

Mr. Kennison took off his cap and chased George across the meadow, swatting at him as though he were a bothersome fly.

Mrs. Kennison hooked arms with Inez and Jennie. "Both of them—children," she announced, shaking her head and laughing. "Come along, sisters, let's go eat up all the ginger biscuits so that Brother Kennison gets nary a one."

"*Brother* Kennison. I like the sound of that," Jennie said.

Sister Kennison beamed at her. "So do I, Sister Brimhall. I like it very much."

Chapter Thirty-Nine

To the Knight Household

My dear family,

Today is October 1, and the weather has changed in an instant. It seems the trees abandoned their green overnight as the warmth gives way to icy wind and rain from the North. Jennie and I wear both a sweater and a shawl while in the apartment, and our small pot-bellied stove is often called into service. Jennie has a slight cold, but it does not stop her. Yesterday we handed out fifty first tracts and spoke at a street meeting. Our numbers were few because of the chill, but at the end, a gentleman approached Will for a cottage meeting. It is hard to think that my dear brother will be gone before Christmas. I will miss him, and I know Sister Brimhall tries not to think about the separation.

We traveled to Bristol last week and returned filled with the spirit of missionary work. The Kennison family was baptized! It was amazing to see the change in their lives. They came from knowing nothing about the gospel to loving the idea of an existence of life spread out through the eternities.

At the service prior to the baptisms, I gave a talk on dedication to gospel principles. I had doubts about my ability and the subject matter, but the Spirit guided me to Proverbs 3:5–6, and I used that as the foundation. If questions arise about the doctrine, then trust in the Lord to direct your path. Do no lean on your own understanding. I also used Moroni 10: 4–5—how by the Holy Ghost you can know the truth of all things. The congregation seemed to accept the words, and I did not faint, so that was heartening.

Jennie Pearl and Addie, I know that being in front of a group does not frighten you, as you are always singing and reciting in front of others. I would suggest that now is the time to memorize your scriptures so you can be brave missionaries in the future. I wish I had been more diligent in my gospel study. I am afraid I was more interested in dress patterns and hats. There! Now I have made my confession in order to set you on a better path.

After the baptisms, Mrs. Boyers, our landlady, surprised everyone with a splendid picnic. Every heart was light, and every stomach satisfied. I sampled all the fare and was pleased with everything but the mutton pies and barberry tart. The tart was too sour for my taste. Mother, I will send you the recipe for the baked apple dumplings. They were my favorite.

Dear parents, remember when we met up with Sister Winslow on the ride to the train station and she said that as women our minds and our bodies were not fit for the pressures of a mission? I admit that on some days I agree with her, but in truth, Jennie and I are growing into our calling. Every day our hearts gain confidence. Our bodies are strengthened by miles of tracting, our brains stuffed with doctrine and scripture, and our knees worn out in prayer.

The mission is difficult. It is so difficult that sometimes Jennie and I go to bed weeping. Jennie made me laugh the other night. We were lying in bed feeling melancholy, and she said, "I wonder if the elders ever cry themselves to sleep?" We laughed hard at that and then spent the next while imitating how we thought each elder would cry. We were kind to Will and Ray—we just had them sniffling and clearing their throats.

It is difficult to believe that we have been in England six months. If we follow the timetable of the elders, we will have another eighteen months to serve. It may seem like a long time but look how quickly the six months have passed.

Be well, my beloved family. I miss you.
Love,
Your Amanda Inez

BAKED APPLE DUMPLINGS (A PLAIN FAMILY DISH)

INGREDIENTS— 6 apples, ¾ lb. of suet-crust or puff paste, sugar to taste.

MODE— Pare and take out the cores of the apples without dividing them, and make suet crust. Roll the apples in the crust, previously sweetening them with moist sugar, and taking care to join the paste nicely. When they are formed into round balls, put them on a tin, and bake them for about ½ hour, or longer should the apples be very large; arrange them pyramidically on a dish, and sift over them some pounded white sugar. These may be made richer by using one of the puff-pastes instead of suet.

TIME— From ½ to ¾ hour, or longer.

Sufficient for 4 persons.

Dear Mother,

Hint: You could try adding cinnamon to the sugar. Also, I think these would be delicious served with Queen Victoria's vanilla custard.

CHAPTER FORTY

Inez and Jennie stood and gathered their scriptures and tracts from the conference hall table. Inez stretched her back, and Jennie yawned. "It has been a very long day," Jennie said, yawning again.

"We had better get to bed before we fall asleep on our feet," Inez moaned. She glanced over and saw all the elders standing at their places, observing them. Inez sighed. "Very gallant, elders," she called to them. "Thank you. Feel free to sit down." They did. "Thank you."

Jennie giggled and moved to leave. "They're only following President Noall's directive."

Inez followed. "I know. I just don't like the extra attention when I feel like curdled milk."

When they reached the doorway, Will's voice rang out.

"Sister Brimhall! Sister Knight! Wait, we'll walk you!"

"Does he think I'm a dog?" Jennie mumbled.

The sisters turned to see Will and Elder Bailey coming from the president's office. Inez watched as Jennie managed a semblance of a smile, and Inez struggled to imitate her. She was sure that instead of a smile, her lips were curved into something akin to a grimace.

"Hello, Elder Knight . . . Elder Bailey," Jennie said in her soft, patient voice. "We are just on our way to bed."

"That is a good idea. You need your rest," Will stated. "You've been over your cold only a few days."

"So why did you stop us?" Jennie snapped. There was no patience in her voice now, and Inez noted her brother's amazed reaction.

"I . . . I . . . we were sent to hand out the mail. I thought we could . . . "

"Why don't you just hand it to me and then go deliver to the elders?"

"Are you angry?"

Jennie took a deep breath. "I am just tired, Will. It's been a long day."

"Of course." He went through the basket and pulled out several letters. She took them and turned to go. "Would you like me to . . . "

"No! No, thank you, Will. I am capable." She shook her head and turned back. "I'm sorry, Elder Knight. I promise to be my own jolly self in the morning." She paused. "Inez?"

"You go ahead. I'll be there as soon as I get my mail."

Jennie left.

Will fumbled through the letters until he found two for Inez. When he looked up, Inez noted the worry in his face. "Did I do something wrong?" he asked.

"Well, a little something," Inez answered, trying not to sound like a sister scolding her older brother.

"I did? What?"

"You have to stop hovering over her, Will."

"Hovering?"

"You are always asking how she's feeling, offering her medicine for this and that, instructing her on what she should do."

"And is that so terrible?"

"She is not a little girl."

"No, she is not a little girl, but she is my fiancée."

Inez held up her hand. "This we know. But Jennie is not the same Jennie you left in Provo. She . . . we have both learned much since being on our mission."

"What does that have to do . . . "

Inez held up her hand again. "Ah! Do you want my advice or not?"

Will hesitated, then nodded. "Yes, I want your advice."

"She's stronger, Will. Jennie has been standing up to ridicule and aggression for six months, working diligently for six months, figuring out her own life for six months. It's made her independent."

"And what of her bout with pneumonia?"

"She knows."

"Does she? Cold English winter is just around the corner, Inez."

"You have to let her figure it out."

"So she's angry at me for caring about her?"

"Don't be petulant, Elder Knight. Jennie loves that you care about her. I just don't think she wants you to smother her."

His look turned wounded. "Smother her?"

"Well, perhaps *smother* wasn't the correct word."

"I see," Will said, clearing his throat. "Well, I . . . I see. Thank you, Inez, you've given me much to think about." He turned and headed to deliver mail to the other elders.

She called after him. "Will! I didn't mean that you were . . . Oh dear."

"Never mind," Elder Bailey encouraged. "I'll speak with him. He is just very worried about her—afraid she's caught up in the work and neglecting her own health. Maybe you could tell her that."

"I will, Elder Bailey. Thank you."

Elder Bailey stepped forward and laid his hand on Inez's shoulder. "We can't help worrying about you."

"Elder Bailey . . . "

"I've noticed that you're not wearing the locket I gave you. Don't you like it?"

Inez stepped back. "I love it—it was very kind, but it wouldn't be appropriate."

"Inez, I care for you."

"I know, Elder Bailey, but now is not the time."

"Do you not have feelings for me?"

Inez gave him an even look. "You are my friend. You make me laugh, and you've given me kind advice."

"And nothing else?"

"Now is not the time. We are not here for ourselves, Elder Bailey. We are here to serve the Lord by preaching to our brothers and sisters in England."

"And what of later?"

"You finish your mission in six months. I will probably finish a year after that. If when I return to Provo you are not married . . . " She gave him a sisterly smile. "Then perhaps we can see what the Lord has in store for us. But now is . . . "

"Not the time."

Inez could tell he was working to hide his disappointment. "I mean this sincerely, Harrison. If you are willing to trek from Spanish Fork to Provo to court a plain, clumsy girl such as myself, then I would be flattered."

A smile brushed the corner of his mouth. "You are not plain, Sister Knight."

"But certainly clumsy."

"Well, perhaps you'll grow out of it." She punched his arm. "Ow! You were the one who said that!"

"You don't have to agree with everything I say."

The two chuckled together, and the awkwardness lessened.

"I will hold you to your Utah promise," he said backing away.

"Of course," Inez stated. "I am a woman of my word."

He gave her a little salute and turned to take up his assignment. Inez watched after him for a moment, grabbed her coat off the coat rack, and headed for the apartment.

Inez stood with her head and back pressed against the apartment door. Her eyes were closed, and her lips pursed. She stomped her foot. "Why do men have to complicate everything?" When there was no response, she opened her eyes to find Jennie slumped down at the small table, head on her folded arms. "Jennie?" Inez moved quickly to her. "Jennie, are you all right?" Jennie sat up and handed Inez a letter. As soon as the missive was out of her hands, she covered her face and wept. "What in the world?" Inez said, removing her coat and throwing it on the divan. She unfolded the letter and read silently.

My dear Sister Brimhall and Sister Knight,

I will have Mr. Easton deliver this letter to you as I am required to break off all ties. This is a privation for me, but one must remember one's duty. I will chance this final correspondence as I could not abide separation without explanation. The damage to your conference house is a misery, and I will find a way to pay reparation. Mr. Easton reports that you were not injured in the attack, which eases my mind. You both are women of honor, and I will miss our time together.

Inez looked over at Jennie, who was still weeping. She went back to the letter.

From my heart, I thank you for the peace and illumination you brought to my life. Because of the Book of Mormon, there is light that pours into my reading of the Bible. The Book of Mormon is a sacred book, and it has brought me a deeper understanding of scripture. Thank you, Sister Knight, for gifting it to me that day.

Inez whimpered and dashed at the tears pooling in her eyes.

Because of the doctrines of eternal life, I have hope of holding Mary in my arms again. With this, my heart is mended.

Dear sisters, though we may never see one another again, please know that your effort will not be wasted. I will continue to ponder and pray and read my precious book. I promise that this pearl of great price in my possession will not be squandered.

With great admiration and affection,

Christine Checkly

Inez folded the letter and placed it on the table. It was a long while before she spoke. "I'm worn through. I'm going to bed."

Jennie nodded.

The companions undressed, put on their nightdresses, and slipped into their beds. Sister Brimhall was voice for the prayer that night. It was heartfelt and punctuated with declarations of gratitude, tears, and tender pleading for the good people of Britain. In the end, the missionary sisters for The Church of Jesus Christ of Latter-day Saints recommitted to their calling and lovingly placed Christine Checkly in the hands of the Lord.

CHAPTER FORTY-ONE

THOUGHTS ON MISSIONARY MANAGEMENT FROM SISTER BRIMHALL AND SISTER KNIGHT

Sister Knight and I have suffered a spiritual disappointment. A person we love will not be able to continue her study of the gospel. We wanted to share this because we know during your time of service you will likely face this heartache. Do not despair. Melancholy is the first cousin of disappointment, and we do not want to give it a home. Sister Knight and I have gone through dark times in the mission and have come through the storm bruised but not broken. Here are a few practical remedies to relieve melancholy. Some are authored by Mrs. Beeton and some by us.

Make sure to open the windows of your room twice daily to allow the cleansing properties of fresh air to circulate.

Obtain sufficient exercise. This will stimulate the blood flow and move stagnation from your lungs and heart. A stroll in nature is especially restorative.

Keep up your toiletries. Keep your body and hair clean and your hair kempt. Keep your teeth polished.

Hold dear the companionship of well-disposed associates. They will cheer you.

Avoid bothersome individuals who agitate. They care nothing for your comfort but only for their own importance.

Speak with the mission president and allow him to give you blessings.

Read scriptures.

Pray.

Read Romans 8:35, 38–39.

Eat nutritious food but also eat ginger biscuits, cream tarts, lemon cake, or Chelsey buns. (We offer Mrs. Beeton's recipe for ginger biscuits below.)

Be assured that the Lord loves you.

Your fellow servants,

Jennie and Inez

DESSERT GINGER BISCUITS

INGREDIENTS— 1 lb. of flour, ½ lb. of butter, ½ lb. of sifted sugar, the yolks of 6 eggs, flavouring to taste. Ginger, or cinnamon, lemon, currants.

MODE— Put the butter into a basin; warm it, but do not allow it to oil; then with the hand beat it to a cream. Add the flour by degrees, then the sugar and flavouring, and moisten the whole with the yolks of the eggs, which should previously be well beaten. When all the ingredients are thoroughly incorporated, drop the mixture from a spoon on to a buttered paper, leaving a distance between each cake, as they spread as soon as they begin to get warm. Bake in a rather slow oven from 12 to 18 minutes, and do not let the biscuits acquire too much colour. In making the above quantity, half may be flavored with ground ginger, and the other half with cinnamon or the essence of lemon or currants, to make a variety. With whatever the preparation is flavoured, so are the biscuits called; and an endless variety may be made in this manner.

TIME— 12 to 18 minutes, or rather longer, in a very slow oven.

Sufficient to make from 3 to 4 dozen cakes.

Seasonable at any time.

Chapter Forty-Two

"I am sorry Sister Knight, but I have had a revelation of Joseph Smith the Prophet, and I believe that if one has not had the same manifestation, they are not truly able to testify of the event."

Inez stared at Elder Forester with no words to respond. She did not need this fly buzzing in her ear. She had sequestered herself in a corner of the conference hall to study and memorize scripture. She was enjoying the solitude when Elder Forester approached with the desire to discuss certain doctrines of the Church. She wished Jennie were by her side. *She* would have known what to say to such an outlandish statement, but she and Will had gone for a stroll to sort out their disagreements, so Inez was left to her own spiritual reasoning.

She took a breath. "I believe most of us testify of things through the Holy Ghost, Elder Forester. Didn't the Lord say to Thomas, 'Blessed are they who have not seen, who believe'?"

He gave her a look of disdain. "Yes, but we are missionaries now, Sister Knight. We have been called to testify to the people the truths of the Restoration. We are not in our little sewing circle in Provo, chatting with our Church friends of gospel stories. If you do not have enough faith to see Joseph in the grove of trees, then should you even be here?"

Inez stood quickly, her scriptures thumping to the floor. "Are you questioning my faith?"

Elder Forester was momentarily taken aback but recovered quickly.

A half grin imprinted itself onto his mouth. "My, my. Seems as though I touched a nerve."

"If you are questioning if I should be here with my *puny* faith, Elder Forester, then you are questioning the First Presidency. They are the ones who called me on this mission. Perhaps they thought my faith was sufficient."

"So typical for women to get emotional at the drop of a hat."

Just as Inez was about to respond, Elder Abernathy came to her side.

"How may I assist you, Sister Knight?"

Inez took a deep calming breath and unclenched her fists. "I . . . I am fine, Elder Abernathy. It just seems that Elder Forester and I have a different opinion on faith."

"His vision of the Prophet Joseph Smith?"

Inez turned abruptly to the English elder. "You know about that?"

"Oh yes indeed, Sister Knight. He has been spouting it to all the elders—calling us to a higher level of spirituality."

"How dare you!" Elder Forester blustered. "Do not mock me, Elder."

Elder Abernathy turned and addressed his companion with such elegant British grace that Inez had to cover a smile. "My dear friend, I have no intention of mocking you. No, indeed. In truth I have made an appointment for us to meet with President Noall."

Elder Forester frowned. "President Noall? Why?"

"Well, it is incumbent on the senior companion—me—to alert the president to any miraculous gifts, visions, or manifestations exhibited by the junior companion—you." He smiled openly. "I believe he will be stunned by your visionary acumen."

Elder Forester's boldness faded. "I . . . well, I . . . "

"So I would suggest you finish up your gospel study. I will come and fetch you in about ten minutes."

Elder Forester turned abruptly and left the hall.

"Oh my," Inez giggled. "That took the wind out of his sails."

"Indeed. I'm afraid his ship may be floundering," Elder Abernathy remarked, a hint of sadness in his voice.

"Are you sorry for him?"

"I am, Sister Knight. And for myself. I feel I have failed him. I knew from the first he would need a course correction, but it seems my tactics have proven ineffective."

"Piffle," Inez stated. "If anyone could have helped him, it was you."

The front door of the conference house opened, and Jennie and Will entered.

"I hope they've mended fences," Inez mumbled.

"Difficulties?"

Inez was surprised that Elder Abernathy had heard her. "Oh! Ah . . . just a small misunderstanding."

"Well, I hope they *have* mended it," Elder Abernathy stated. "Elder Knight needs his wits about him to keep us all in line."

"I think his wits are just fine," Inez defended.

Jennie and Will hung their coats on the wall pegs and parted ways, with Will going to speak with the elders studying at the long table and Jennie coming to Inez's side. Inez began to ask her a question, but Jennie cut across her.

"Shall we eat dinner in the kitchen today? I do not feel like eating with the elders."

"That suits me," Inez said.

"Inez, why are your scriptures on the floor?"

"Oh!" Inez remarked, bending down to retrieve her scriptures. She stood. "Actually, it's a very interesting story."

"Wonderful. Tell me while we're eating." Jennie turned and walked toward the kitchen. She made a wide arch around the table, avoiding eye contact with any of the table's occupants.

When they reached the kitchen, Inez breathed in the savory smell of onions and meat. "Is it stew, Mrs. Wilkey?"

"It is, Sister Knight."

"Mrs. Wilkey?" Jennie questioned. "Would it be all right if Inez and I ate dinner in the kitchen today?"

Mrs. Wilkey gave them a smile and a wink. "What do you think, Mabel?" she called to the cook. "Shall we let the girls escape those tiresome elders for a time?"

Mabel nodded and ladled stew into a bowl.

"Thank you," Jennie said, obvious relief in her voice.

"Sit at that wee table there, and I'll bring you some food. You two looked stretched thin."

Jennie plopped down in her chair. "Stretched thin. That is exactly how I feel."

Inez wanted to ask her companion if she felt another illness coming on but decided she had been pestered enough with questions about her health. "I'll tell you who stretches me thin," Inez growled. "Elder Forester. He could be a good missionary, but he is a pudding head."

"What has he done now?"

Over bowls of stew, Inez told the story of her argument with Elder Forester, his claims of a personal vision, and his belligerent dismissal of any other views on faith. "If Elder Abernathy hadn't come along at that very moment, I'm afraid a certain elder would have gotten a punch on the nose," Inez stated, vigorously jabbing a piece of meat with her fork.

Jennie laughed, and Inez was glad to see a modicum of distress leave her face.

"Here is what I think," Jennie said, buttering the last of her bread. "I think we should skip the street meeting this afternoon and go for a bath."

"Really?" Inez questioned. "But we've never missed a meeting without good cause."

"I say a little time for us to breathe is a very good cause," Jennie said, sitting straighter. "Besides, I need to buy a knit hat for winter. Something to cover my ears."

Inez heartily agreed with the plan, and she and Jennie spent a lovely hour in the kitchen doing the dishes and chatting with Mabel and Mrs. Wilkey, which filled their souls with the sound doctrine of womanhood.

NOTE

Elder Forester's revelation of the Prophet Joseph: Although Elder Forester is a fictional character, Inez's journal names an elder who claimed revelation concerning Joseph Smith and who chastised the other missionaries if they had not received the same experience.

Chapter Forty-Three

NOTES ON MISSIONARY MANAGEMENT

There will be times when you will feel stretched thin. When this occurs, there are four things we suggest:

Eat a bowl of stew in the kitchen.

Cook or bake something.

Go for a bath.

Find a topic of amusement, and laugh with your companion.

Sister Brimhall and Sister Knight

MRS. BEETON'S STEWED BEEF

INGREDIENTS— About 2 lbs. of beef or rump steak, 3 onions, 2 turnips, 3 carrots, 2 or 3 oz. of butter, ½ pint water, 1 teaspoonful of salt, ½ do. of pepper, 1 tablespoonful of ketchup, 1 tablespoonful of flour.

MODE— Have the steaks cut tolerable thick and rather lean; divide them into convenient-sized pieces, and fry them in the butter a nice brown on both sides. Cleanse and pare the vegetables, cut the onions and carrots into thin slices, and the turnips into dice, and fry these in the same fat that the steaks were done in. Put all into a saucepan, add ½ pint of water, or rather more should it be necessary, and simmer very gently for 2½ or 3 hours; when nearly done skim well, add salt, pepper, and ketchup in the above proportions, and thicken with a tablespoonful of flour mixed with 2 of cold water. Let it boil up for a minute or two after the thickening is added, and serve.

TIME— 3 hours.

Sufficient for 4 or 5 persons.

Seasonable at any time.

Chapter Forty-Four

"It's a fairy-tale castle," Inez whispered.

"I can't believe I'm seeing this," Jennie added, staring up at the pinnacles and turrets of the Stratford Theatre.

"Your father would love it, wouldn't he?"

Jennie nodded. "I'm sure he would stand on this very spot and quote *Hamlet*."

"To be, or not to be," George Kennison quoted, sneaking up behind them. Inez and Jennie jumped.

"Oh, George! You frightened the wits out of us!" Inez scolded. "I thought you were with your parents, buying tickets."

"That was boring. I'd much rather be here with you two, admiring the theatre."

"It's a new building, is it not?" Jennie asked.

"Oh no," George refuted. "It is nigh on twenty years old."

Inez and Jennie laughed at his antics.

"Pardon our mistake," Jennie mocked. "I suppose we have become accustomed to things being hundreds of years old."

"It really is a fine building, isn't it?" George questioned, setting aside his teasing.

"Other than the Salt Lake Temple, it is the most beautiful building I've ever seen," Inez answered.

A few feathery snowflakes drifted around them.

"Snow!" Jennie exclaimed. "My first snow in England!"

Inez reached out a gloved hand, trying to capture one of the elusive flakes. "It's magical."

"Magical and cold," Mr. Kennison said, coming to join the group.

"Where's Mum?" George asked.

"She's gone to get us a table at the inn," Mr. Kennison answered. "Teatime is fast approaching!" He said this with such glee that Inez and Jennie laughed. "What? Ah, you may laugh at me now, but wait until the sausage rolls, jam roly-poly, shepherd's pie, and sticky toffee pudding come along. You will not be laughing then!" He began walking. "On we go!" Jennie and Inez fell in behind.

"So were you able to get tickets for tonight's performance, Da?" George asked, striding along with his father.

Mr. Kennison brought tickets from his breast pocket and held them high in the air. "Five superb tickets for a whimsical tome by Mr. William Shakespeare! *The Comedy of Errors*!"

Inez stopped short. "*The Comedy of Errors*?"

Mr. Kennison halted and turned back. "Is it not to your liking? I could go back and return them for tomorrow's production of *Julius Caesar*."

"Oh no. We love *The Comedy of Errors*!" Jennie insisted. "In fact, it is my father's favorite Shakespearean comedy." She turned to Inez with a smile. "It's just that Sister Knight once said her mission would probably be a comedy of errors."

Mr. Kennison gave her a discerning look. "Well now, that has proven to be totally false, has it not?" He started on his way without waiting for an answer.

Inez and Jennie hurried to keep up.

"But there's still time ahead for disaster!" Inez called.

Mr. Kennison's hearty laugh drifted back to them with the swirling snow.

"Going off on a train again," George Kennison grumbled, stomping snow from his boots and giving the sister missionaries a frown.

Amanda Kennison ruffled her son's hair. "We have already made plans for them to come to Bristol for Christmas holiday, Son. Be content."

"Yes, ma'am."

"As much as we may like, we cannot have them all to ourselves," Mr. Kennison said. "They have their work to do."

The train whistle sounded.

"It has been a miraculous three days," Jennie said. "How can we ever thank you?"

"Try not to forget us," Mr. Kennison said with a wink.

"We could never do that," Inez stated.

Mrs. Kennison embraced each of them. "Off you go now. We'll see you at Christmas."

Emotion caught in Inez's throat as she noticed Jennie lingering in Sister Kennison's embrace. Jennie's own mother had lost awareness of her children in her mental shadowland, and though Flora was a splendid stepmother and organizer, she was not overtly affectionate.

The train whistle sounded three short blasts.

"Run, sisters!" Mr. Kennison barked. "President Noall will chide us if we keep you another day." His booming laugh echoed around the platform, causing several people to turn.

The sisters ran for the train, waving and calling words of connection as they went. The Kennison's returned the same. On the train, Sister Knight and Sister Brimhall settled themselves, pressing their faces to the window for one last glimpse. George ran beside their window, saluting and waving until the steam engine pulled them out of view.

Jennie sighed. "Why can't Christmas come at the beginning of December?" She slumped into her seat and reached into her satchel, retrieving the leather-bound book she'd purchased at the vintage bookseller's. Her fingers drifted slowly across the soft russet leather. "Do you think he'll like it?"

"What? That old thing?" Inez teased. "A copy of his favorite Shakespearean comedy from a bookseller in Stratford, England?" She gave Jennie a warm smile. "I think he will treasure it forever."

Jennie held it to her chest, laid her head back and closed her eyes. "I miss him," she whispered. "I hope he's well."

Inez turned her head to gaze out the window. The waning sun cast a golden shimmer over the snow-crusted fields, reminding her of the harvested fields at home. She pulled her mind from those pictures and focused on the delightful three days in Stratford with their friends. She had loved the play with its zany characters and madcap misadventures, visiting the home where Shakespeare was born, the chilling snowball fight with George, the three-hundred-year-old inn with its cheery fire, eating sausage rolls and sticky toffee pudding, strolling along the banks of the River Avon within a lacy swirl of snow, and exploring the enchanting old bookshop where Jennie happened upon the precious book for her father. These memories, along with a hundred others, made Inez smile and filled her heart with England. She knew there would be days in the dry, parched summers of Utah when her soul would be called back by the sounds of English accents to wander among stone cottages and green glades. Inez accepted the ache of kinship and recognized that she would never be the same.

NOTES

Stratford, or Stratford-upon-Avon: This market town is in the county of Warwickshire, England, and was established in 1196. Poet and playwright William Shakespeare was born here in 1564.

Kinship with members: In her journal, Inez often mentioned spending time with Church members and the treasured kinships she formed. Present-day missionaries often bear testimony of these tender ties of attachment to investigators and local members.

Chapter Forty-Five

Inez's attention wandered as President Noall conducted the priesthood meeting. There were reports and procedural discussions and logistical concerns, and to Inez, it seemed each point was restated three or four times. Her mind was on the verge of shutting down when President Noall moved to the subject of mission transfers. She sat up straighter and leaned slightly against Jennie. "Transfers!" she whispered.

"I'm aware," Jennie said. "Unlike you, I have been paying attention."

"Do you think we're staying or going?"

"No idea."

It was true. The missionaries of the Cheltenham Conference were never alerted beforehand to the changes; therefore the meeting was now filled with anticipation and angst. Inez was unfamiliar with the elders being transferred from other towns and cities, so she paid scant attention, but when Elder Bailey's name was put forward, she listened to every word.

"Elder Bailey and Elder Forester will be companions in Birmingham."

Inez looked over at her friend, but his head was bowed, and he would not look up. *It's because of me,* she thought. *Because of what I said to him, and now he is going away to a big city with Elder Forester.*

"Therefore, Elder Abernathy and Elder William Knight will be serving together in Cheltenham along with Sister Knight and Sister Brimhall."

"I'm so glad we're staying," Jennie whispered, but Inez only nodded, her mind still on poor Elder Bailey and the difficulties in his future.

"Inez, aren't you happy?" Jennie whispered again. "And my Elder Knight will be staying as well."

"Yes, it's wonderful. I am just upset that Elder Bailey has to work with Elder Forester."

"Elder Ray Knight and Elder Davis will be going to Bristol," President Noall announced.

"What?" Inez exclaimed without thinking.

President Noall chuckled. "Yes, Sister Knight—Bristol. I have received several requests for missionaries from people interested in the Church. It seems you and Sister Brimhall planted some seeds."

"Not to mention the influence of the Kennison family," Elder Davis said, giving an open smile to the sister missionaries.

Inez stood. "Then Sister Brimhall and I should also return."

President Noall gave her a knowing smile. "Perhaps at some point, Sister Knight, but it is not what the Lord has instructed at this time."

Jennie tugged at her sleeve. "Inez, sit down."

She grumbled as she did. "But if we planted the seeds . . . "

"Then others will water," Jennie instructed.

"And harvest," Inez added bitterly.

"Inez, you're being peevish. Just think of Elder Bailey. He won't be here when Mrs. Fletcher is baptized, and he was asked to perform the ordinance."

Inez's attitude changed in an instant. "Oh, Jennie, you're right. How could I not think of poor Elder Bailey? What disappointment he must be feeling."

The sisters' whispered conversation had been covered by questions from the elders to President Noall. Finally, he held up a hand. "I think we should end the meeting so you can get out to your fields of labor. Those being transferred, please come to my office, and we will discuss the details of your travel." He scanned the group. "Elder Abernathy, will you give us our prayer?"

"Of course, President."

After the prayer, Inez went directly to Elder Bailey. "You are being forced to transfer because of me, aren't you?"

"Yes," he said with a shrug. When a dejected look printed itself onto

Inez's face, he relented. "No, Sister Knight, I am not being forced." He looked at her straight on. "I requested it."

"You did? Well, that makes me feel even worse."

"It shouldn't. Everything you said the other night was absolutely proper. Neither of us wants to be distracted from the work, so I requested to serve in another part of the vineyard."

"But Birmingham with Elder Forester?"

Elder Bailey laughed. "Well, those things I did not request, but I'm calm about it. The Lord has work there for me and Elder Forester."

"What are you saying about me?" Elder Forester asked as he stopped by Elder Bailey's side.

Elder Bailey clapped him on the back. "Just that you and I have a grand work to do in Birmingham!"

"As long as they don't chuck you in the cut," Inez said.

"What does that mean?" Elder Forester asked with a frown.

"It's just a rumor," Elder Bailey deflected.

"Really?" Inez persisted. "I heard the Anti-Mormon League in Birmingham likes to toss the elders into the deep Birmingham canals, whether or not they can swim."

The color drained from Elder Forester's face. "I . . . I don't swim."

"Sister Knight is only joking," Elder Bailey assured.

"Well, that's mean-spirited of her. I would have hoped for better." He turned his back on Inez and addressed Elder Bailey. "We need to be in the president's office."

"You go on. I'll be there in a minute."

Elder Forester cast a glaring look at Inez and moved away.

"I'm sorry. That *was* mean-spirited of me, Elder Bailey. Especially when you're obviously trying to be the ideal senior companion."

"Then go and repent, Sister Knight!" Elder Bailey roared in the voice of a Baptist preacher.

Inez started laughing, and Elder Bailey joined her. "Oh, I am going to miss you, my friend," she said.

"Now, none of that. We both have work to do. Off you go to your cottage meeting, and I will go and secure my marching orders."

Inez held out her hand, and Elder Bailey shook it. She smiled at him. "I will pray for you."

"You'd better," he said with a half grin. "Because I do not know how to swim either." Reluctantly he let go of her hand.

Jennie came from speaking with Will and Elder Davis. "Congratulations on your transfer, Elder Bailey. I'm sure you are much needed in your new assignment."

"Thank you, Sister Brimhall. And you two carry on with your marvelous work here in Cheltenham."

"We will try." Jennie answered. "It would help if I could get Sister Knight to hold to the rules."

Elder Bailey laughed. "She tends to be a floss-in-the-wind, doesn't she?"

"Very funny," Inez said. "Are you not supposed to be in the president's office?"

"On my way," Elder Bailey said, moving off. "Success with your cottage meeting!"

"Success with . . . success with . . . everything!" Inez stammered.

Jennie sighed. "Birmingham. Will told me that a big city is always more difficult. I will pray for him."

"I will pray for both of them," Inez added.

Jennie gave her a surprised look. "Really?"

"What?" Inez asked.

"I understand your prayers for Elder Bailey, but Elder Forester?"

"Of course. He needs more prayers than anyone, doesn't he?"

Jennie shook her head. "I thought your kindness was too good to be true. Just for that, Sister Knight, I think you ought to give the lesson at the McKees' home."

"I would be pleased," Inez said, picking up her satchel and grabbing her coat.

"Are you feeling well?" Jennie asked, putting on her coat and following after.

"I am! I have just decided to embrace change," Inez said as she opened the conference house door and stepped out into the cold day.

Chapter Forty-Six

Sisters Inez Knight and Jennie Brimhall stood in front of the cast-iron stove, reaching out to its warmth like schoolgirls to a kitten.

"Cold. Cold cold cold," Jennie stammered as she inched her fingers closer to the warmth.

"Ah! Don't burn yourself," Mrs. Wilkey warned as she took the kettle from the flat.

Jennie pulled back her hands but only slightly. "Maybe I'd get warm if Mabel put me in a pie and popped me in the oven."

The cook chuckled.

"You should be very warm," Inez teased. "You still have on your coat and knit hat."

"And I may not take them off all day," Jennie pronounced. "I'm so glad you use the wood stove in the winter," she called to the cook.

"Well, she prefers it," Mrs. Wilkey stated. "Says the gas stove gives everything a peculiar flavor. Isn't that right, Mabel?"

"New-fangled invention," Mabel grumbled.

Mrs. Wilkey leaned toward the girls. "It has been in the kitchen for nearly ten years." She set two mugs on the kitchen table. "You girls have a seat. Here's some hot lemon water. Put honey in it. Good for your throats."

"Oh, thank you!" Jennie said, taking off her coat and reaching for the honey jar. "My throat is a little scratchy." She sat down and put two globs of the amber sweet into her drink. "I might just thaw."

"You two could have stayed in today," Mrs. Wilkey said as she placed a plate of scones and clotted cream on the table.

As Inez smiled up at Mrs. Wilkey, Jennie shook her head. "We had tracts to hand out."

"Oh, and I suppose there was a crowd out today just waiting for you to pass by."

"Well, no, not a crowd," Jennie admitted. "But we did give out twenty tracts."

"Twenty-two," Inez corrected. "And one man stopped to talk with us. He was curious what two single American girls were doing so far from home."

Mrs. Wilkey gave them a tender smile. "You two are an oddity, no mistaking." She went to take her coat off the peg. "Now, Mabel and I are off for shopping. Stay as long as you like. Clean up after yourselves."

"We will!" Inez called. "Thank you for the scones!"

Mrs. Wilkey hesitated at the door. "Oh! I almost forgot. The elders brought down the mail. They left yours on the side table." She exited with a wave.

"Mail!" Inez said, standing. "I'll get it!" She went to retrieve the letters, coming back with a smile. "Two for each of us!"

"Rewards for our hard work," Jennie remarked, taking her letters and perusing the addresses. "Another letter from Father? I received a message from him only a week ago. Odd." She set it down and opened the other. "Something from my sister Alsina."

"And I have one from Elder Bailey in Birmingham!" Inez announced. She took the butter knife and sliced across the top of the envelope. They both took a sip of tea and settled back to read. Inez chuckled several times and said, "Oh my," several times.

Jennie finished the letter from her sister and went to open her father's missive.

"Wait! Wait! Listen to this," Inez insisted. She located the place in the letter and read: "I guess firsthand experience is the best teacher of all, dear friend, for Elder Forester now has a black eye. It was not received from one of the thugs of the Anti-Mormon League. Oh no! It was compliments of the bishop's fifteen-year-old daughter, Ellie. Elder Forester tried to convince her of his revelation and her lack of faith, and she busted him in the eye!"

Jennie and Inez burst out laughing.

"Oh dear," Jennie said in a repentant voice. "I guess we should not be laughing at Elder Forester's misfortune."

"Piffle," Inez said, still giggling. "I hope we meet Miss Ellie sometime on our mission. I want to shake her hand."

"Inez."

"I do. Didn't Elder Bailey say his companion needed to learn a lesson? Well, if he was still spouting that nonsense after receiving counsel from President Noall about it, then Ellie showed him the way of things."

"We don't know exactly what the president said to him."

"Oh yes, I do." She attempted to imitate President Noall. "Elder Forester, you are a dunderhead! Jolly good if you have received spiritual insight but hold it sacred and do not go judging others about their faith. If you keep it up, Son, I will have to boot you back to Utah."

Jennie tried hard not to laugh at her companion's antics, but it was impossible. "Stop it, Sister Knight! Stop! You are a bad influence on me."

"'Boot you back to Utah.' I am sure those were the president's exact words."

Jennie took off her knit hat and threw it at Inez. "Stop!" She took her father's letter from the envelope and waved it at Inez. "Go back to reading your letter—silently."

"You don't want me to share any more of . . . "

"No!" Jennie said with a grin. She took a sip of tea and disappeared behind her own letter.

Inez munched happily on a scone and silently reread the part about Elder Forester being punched in the eye.

"Oh no, Father. Oh no no no no," Jennie muttered.

Inez looked up to see her friend's stricken face. "Jennie, what is it? Is your father ill again?"

Jennie crumpled the letter and threw it down. She stood abruptly, bumping the table and knocking over her drink. Inez grabbed for the letters.

"I have to find Will."

Inez grabbed her wrist. "Jennie, wait."

Jennie glared at her. "Do not tell me what to do! Everyone, stop telling me what to do!" She wrenched her arm away and headed for the stairs.

Inez grabbed a towel and threw it on the table. She set the letters safely on the dry part of the table and smoothed the one from Jennie's father. She read.

Dearest daughter,

As you know we pray for you every day. I pray for you. Your well-being is constantly on my mind. Normally the Spirit reassures that all is well, and I go about my day without concern, but lately the prompting has been one of warning. I realize the damp cold of an English winter is fast approaching, and the memory of your fight with pneumonia lies heavy on my heart.

Flora and I have spent many days fasting and praying, and the answer is that you end your mission early and come home with Elder Knight in November.

Inez stopped reading.

Time seemed to hang for a moment, suspended between disbelief and sorrow. Inez stared at the paper in her hand. *They are just words—a few small words*, she told herself. *Maybe I read them wrong. Desolation cannot live in a few small words.*

She felt frozen in place, unable to speak or move, until Jennie's upraised voice from the conference hall shook her from her stupor. She raced up the stairs to find Jennie confronting Will at the front doorway. It was obvious that he and Elder Abernathy had just stepped into the room—coats on, hats in hand, looks of astonishment and dismay coloring their faces. As Inez approached the trio, she watched as Will reached out and Jennie recoiled.

"Jennie, I don't understand," Will pleaded.

"How? How could you tell my father about my illnesses?"

"Jennie, what happened?"

"You wrote to him, didn't you? You wrote that you were worried about me."

"Jennie, I . . . "

"And now he's sent a letter insisting that I return home. That I leave my mission and come home with you."

Will stepped toward her, and Jennie stepped back. "Jennie, please. I did not write to your father." She gave him a defiant look. "I didn't. I wrote my concerns to my father for his advice."

"How could you, Will? You know they are close friends. You knew your father would share those concerns."

"I'm sorry."

"In fact, it's exactly what you hoped, wasn't it? Exactly what you wanted."

"I was worried about you."

"And now I have to go home. I have to leave my mission! How could you do that?"

"Jennie . . . "

"No! I do not want to talk to you anymore." Inez could tell her friend was on the verge of tears as she turned to leave. Jennie stopped short and blinked at Inez, belatedly realizing that her companion and Elder Abernathy had been witnesses to the quarrel. "I want to go to the apartment."

"Of course."

They headed off to the kitchen to get their coats. Inez turned back once to see her brother staring after them—devastation written on his face.

NOTE

Jennie Brimhall leaving her mission: Several histories state that Sister Brimhall's family requested that she come home early over fears for her fragile health and the coming of the cold, damp English winter. There is a break in Inez's journal from September 19 through November 11. On the day of Jennie's departure, November 11, Inez writes, "After leaving Jennie and Will in Liverpool went with Ray to Hull where we stayed in quiet lodgings. Walked out on the pier of the docks where the sight of the ships seemed to fascinate me, but at the same time caused me to feel what a long way I was from home and my lonely condition more than ever before."

Chapter Forty-Seven

"The Cheltenham Women's Gymnasium," Inez read from the card. "This seems to be the place." She looked up at the ornately scrolled façade, admiring the carvings of Greek women in graceful poses holding grapes or pomegranates or baskets of bread. She looked expectantly at Jennie, hoping to see a smile, but was met with a vacant visage. "Well, shall we venture in and see if we can find Mrs. Fletcher?"

They moved up the wide stone steps and into the building, Jennie tagging along a step behind. The week since her father's letter, Jennie had gone from despair to gloom to a numb acceptance. She and Will had spent many hours repairing their torn relationship, and many tears had been shed. Inez was going through many of the same feelings of gloom and loss but chose to show Jennie only a positive face. For days, she knew her smile had merely been painted on, but recently the optimism felt more genuine. Perhaps it was the change in her personal prayers. One night while praying for Jennie and Will's safe travel, Inez imagined herself with them, crossing the ocean together, stopping to see Niagara Falls, coming into Provo on the train, and being greeted by her mother and father. The more she thought about the prospect, the more it appealed to her. Hadn't she and Jennie worked diligently for the past months, opening a trail for other sisters to follow? Hadn't they compiled their book of missionary management as a guide for future sister missionaries? Hadn't their experiences provided valuable information for mission presidents and the First Presidency? Perhaps their work was finished.

Inez was so lost in thoughts of leaving, she passed the greeter's desk without stopping.

"Excuse me, miss," the greeter called in a pleasant voice. Inez turned, and the woman gave her a smile. "I am afraid one must stop here before being admitted."

"Sorry," Inez said, hurrying back to stand by Jennie. "I . . . I was thinking about other things."

"As one often does," the greeter said. "Have you your card?"

"We do," Inez answered, retrieving the card from her coat pocket.

The woman examined it. "Oh, from Mrs. Fletcher. Wonderful. You will be in attendance today in the swimming area. Straight down that hallway to the very back."

"Thank you," Inez said, and they started off.

"I wish I were staying longer if only to learn how to speak in that elegant fashion," Jennie said.

Inez agreed. "That woman could be the greeter for the queen." She attempted an imitation. "Have you your card? Queen Victoria will be charmed that you took time from your demanding missionary work for a visit."

Jennie laughed. "You would probably try and give the queen a Book of Mormon."

"I would," Inez confirmed. "Although, I heard Wilford Woodruff presented one to her when he was here as a young missionary."

"Legend," Jennie said with a grin.

Inez was surprised and pleased by Jennie's involvement. "Are you feeling more cheery?"

Jennie stopped at the door of the pool area and took a deep breath. "This is not my day, Inez. It belongs to Mrs. Fletcher, and she deserves to see our faith and joy in the gospel."

Inez felt tears pressing at the back of her throat but counteracted the emotion with a smile. "About time you thought of someone other than yourself," she said, making Jennie chuckle.

As the sisters stepped into the swimming pool area, their mouths dropped open. "Oh my goodness!" Jennie whispered.

The arched dome of the swimming area was made of opaque glass and soared forty feet above their heads. The muted sunlight played in waves on the surface of the pool water and the surrounding blue tiles.

"I have never seen anything like this," Inez said in awe.

"Remarkable," Jennie said, her gaze roaming over the Grecian statues and large potted plants. "I understand there are a few places like this in the Eastern states, but we'll never see them."

"And Mrs. Fletcher and Mrs. Checkly swim here?"

"We do indeed," Mrs. Fletcher said, coming to greet them. "You seem to be carried off in your imaginings."

"It is a place for flights of fancy," Jennie confirmed.

"I am so glad to have you both here," Mrs. Fletcher said.

Inez tried not to stare at Mrs. Fletcher's appearance. Gone was the tailored dark suit with exquisite hat and stylish shoes. The elegant woman was barefooted, and she wore a cream-colored dress that could have easily passed for a refined nightgown. Inez pulled her thoughts to the present. "Ah . . . where are the others?" she questioned.

"I believe the gentlemen are off in a room somewhere discussing whether or not to let me in."

Inez giggled. "That will be a short meeting."

"And Christine has not yet arrived."

"Mrs. Checkly is coming?" Jennie asked excitedly.

"She is. My dearest friend must be in attendance, if for nothing more than to ensure that I do not drown."

At that moment the door to the swimming area opened and Christine Checkly and Mr. Easton entered. The girls rushed to her and wrapped their arms around her, expressing their joy.

"What a glorious surprise!" Jennie rejoiced.

"And Mr. Checkly let you come?" Inez blurted.

"Inez!" Jennie scolded.

"Sorry," Inez said, pressing her lips together.

Mrs. Checkly gave Inez a gracious smile. She stepped back and beamed at them. "Oh, how I have missed you two." She turned to Mr. Easton. "To answer your question, Sister Knight, let us just say that Mr. Easton escorted me here for swimming lessons."

"Well done, Mr. Easton," Inez said. Mr. Easton gave a slight grin. "Look there! He almost smiled."

Jennie shook her head as Mrs. Fletcher took Christine's hand. "Welcome, dear friend. Thank you for coming. I had them set up a few chairs at the west end of the pool." As the entourage started off, Mr. Easton held back. Mrs. Fletcher stopped and extended her hand. "Please join us, Mr. Easton. You have been a true friend to your mistress, and I thank you." He nodded and joined. As they approached the sitting area, President Noall, Elder Knight, and Elder Abernathy emerged from a side door. Will had on light summer pants and a white shirt, and his feet were bare.

"Will is going to perform the ordinance!" Jennie whispered as she took off her coat and tried to make herself comfortable in the gilded chair. "How tender—just before he leaves the mission."

Inez's heart lurched at the "just before he leaves" sentiment, until she remembered that she would probably be going home with him. She took a breath and watched as Mrs. Fletcher sat down next to Mrs. Checkly and President Noall stood at the front of the group.

"This lovely place makes me feel as though we are performing this ordinance in the terrestrial kingdom—a place apart from the troubles of the world. We are grateful for Mrs. Fletcher, who made this possible. Elder Bailey could not be with us today as he is working mightily in Birmingham, but he sent along a letter that he would like me to read to you, Mrs. Fletcher, if that is satisfactory?"

"What a dear lad. Of course, President Noall. I would be pleased."

The president took the letter from his coat pocket, opened it, and read.

Dear Mrs. Fletcher,

This must be your baptism day, and I wish to express my joy. I also wish I were there in person so you could see my smiling face, but one thing we learn as a missionary is that some plant, others water, and others harvest. I think Elder Knight will be performing the ordinance, and I hope he will do a good job.

The gathering of people chuckled at that sentiment as President Noall continued.

Remember, as we have taught you, he holds the priesthood of God and therefore has the power to unlock this gate to the pathway home—your pathway home to heaven. I know, dear Mrs. Fletcher, that you will walk this path with great confidence. I always admired your study of gospel principles and your astute questions. You will also receive a great gift—the gift of the Holy Ghost, which is given to lead and guide you on your path. You will then be a member of The Church of Jesus Christ of Latter-day Saints. Be diligent.

I bear my testimony that the Church of Jesus Christ has been restored with all the gospel keys necessary to tie us together and get us home.

Know that I will be there in spirit.

Elder Harrison Bailey

President Noall put the letter in his pocket. "We all bear the same testimony, Sister Fletcher." He turned to Jennie and Inez. "We will now have Sister Knight, Sister Brimhall, and Elder Abernathy sing 'Hail to the Brightness of Zion's Glad Morning,' after which Elder Knight will perform the baptismal ordinance, and you will be the newest member of the Lord's Church in Cheltenham."

As Will led Mrs. Fletcher into the water, Inez noted that Mrs. Checkly moved to the edge of her chair and paid earnest attention.

When Mrs. Fletcher went to change her clothing, Inez, Jennie, and Mrs. Checkly stood in the swimming area of the Cheltenham Women's Gymnasium, talking and reminiscing about the baptism, gospel principles, and their times together. Adventures from the day at Sudeley Castle came into the conversation several times.

"I want you to know, Sister Knight, that I am on my second reading of the Book of Mormon."

"Wonderful!" Jennie said. She turned a critical eye on Inez. "Now you won't have to scold her into reading."

Inez's face reddened. "I may have been a bit enthusiastic."

"I am glad you were. That book is one of the treasures of my library." She sighed. "Perhaps later, if Richard ever relents, we can meet together again. That would be a great joy for me." There was an awkward silence as Inez and Jennie shared a look. "What is it? Do not tell me you two are being transferred like Elder Bailey."

"I actually will be leaving for Utah in a few weeks," Jennie said. Inez could tell she was working desperately to keep sadness out of her voice.

"A few weeks? But Sister Brimhall, you have been in England only a short while. Do you not stay as long as the male missionaries?"

"We have not been given a time of service from our Church leaders," Jennie explained. "I am going because of health reasons."

"Oh, my dear! Are you ill?"

"No, I'm fine." Jennie insisted. "It's just that not long ago I had pneumonia, and my father is worried about the cold, damp English winter."

Mrs. Checkly took her hand. "He is right, my dear. As much as I will grieve to lose you, you must stay safe."

Jennie lowered her head, dashed away a few tears, and then looked directly into Christine Checkly's face. "I have been so angry about this change. I love my mission. I do not want to leave. I have been praying to feel calm—to know from another source that the decision others have made for me is right. You were the answer to my prayer, Mrs. Checkly. Thank you."

Mrs. Checkly nodded and patted Jennie's hand. Inez knew that words were unnecessary. Then Mrs. Checkly turned her attention on Inez. "And what about you, Miss Knight? Are you going home too?"

"Well, it is likely that . . . "

"No," Jennie said. "Inez will be staying. They will send her another companion, and the work will go on."

Inez started to protest, then closed her mouth. The Spirit testified that she was indeed meant to stay and serve out her mission.

Inez looked earnestly at her companion and nodded. "Yes, I will be staying."

NOTE

Queen Victoria: Alexandrina Victoria ascended the throne of Great Britain and Ireland at age eighteen on June 20, 1837, and served until her death at the age of eighty-one, on January 22, 1901. Inez noted in her journal that some of the sister missionaries, after Sister Brimhall's departure, had the opportunity to see the queen in her carriage.

Chapter Forty-Eight

A WORD TO FUTURE SISTER MISSIONARIES ON MISSIONARY MANAGEMENT

In the preface to her monumental book on cookery, Mrs. Beeton makes a statement of her feelings, which Inez and I find parallels our thinking: "I must frankly own, that if I had known, beforehand, that this book would have cost me the labour which it has, I should never have been courageous enough to commence it. What moved me, in the first instance, to attempt a work like this, was the discomfort and suffering which I had seen brought upon men and women by household mismanagement."

Did Inez and I have any idea what lay ahead for us when we sat in the parlor of the Knight home and heard the call to come to England to preach? We did not. If we had, we would never have been courageous enough to commence our mission. Rejection, toil, bedbugs, blisters, lack of sleep, illness, dismissal by some of the male missionaries, speaking to mulish individuals, addressing large congregations, and being threatened by mobs—a list of just a few of our experiences.

But please know, dear fellow sister missionaries, we do not tell you this to dissuade you from the work, but to let you know that we encountered these things and survived! So far, with the Lord's help, we have survived! We were moved to attempt this work because of love for our brothers and sisters. And, since arriving, we have seen the discomfort and suffering brought upon men and women by life mismanagement. It is a dreary world without the light of the gospel and the guidance of the Spirit. Believe us when we say the work is worth your effort.

And you must not imagine that it is all toil. There are picnics in the lovely English countryside, sightseeing, attending the theater, tea and suppers with members of the Church, amusing times with the elders, choir rehearsals, book reading, and long gospel conversations with people whose parched souls long for the water of truth.

So, carry on!

Sister Brimhall and Sister Knight

Chapter Forty-Nine

"The ivory petticoat or the ivory petticoat?" Jennie asked, holding up her one and only petticoat, tattered and permanently dirty on the hem.

"You'd better wear it since it's the only one you have."

"Capital idea," Jennie said, laying the garment aside with her traveling clothes.

"At least it's clean," Inez teased. She sat on her bed, watching the packing process and putting on a brave show of fortitude.

Jennie looked around. "Well, I think that's done it."

"Except for one thing," Inez said, popping up and snatching a book from the desk. She handed it to Jennie.

"Mrs. Beeton's book?"

"I want you to take her with you."

"But what will you do without her? You need her for the missionary management book."

"I'll purchase another copy. I am in England, you know, where there is a bookseller on every other corner."

Jennie ran her hand across the worn paper cover of the book. "Thank you, Inez." She sat on the bed and flipped through the pages. "Ah! Look here! We never got to the general observation on wild game," Jennie lamented. She turned a page. "My goodness, there are a lot of laws connected to hunting." Inez gave her companion a look—a mixture of amusement and understanding. She wanted to lengthen out the parting as well. Jennie sighed and continued with her review of the book. "Oh, Inez, we haven't done soups or soufflés or omelets . . . "

Inez laid her hand on her companion's. "We've done what we could, Jennie. We've done well."

"Do you think so?"

"I do."

"I don't want to go."

"I know."

"Are you going to be all right without me?"

"No."

Jennie shut the book. "Pushing against the waves."

Inez gave a weak smile. "Pushing against the waves. No success in that."

Jennie looked into her friend's eyes. "You *will* be all right, Sister Knight. You are a good missionary." She hurried on as Inez began to protest. "Besides, I will be praying for you every day."

"Pray for my new companion," Inez said with a half grin. She watched as a tear slid down Jennie's cheek. Inez stood abruptly. "No time to waste! Pack Mrs. Beeton away and shut up the trunk. President Noall will be sending the boys over shortly for the luggage, and we do not want to be caught in our nightgowns."

The platform of Cheltenham train station was the normal hustle and bustle of people, luggage carts, and vendors, but Sister Inez Knight and Sister Jennie Brimhall were oblivious to any of it.

"Please tell Mabel and Mrs. Wilkey thank you for the Chelsea buns."

"Thank *me*," Inez said. "I ordered them."

"Thank you," Jennie said softly. She glanced over at Will and Ray, who were talking with President Noall. "I am glad the president brought Ray up from Bristol to be with you."

"And lucky Elder Abernathy gets to go to Bristol and be a companion to Elder Davis."

"And associate with Brother and Sister Kennison."

"And George," Inez said with a chuckle.

"And George. How could one ever forget dear dear George?" The train whistle sounded. "Oh, be quiet!" Jennie barked, laying her hand on her heart. She took a deep breath. "I've written the Kennisons a long letter, but will you please give them my love the next time you see them?"

"Of course."

"So when does your new companion arrive again?"

"December 2nd. Miss Liza Chipman."

"Sounds very British. She should fit right in."

"We will see about that," Inez scoffed. "I'll have to bring her up to our high standards."

Jennie laughed. "Oh, you're so very intimidating. All that bluster will be gone the first time she sees you fall down."

Inez laughed. "Perhaps I'll never fall down again. I've changed a lot since the beginning of the mission."

"Indeed, you have," Jennie said, her voice a mix of certitude and affection.

"I hate that I will miss your wedding," Inez said.

"I promise to have the photographer take lots of photographs, and when you get home, we will look at them together and discuss every detail."

The train whistle sounded again, and Inez glanced over to see Will pacing and looking anxious. She clasped Jennie's hands. "Did you remember your teeth-polishing kit?"

"Yes."

"Your umbrella?"

"Yes."

"Your . . . " The men approached. Inez threw her arms around her companion. "Your scriptures?"

"Yes. I always have my scriptures."

"It is time to leave," President Noall said, his voice low and gentle.

Inez stepped back, her focus on Jennie. "All right. All right, then. As long as you've remembered your scriptures."

Will came and gave Inez a hug. "I promise to take good care of her," he whispered.

Inez pushed away. "And don't smother her."

Will laughed. "I won't. I am very aware of what she's become." He looked at his sister straight on. "What you've both become. I'm proud of you, Sister Knight. I will be able to give Mother and Father a glowing report."

"So you think we've done a passing job?"

"I think you and Sister Brimhall have changed mission service forever."

President Noall approached and took Jennie's hand. "The mission will be a little less bright without you, Sister Brimhall, and probably a little less organized without you, Elder Knight. You have both served well. And, Sister Brimhall, I could use a dozen more like you."

"Well, we will just have to work on that, won't we?" Inez stated. "You could write a note to the First Presidency."

The train whistle blew three short blasts, and Will took Jennie's hand. As the group made their way to the train, Jennie moved close to Inez and whispered, "Remember to say your prayers."

"I will."

"Think of me when you eat Chelsea buns or sausage rolls."

"I will."

"Promise to write me about . . . everything."

"Of course."

The company reached the train, and Will and Jennie stepped aboard. Jennie turned and waved. "Faces to the future."

Inez waved back. "Faces to the future."

Sister Brimhall and Elder Knight disappeared into the train's shadowy interior.

President Noall turned to Ray and Inez. "Goings and comings. It's the way of things." He cleared his throat. "I have work at the office. I will see you two back at the conference home."

"Yes, President," they chorused.

Ray focused on the train as the steam billowed and the gears engaged. "What can I do for you, dear sister?"

Inez was quiet as the train pulled away, then she turned to her brother. "Handkerchief." He handed her one, and she wiped the tears from her face. She picked up her satchel. "I think we should spend a couple of hours handing out these tracts."

"A splendid idea, Sister Knight."

"But first . . . ," Inez said, pointing. "See that vendor over there? I believe he's selling sausage rolls."

AUTHOR'S END NOTE

Photo courtesy of the Church History Library

Lucy Jane (Jennie) Brimhall and Amanda Inez Knight, Manchester Conference, British Mission.

Lucy Jane (Jennie) Brimhall and Jesse William Knight left England November 11, 1898, and arrived home to Provo, Utah, on December 8 of the same year. They were married January 18, 1899, in the Salt Lake Temple. Shortly after their marriage the couple moved to Raymond, Alberta, Canada, where they helped colonize that region for the Church. They adopted two sons: Richard and Philip.

After Sister Brimhall's departure, Amanda Inez Knight went on to serve another eighteen months in England, Scotland, and Wales. Several early sister missionaries to Great Britain were trained by Sister Knight. She returned home to Provo in May 1900. In 1902 she married Robert Eugene Allen, a prominent banker and developer. They were the parents of five sons.

ACKNOWLEDGMENTS

Thank you to Matthew McBride in the Church History Department, who answered my questions and supplied historical information. To Breanna Olaverson for her wonderful historical book about the early sister missionaries. To Robert Preston, an English gentleman who suggested contacts and pointed me in the right direction. To Peter Fagg of Chorley, another English gentleman who welcomed me into his church history museum and shared valuable information about the early missionary work and structure of the Church in England. To the delightful British people who added depth and color to the characters. To my editor, Alison Palmer, for her perceptive evaluations and encouragement, and to the able team at Deseret Book. To Teri Boldt for direction and support as an alpha reader. To George, who is my research buddy and forever friend. And a tender thank-you to the sister missionaries in Rome with whom George and I served. Thank you for your insights and escapades, your devotion and courage, and your valiant testimonies of the gospel. (You didn't know I was taking notes, did you?)

Bibliography

BOOKS

Beeton, Isabella. *The Book of Household Management*. First published in bound edition, 1861; reproduced in facsimile, 1968, by Jonathan Cape Limited; printed in the United States of America by Farrar, Straus and Giroux, 1969.

Black, Susan Easton, and Mary Jane Woodger. *Women of Character: Profiles of 100 Prominent LDS Women*. American Fork, Utah: Covenant Communications, 2015.

Dickens, Steven. *Oldham through Time*. The Hill, Stroud, Gloucestershire: Amberley Publishing, 2018.

Jarman, William. *U.S.A., Uncle Sam's Abscess; Or, Hell Upon Earth for U.S., Uncle Sam*. Exeter, England: H. Leduc, 1884.

Olaverson, Breanna. *Sweet Is the Work: Lessons from the First Sister Missionaries*. American Fork, Utah: Covenant Communications, 2017.

Paul, David. *Illustrated Tales of Lancashire*. The Hill, Stroud, Gloucestershire: Amberley Publishing, 2018.

Roberts, B. H. *A Comprehensive History of The Church of Jesus Christ of Latter-day Saints, Century One*. 6 vols. Salt Lake City: The Church of Jesus Christ of Latter-day Saints, 1930.

Whitney, Orson F. *History of Utah*. Vol. 4. Salt Lake City: George Q. Cannon & Sons, 1904.

FAMILY HISTORIES AND JOURNALS

Allen, Amanda Inez Knight. Diary, 1898–1899. L. Tom Perry Special Collections, Harold B. Lee Library, Brigham Young University, Provo, Utah.

Brimhall, G. H. Diary, 1885. L. Tom Perry Special Collections, Harold B. Lee Library, Brigham Young University, Provo, Utah.

ARTICLES

Britton, Davis, and Gary L. Bunker. "Double Jeopardy: Visual Images of Mormon Women to 1914." *Utah Historical Quarterly* 46, no. 2 (1978).

Cannon, George Q. "Address." In Conference Report, April 1898, 8.

"Cheltenham and the Cotswolds Heritage of Wool and Stone." Cotswolds Tourist Information. www.cotswolds.info/cotswold-heritage.shtml.

Maki, Elizabeth. "Real Live Mormon Women." Women of Conviction. The Church of Jesus Christ of Latter-day Saints. https://history.churchofjesuschrist.org/article/inez-knight-ambassador?lang=eng.

McBride, Matthew. "'Female Brethren': Gender Dynamics in a Newly Integrated Missionary Force, 1898–1915." *Journal of Mormon History* 44, no. 4 (October 2018).

"Orchards and Farming in England." Garden Focused. www.gardenfocused.co.uk.

Perry, James. "LDS British Mission Headquarters in Liverpool (1842–1929): A Brief History." 2014. *British LDS History—A History of the Latter-day Saints in the United Kingdom,* https://britishldshistory.wordpress.com.

"Queen Victoria." Biography, www.biography.com/royalty/queen-victoria.

"Wilford Woodruff: Fourth President of the Church." In *Presidents of the Church: Teacher Manual, Religion 345.* Salt Lake City: The Church of Jesus Christ of Latter-day Saints, 2005.

Woodger, Mary Jane, and Joseph H. Groberg. "George H. Brimhall's Legacy of Service to Brigham Young University." *BYU Studies* 43, no. 2 (2004).

About the Author

GALE SEARS is an award-winning author, known for her historical accuracy and intensive research. Gale received a BA in playwriting from Brigham Young University and a master's degree in theater arts from the University of Minnesota. She is the author of the bestselling *The Silence of God*, *Letters in the Jade Dragon Box*, and several other novels including *Belonging to Heaven*, *One Candle*, *The Route*, and *The Fifth Favorite*. She and her husband, George, are the parents of two children and reside in Salt Lake City, Utah.